To Roger

POSING FOR PICASSO

SAM STONE

love Sam Stone x

POSING FOR PICASSO

SAM STONE

PRAISE FOR SAM STONE

A novel that is dark, disturbing, and utterly tremendous entertainment.

—Ken Bruen

Confidently blends the supernatural and the Gothic with the crime novel. Satisfyingly gruesome; genuinely spooky.

—Mike Ripley

Stone's trademark imagination runs riot as the traditional spooky chiller meets hard case crime head-on. Intriguing, smart and very entertaining.

—Paul Finch

Posing for Picasso

ISBN: 978-1-61475-622-4

Cover painting by Marcela Bolivar

Cover design by David J Howe

Edited by Manny Frishberg

Kevin J. Anderson, Art Director

Published by
WordFire Press, an imprint of
WordFire, LLC
PO Box 1840
Monument CO 80132

Kevin J. Anderson & Rebecca Moesta, Publishers

WordFire Press Trade Paperback Edition January 2018
Printed in the USA

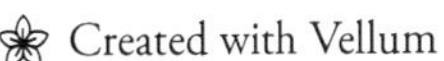

DEDICATION

For David and Linzi and for the love of artists all over the world.

Thanks to Hazel Latus, David J. Howe, Kevin J. Anderson, and Manny Frishberg

A NOTE FROM THE AUTHOR

Within these pages lies an alternative history and universe. Although the name and history of Pablo Picasso have been referred to in this novel, please note this is a complete work of fiction and the author makes no claim that these events actually occurred.

PROLOGUE

Pablo Picasso was rarely alone, but when he was working, the usual hustle and bustle of having his friends around was a constant distraction. For this reason, he never allowed anyone in his studio unless they were his chosen model for the day. However, that day he had picked no one, opting to work alone in silence on a realism piece that he had almost finished. It was a commission, and therefore was worth completing in order to get paid.

There was a clock on the mantelpiece and Picasso was aware of its loud, rhythmic tick in the background. It was soothing and it kept him grounded in time, aware that the day was passing and the working hours, and natural daylight, would soon be over. The clock reminded him that his friends waited in the salon, drinking his wine, eating his food, longing for his attention. It made him feel in control of everything, including time—because he never raced against its passing, but merely worked with it.

He stepped back from the canvas, pleased with the results of his hard work. Yes, the client would be happy with this portrait. He had appealed to the vanity of the wife, thus pleasing the husband, by making the woman appear thinner, prettier, even though she was somewhat plain and plump. He expected a generous monetary reward for his efforts from the husband. He washed his brush in a jar of spirit. The metallic smell wafted up to his nostrils, reminding him of the heady night he had spent the previous evening in the arms of a baffling woman. They were all mysterious to him until he unraveled them with his art, his passion, his obsession; she would be no different from the rest in the end.

"You're Picasso?" she had said. "Pablo Picasso?"

"Yes," he had laughed. "Who else?"

She was stunning and Picasso had wanted to paint her from the outset.

"Paint me then," said a voice behind him now. "Paint me as if your very life depends on it."

He turned around and looked at her. Perfect skin, pale blue eyes with the purest whites he had ever seen. Long blonde hair that flowed over her shoulders. She appeared to be an amalgamation of all of the various parts he had loved in other women. Long legs, small waist, swollen breasts that pressed against the sheer fabric of the robe she wore. Her voice held a musical quality unlike any other woman he had known.

She stepped around him and placed herself before his easel in the position reserved for his models. Then she took up a natural pose. She was not Diana, or Aphrodite, or any other contrived goddess that he had painted before. She was merely a woman and everything about her was sensual, earthy, beautiful.

Perhaps she was Gaia, because surely, she exuded nature and nurture and all that Mother Earth was known for.

Picasso shook away all of these excessive thoughts and replaced the canvas on his easel.

He began to outline her perfect shape. The ticking of the clock became muffled in his ears and then receded to nothing. It was as though all sound had been taken from the room, and the silence that remained was startling and loud. It cocooned him, allowing him to sink completely into his work with no thought of the outside world.

The brush swirled and flowed over the canvas with flesh tones and pastels and all manner of colors in between, and yet Picasso did not deliberate on them as he usually did. Nothing could hold him back. For once there were no fears of failure, no torturous decision making on tones, no worry of inappropriate shading. All he thought about was that he must show her as she really was.

As the last stroke flowed over the canvas, Picasso closed his eyes. This was the masterpiece that he had spent his whole life striving for. This was perfection. This was a moment to savor.

He opened his eyes and stared at the canvas. For a moment, he could not make sense of what he saw.

He glanced back at his new model. Piece by piece.

When Picasso realized what he had done, he dropped his brush to the ground and turned toward the door of his studio with the intention of fleeing.

Blood pumped hard through his veins, his heart hurt, and revulsion stole the sound that tried to screech past his lips. Sickness rose with acidic bile into his throat. He swallowed, barely keeping it down.

A hand caught him from behind.

"You will not turn away from me," she said.

Picasso was spun around by impossibly strong hands to face the object of his terror.

The bile pushed forth and the sickness took him.

Released, he collapsed into the pool of his own vomit even as his bowels gave out. He sat in that vile smelling pool, reeking of shit and piss and sickness, unable to move.

"Look at me," she said.

His eyes burned behind his tightly closed eyes. He didn't want to see her again.

"No."

He shook his head even as her hands clawed at his face. He couldn't fight her.

His eyes opened as though with a will of their own and Picasso found himself face to face with what he knew was the darkness of his own soul.

"What do you want?" he croaked.

His acid-seared throat hurt and he wondered if he would ever whisper words of passion to any woman again. For what was seen could not be unseen.

"You're going to help me," she said.

Anxiety took him then, and he fell mercifully into a dark place inside himself.

When he awoke he was alone, and the canvas before him was blank.

He pulled himself to his feet. Glancing down he expected to find himself still in his own stink, but he was clean and there was no sign of sickness on the floor.

He stroked his forehead. The night before had clearly taken its toll. Relief flooded his cheeks red, even as the image of the woman, and the painting, flashed behind his eyes. It had been so vivid but it had been a hallucination. There was no woman, he was alone, and had blacked out.

He staggered to the door, reached for the handle, hands still trembling.

"I've been working too hard," he murmured but his voice cracked around the words.

For the first time Picasso was aware that time was no longer his friend. The clock started ticking again on the mantelpiece, louder, faster than it ever had before, as though to illustrate that he had so little time left.

CHAPTER ONE

Sun streamed through his roof window offering Avgustin Juniper the perfect lighting. He was painting Annabel's portrait again. She was his muse: he really believed it. Hadn't everything just fallen into place as soon as he had met her?

"I've almost finished my degree," she told him. "I want to thank you. You have helped me develop so much as an artist, Avgustin," (she pronounced it *"Awgustin"*) "and … in other ways too."

The portrait evolved while she spoke, and it appeared to be so photographically perfect that Avgustin could almost believe he had imagined painting it. Sometimes the creativity rode him, instead of him riding it. A spine-shuddering sensation would come over him, and he would feel as though he were being watched. At these times, a faceless being appeared to be standing beside him, hand swirling in the air in rhythm with his own brush strokes. Juniper felt that presence on this day too. Something was beside him, just flickering in his peripheral vision. Otherworldly hands turned and moved, painting in the air, and he was driven to work harder, faster, more intensely.

Annabel left her place—moved from the pose he had set her in. It didn't matter though, her image, her position, and the fall of the light was all still there: burnt into the back of his eyes like a photograph that would never fade.

"I love you, Avgustin," she said.

He came out of his trance to find her beside him. The paintbrush dropped from his fingers as she pressed her warm soft lips against his.

They went to bed. It wasn't frantic; it was slow, loving, beautiful. Everything he had imagined it would be.

Afterwards they lay side by side until the light outside faded.

The obsessive rollercoaster stream of consciousness had left him the minute Annabel kissed him, and so he had no urge to return to work. Still he climbed out of the bed and pulled on his jeans. Then he reached for his crumpled tee-shirt. It was lying on the floor where he had dropped it. He didn't notice the creases as he pulled it over his head.

"Where are you going?" Annabel asked sleepily. "Come back to bed."

"To get us some food, and vine too, if you like?" he said. His accent was heavily Russian, but his English was good.

"I'd love it. Maybe I'll use your shower while you're gone."

"Okay. I von't be long. Just a short walk to the bodega …"

Juniper looked at her lying on the bed.

Street light filtered through the curtains illuminating her wonderful face. Juniper saw shadows and lines that he wanted to paint: another story for the canvas, another work of perfection that Annabel inspired. The compulsion to work surged up inside him again but he quashed it.

No more work today: he deserved a rest.

He placed a kiss on Annabel's lips. Then he hurried out, taking his wallet and keys from the bureau beside the front door.

At the store Juniper bought some wine, cheese, pâté and bread.

We'll have a picnic on the balcony, he thought as he hurried back through the sodium-washed streets towards his apartment building. He had some candles in a drawer in the kitchen and he could make the evening's romance last until they both wanted to make love again.

When he reached the street front door, he noticed that someone had left it on the catch again.

"No idea about zecurity!" he muttered, throwing the door properly closed behind him. It was probably the old lady on the first floor, leaving the door ajar for her son and daughter-in-law to visit. He just wished she would give them a key. It wasn't the safest of neighborhoods and it was only a matter of time before a local *bor*, a thief, realized that he could gain access to the building.

With the paper sack grasped against his chest with one arm, Juniper pressed the call button with his free hand and he waited in the small reception for the elevator to come. The mechanism made a noise but nothing happened. It was an old-fashioned contraption that was prone to breaking down. Juniper cursed under his breath.

A sense of urgency, a feeling that he needed to hurry, overcame him. Already his infatuation with Annabel was making him obsess.

"Soon I'll be able to afford a new place," he murmured. "Give her everything she deserves to have. Nothing but the best for Annabel."

But Juniper loved his studio and wondered if a better location could ever be found for him to work in.

As he climbed the stairs he considered how his life had changed. A few months ago, he had met an art agent and gallery owner by the name of Joy Awen, and now his first exhibit was planned. Everything was falling into place, his work, love life, and finances had dramatically improved. And it was all down to Annabel and the way she inspired him.

He reached the third floor and began to climb the stairs to the fourth and final level that led to his loft apartment.

Already there had been reserves of some of his paintings at the gallery, and Juniper had let his imagination and ambition run for the first time in his life. With Annabel by his side, his life would be fulfilled. They would make a great team. The Joy Awen Gallery would sell all of his finest works. People would pay for commissions. There was much to celebrate. Not many artists achieved that kind of success in their lifetime.

Juniper reached the top of the stairs and began to walk down the landing towards his apartment.

The front door was slightly ajar.

How careless! Juniper thought. *Idiot*! He cursed himself for being too distracted. *I'm probably in love. I'm entitled to make some mistakes.* Besides, no one ever came up this far. Juniper only had models calling, no one else. Until recently he hadn't had much money, but was careful not to get into debt. He had no enemies. And, although New York was known for crime, he hoped there was nothing of interest in this old building that might attract the wrong sort to come snooping—especially this far up. Despite his earlier irritation about the front door being left ajar, he had always felt safe here.

Juniper walked inside his apartment. The door opened up onto his working space. The lights were off, but moonlight poured through the starlight window. It illuminated the picture on his easel. The painting he was working on of Annabel, glowed with the same ethereal quality that she had when he looked at her. It really was perfect—*almost* finished. Just a few more strokes of the brush and it would be there.

He closed the door behind him, then placed the bag of wine and food onto the bureau along with his keys and wallet.

Juniper approached the easel. He almost stepped on the paint brush that he had dropped earlier. He smiled at the memory and then bent to retrieve it. He dipped the brush in spirits, rinsed through the hardening paint, cleaning it. Then he selected another brush from the jar next to the spirits and picked up a tube of dark blue oil paint. He squeezed a little onto his palette, ran the brush into it, then added a little white to lighten the color until he was happy that the shade matched the one he had used on the canvas.

The brush twitched in his fingers. The air beside him moved. Pressure built between his eyes as he tried to resist. He knew Annabel would be waiting in the bedroom for him, yet he had to do this. Just one, two, three, strokes. *There*! It was done. Now he could forget this until tomorrow.

A stifled sound, almost a cry, came from the bedroom. Juniper froze, startled, but also because he was unsure what he had heard. Maybe Annabel had turned off the radio beside the bed. Maybe it was the groan of the shower as the stop button was pressed. This old building often emitted sounds that Juniper had learned to live with but that sound, he couldn't quite place.

Juniper put the paint brush down on the table beside his easel. Then he walked down the narrow corridor, past the empty, dark bathroom and opened the door to the bedroom.

The bed was empty. Annabel was on the balcony outside, or at least that was what he thought. There was a shape there, strangely dulled, not illuminated at all in the street lights.

"I'm back!" he called.

The shape moved. Juniper knew that eyes watched him. The hair on his arms and the back of his neck stood up.

"I hope you missed me …" Avgustin said. His voice was soft, teasing.

A prickle of anxiety crept along his spine as Annabel didn't answer. A peculiar lethargy consumed his limbs. He stopped in the middle of the room as overwhelming tiredness swept over him. His eyes dulled, as though he was wearing sunglasses in the dark, but he could still make out a second shape. And this one he knew without doubt really was Annabel. Juniper blinked. He forced his arm to move, rubbed a softly clenched fist into one of his eyes. There was a blur, a flurry of movement and then a dull thud: a sound that would replay over and over in his head.

The tiredness began to leave him. It was as though some

miasma had enclosed his body, but now the fog was clearing. Juniper crossed the threshold onto the balcony. The whole space was lit up now, not only by the streetlight below, but also by the side light on his wall outside.

There was no one there.

He experienced a sense of confusion and then the sounds of hysteria floated up to him as though he were waking from a drug induced sleep.

He staggered to the railing, every step forced the paralysis farther away, and his eyes cast downwards, into the street below.

It was hard to make sense of what he saw at first. A weird shape in a robe. A twisted body—arms and legs at painful angles. And a face turned upwards that was somehow incomplete.

Four stories up, Juniper could not make out all of the detail and so he later told himself that his hysterical mind had created this bizarre image. It was as though something was gone—like a jigsaw puzzle awaiting its final piece. A part that had been lost. No! *Stolen.*

But it wasn't a puzzle that lay below him. It was Annabel, and something was wrong with the features that had inspired him. He thought he saw a triangle, not an irregular jigsaw shape after all. And it was missing from her face. As if a sharp pastry cutter mold had been stamped through her features.

"Annabel!" he screamed.

Below a man looked up and shouted. Juniper didn't understand his words. They did not make any sense at all because what the man was saying was wrong. Impossible.

"It was him!" shouted the man. "He threw her over."

Darkness swamped his vision again. Tears seeped like black rain. Juniper was blind. His heart a cold mass that hurt beyond endurance but still somehow continued to pump blood through his icy veins. He slumped to the ground and he stayed there until the uniformed police arrived to take him away.

CHAPTER TWO

Detective Jake Chandler stared at the monitor showing Interview Room 3. It was midnight and the station was quiet—which meant that there was marginally less chaos than the dayshift. It was quiet because it was early; the trouble usually started around two am. The nightshift hadn't brought in any hookers, or drunks that had got a little carried away when placing money into one of the girls' G-strings at the local strip clubs. Fortunately, this gave Chandler time to contemplate his interview with Avgustin Juniper.

He turned back to the computer screen on his desk, pulling up the forensic photographs that had already been downloaded onto the system. Now he sent them all to the color printer in the corner of the room. He had a use for them.

Of course the autopsy and forensic analysis of Juniper's and the body were not yet available. Forensics would get to it, though and then, Chandler knew, he would have a clearer picture of what had happened. Even so, he couldn't imagine what weapon had been used to do the damage to the girl's face. Nothing obvious had been found at Juniper's. Nor in the garbage which was quickly examined.

Chandler watched Juniper. The man was catatonic. He hadn't said a word, just kept crying. If it hadn't been for the purse they had found, with the girl's ID inside, then they wouldn't, as yet, know her full name.

Chandler ran a hand through his pale, almost white, blond hair. He was tired. Weary of the treadmill that he could never get off. And now there was Juniper, and the death of Annabel Linton.

In his early forties, Chandler had been a cop since graduation some twenty years ago, quickly advancing from uniform to plain clothes when he showed a proclivity for analyzing the *modus operandi* of a high-profile serial killer. His investigation on that one particular case had been a career-maker.

Since then Chandler was the cop they brought in to work on media-focused cases, which meant that every new potentially prestigious case in his precinct was automatically placed in his hands. It also meant a great deal of unrelenting pressure: a pressure that he used to help focus his mind.

The printer stopped and silence fell before Chandler even registered that there had been noise. He picked up the photographs and placed them in a brown folder.

Chandler had studied killers. Most had an unrelenting narcissistic streak and were sociopaths who believed that they were always right: the world revolved around their needs. Few showed any signs of remorse.

One death, hardly made a serial killer, but the bizarre nature of this murder was why Chandler had been called in. Chandler knew what made most of these types tick. There was a pattern to it that could be found, just as certain as there was a trigger in most cases that made them repeat the act over and over again. They liked what they did, or found some logical justification that made it all acceptable.

Juniper didn't fit into any normal pattern. Not even a crime of passion. In fact, the death of Annabel Linton made no sense at all. This very fact alone made Chandler wonder if the world around him had suddenly changed overnight making the logic he lived by meaningless.

Chandler picked up the folder. The newly printed photographs weighed heavy in his hands. He wondered what he would learn from Juniper and if his gut instinct—that the man was innocent—could be wrong.

"You ready?" said Gemma Sarasvatī as she opened the door. "He's ripe for the picking—we've left him alone for quite a while."

Chandler nodded. He opened the folder.

Sarasvatī looked down at the pictures. She didn't react and Chandler thought how cold she was. He immediately rejected his own misogynistic opinion as soon as he had thought it. Sarasvatī had to be frosty; policing was still very male-dominated. A female officer wouldn't get far if she showed even the slightest sympathy. A ridiculous reality because Chandler felt no need to hide his revulsion at a crime scene: it was natural to react to horrific circumstances. Sarasvatī, however, never gave anything she was feeling away.

Sarasvatī was from an ethnic family and Chandler thought that she was probably fighting against other stereotypes because of this too. Chandler never asked her origins, but it was rumored her parents originated from Nepal. She had an East Indian look, with dark skin, brown eyes, and delicate features. But Sarasvatī was taller than the average woman at around five feet ten. She was also fully westernized in her manner and dress. She rarely smiled and because of her constant frown, Chandler found it difficult to determine whether she was pretty or not. Not that he ever looked at his female colleges this way intentionally. But Sarasvatī intrigued him more than some of the others, who were either obviously feminine or attempted to be "one of the boys." Sarasvatī tried to be neither. She was somewhat sexless if anything, though not from any obvious intention.

"If that doesn't get him talking, nothing will. How he did it; that will be a tale worth listening to," said Sarasvatī.

Shaken back into the present, Chandler glanced at Sarasvatī. Her expression hadn't changed and her voice had been emotionless, as though she didn't care one way or another how the murder had happened.

"I'm not sure he did anything," Chandler said. "But his reaction to this will be telling."

Avgustin Juniper had his head down on the desk when the door to the interview room opened. Nausea swirled around in his stomach. They had offered him coffee, but, so far, he could barely even choke down a mouthful of water. All he could see was the image of Annabel lying beneath his balcony, horribly mutilated.

"Mr. Juniper," said Chandler as he pulled out the chair on the other side of the table. "I'm Detective Jake Chandler. And this is my co-worker, Detective Gemma Sarasvatī. This case has been assigned to my team. I'm going to interview you now and everything we say is being recorded here."

Chandler placed a small recording device on the table between them.

"Can I get you anything? Coffee? Tea? Have you eaten?" said Sarasvatī.

Juniper looked up at her. He saw no kindness in Sarasvatī's dark brown eyes. Offering him refreshment was merely a way of making sure they couldn't be accused of maltreatment.

Juniper shook his head. "I don't vont anyzing."

Chandler sat back in his chair. He didn't know why but he hadn't been expecting Juniper, despite his unusual name, to be foreign.

"Where are you from?"

"I'm an American zitizen."

"I realize you do have a visa to be here–"

"Not visa … full zitizen."

"But you're from Russia originally, right?"

"Yez. Moscow."

"What brought you here?"

Juniper didn't answer.

Chandler placed the folder down on the desk. He sighed as he wondered if Juniper, like most immigrants, was going to close up about his status. They always feared deportation despite being legal, and he was sure Juniper was legal.

"Tell us about Annabel Linton," Sarasvatī said.

Juniper jumped. The sound of her name, so formal on the cold female detective's lips, brought bile up into the back of his throat. He pushed himself up from the desk, sitting up to look at them both for the first time.

"She is my model."

"You're an artist?" said Chandler.

"Yez. Annabel is fine model."

Sarasvatī blinked. "*Was*. She's dead, Mr. Juniper. But you know that, don't you?"

Juniper's head dropped to his chin. Tears seeped through his long lashes.

"I don't know vat happened."

"Mr. Juniper, Afgustin …" Chandler began.

"It's not Afgustin. Though spelt A-V-G-U-S-T-I-N it is pronounced Awgustin." Juniper mangled the vowels and consonants to get his point across.

"Awgustin," Chandler continued. "It would help your case if you showed a willingness to give information about Annabel's murder."

"I don't know anyzing. I vent out. I come back. It's all strange. I call her name, she doesn't answer, then I zee zomething on zher balcony. Next … there's shouting and I look over zher rail and …"

Juniper collapsed into silent sobs.

"It's so horrible … I …"

Sarasvatī flipped open the folder. "We want to know how this happened. Then we can get you the help you need."

"Vat are you zayin'?"

Juniper's eyes fell on the top photograph. It was a close-up of Annabel's face. Her beautiful face! *Oh God!* He hadn't imagined what he saw—it had been real!

A sharp straight, perfect triangle had been cut out of one side of Annabel's face. The triangle stretched from the top of her lip, took in her entire cheek and nicked a corner of one of her beautiful blue eyes. *Right through!* Juniper's mind screamed as he realized he could see through the hole to the ground beneath.

"You see, on first glance I can't imagine how you did this?" Chandler said. "It's cauterized. Somehow. There's no blood, though we did find some on your balcony. Then there is the missing piece. What did you do with it, Avgustin? And why?"

"I didn't do anyzing!" Juniper cried.

The bile rose further up his throat. His heart pounded in his chest and all the time Chandler was pulling out more photographs. Oh, the horror of it! Juniper thought that he must surely be going insane with grief. He couldn't think straight. His mind ran over those last few moments before Annabel had died. And it made no sense at all. What could he tell the detective that he would believe? He remembered vaguely thinking he had seen someone there, in the shadows, on his balcony but had dismissed it as impossible. "I vas falling in love with her," was all he could say. "I vouldn't hurt her. *Don't you understand?*"

And then he could stand it no longer, he turned his head, and vomited on the floor beside the table. Even while the grotesque photographic images burned into his artist brain. No manner of purging would ever free him from this terrible sickness inside his heart and mind. His photographic memory could never be cleansed.

The mess splashed over the tiles and onto Chandler and

Sarasvatī's shoes. Sarasvatī jumped up in disgust, but Chandler didn't move.

As he wiped his mouth on his sleeve, Juniper barely noticed the cold blank expression on Sarasvatī's face. All he could think about was Annabel. Dead. Really gone. His mind rocked on the edge of sanity.

CHAPTER THREE

Cassandra Moúsa waited by the grille until the prison guard closed the gate behind her. She felt the guard's eyes on her. She was a smart-looking thirty-year-old woman, with streaked blonde hair pulled back into a severe bun. She wore a checked skirt suit and was carrying a brown leather briefcase. The guard was admiring her bottom in the tight-fitting skirt. She pushed her spectacles back up to the bridge of her small straight nose as the gate opened in front of her.

"Please step through and place your briefcase on the table, Ms. Moúsa."

She said nothing while the guard opened her case and flicked through the pockets looking for anything that could be used as a weapon.

"Who are you here to see today?" asked the guard.

"Avgustin Juniper."

"Ah. The artist who murdered his model?"

"May I remind you that my client is innocent until found guilty," Cassandra said.

"Sure. That's your job, lady. But to us he's guilty until we're told otherwise."

The guard closed her briefcase and passed it behind him to another table beyond the security scanner. Cassandra kept her face deliberately blank. Some of the guards were bigoted and arrogant, but most of the ones she had come across at the vast city jail complex known as Riker's Island were respectful.

She made a mental note of his badge number. She didn't like his attitude or his way of looking at her. Sometimes, police officers and prison guards gave off a far more brutal and dangerous vibe than the criminals she represented. She believed that in a few cases, had they not chosen a life of upholding the law, they may well have ventured into crime themselves.

Cassandra had a personal interest in psychology. She had majored in it before she obtained her law degree, and she felt it gave her insight into the human psyche. It helped her to understand her client's motives and gave her an advantage on some of her colleagues. This was why she took the seemingly impossible cases. Some of them had been career-making when she had won what everyone thought to be a lost cause.

Cassandra enjoyed her work. She understood criminals better than normal people who had no interesting features or particular agenda in life. She had learned that publicity helped her win and for this reason she always made every case she was working on "high profile." A few leaked and exaggerated truths here, a suspicion of tampered evidence there: such suspicion *always* reached the jury. Human nature did the rest in raising reasonable doubt.

Sometimes this had gone against her clients, but her contacts were good at hiding "their sources" and, so far, no real stink had returned to haunt her. If it had, though, Cassandra would have weathered the storm. She knew how to manipulate the law to her own advantage. She always had a fail-safe in place: a stooge between her and the leaked evidence—usually a current boyfriend that could be blamed. She never gave the data to the press herself. Nor did she ever admit to previously knowing what had been revealed. But someone close to her always made a believable source with the press, who were far easier to maneuver than people thought. There was always a journalist angling for a great story that could further a career, and Cassandra was an expert at finding them.

She experienced a dull ache in her back and neck as she passed through the scanner and collected her briefcase. It had been a difficult week and she wasn't feeling that well. Her usual vigor had diminished, and all sorts of aches and pains had been plaguing her recently.

I've been working too hard, she thought. But the idea of stopping or slowing down just didn't occur to her.

She passed through another doorway and into a corridor that was lined with interview rooms. She entered the nearest one.

The room was divided into two with a huge barrier of glass. There was a row of booths on one side and an open space with a chair facing each booth on the other side. Each area had a phone. Cassandra extracted a packet of wet wipes from the pocket of her jacket, and, as the door opened on the other side of the screen, she took out one of the wipes and cleaned the handset before placing it to her ear.

Cassandra looked through the glass to see Juniper shuffling forward in cuffs and leg irons, like a zombie newly risen from the grave. He looked bewildered and terrified. He sat down opposite her and stared through the glass without understanding what he should do. Cassandra waved the receiver at him. He turned glazed eyes towards the phone then reached out like a blind man. His hand waved in the air until it found the target. He placed it to his ear and turned his dull eyes back to Cassandra.

Juniper didn't look good. He looked as though he were suffering from shock. Cassandra frowned and glared over Juniper's head at the guard standing by the door. What had those bastards done to the man?

"Mr. Juniper? I'm Cassandra Moúsa. I'm going to get you out of here. Do you understand?"

Juniper didn't respond.

"Mr. Juniper. Are you all right?"

Juniper met her eyes. She could detect no trace of hope.

"All you have to say right now is that you engage me to act on your behalf."

Juniper appeared confused.

"Don't worry. The state-appointed attorney you've seen so far won't mind."

"I can't afford a fancy lawyer …" Juniper mumbled.

"I'm going to work your case *pro bono*," Cassandra said.

"What do you mean?"

"Charity. I'm doing this out of the goodness of my heart. I don't think you're guilty and I want to see justice done."

"You believe I'm innocent?"

"Yes. I'm going to *help* you."

The blank expression left his eyes. He focused on Cassandra as though he were seeing her for the first time. *There.* The faint spark rose, his face lifted.

"That's it," Cassandra said. "Start to believe it because it is going to happen. I'm getting you out of here today. Do you understand?"

"I don't know what to say … Why are you doing this?"

"Just say you accept my help."

"Thank you. I do."

"Good. That's the formality out of the way. Now, let's see about getting you bail. It won't be easy but I know a very friendly judge who owes me a favor."

Within a few hours Cassandra was standing in front of a podium in her office conference room, Juniper by her side, as a group of reporters and television crews set up their microphones and tripods around them.

"Why have you decided to take this case, Ms. Moúsa?" asked one reporter.

"Because my client is clearly innocent and I aim to prove it."

"NYPD say that they have overwhelming evidence. How do you intend to prove that Mr. Juniper is innocent?"

"The evidence is purely circumstantial. I have already obtained witness statements to say that they saw Mr. Juniper outside of his apartment at the time of Annabel Linton's death. Correct me if I'm wrong, but no human can be in two places at once."

The reporter laughed. Cassandra smiled. She was now wearing make-up and had removed her reading glasses. Her hair was loose over her shoulders and fell in shiny blonde waves. She looked down the lens of the camera and she knew it loved her. She had great bone structure. She was oozing charisma and the reporters were already on her side. The write-ups might be prejudiced against Juniper, but they would praise Cassandra.

"When I passed the bar, I promised to uphold justice. My client is innocent. And I have every confidence that the evidence is going to support that. Now, if you'll excuse us. Mr. Juniper is very tired and he has been through a lot in the last few days."

With that Cassandra took Juniper's arm and led him out of the room. A few moments later they were hurrying down the steps of her office building and into a waiting limousine.

As he sat back against the plush leather, Juniper believed he had been swept away by a whirlwind. It was a force he had never before encountered and he didn't know whether he was pleased or not to be in the hands of Cassandra Moúsa. She was an anomaly, and he found her both inspiring and intimidating.

Oblivious to her client's doubts and fears Cassandra pulled open the fridge in the back of the car.

"Champagne is in order," she said.

Juniper shook his head. "I don't drink it."

She poured a clear liquid from a crystal decanter into a glass and added ice. "The champagne is for me. I know that you like vodka. Try this."

Juniper took the glass and sipped the contents. Cassandra's fingers momentarily brushed his. Her touch affected him. He lolled back into the seat finally letting the angst and fear of his situation slide away as a feeling of well-being consumed him, even though his conscious mind knew that the emotion was irrational. In the prison, all hope had gradually dwindled away until he experienced guilt for Annabel, even though he knew her death wasn't his fault. In Cassandra's presence, he was starting to believe that he would be found innocent and that this nightmare would soon be over.

"Now the detective on this: Jake Chandler. He's a tough nut to crack. But the thing is his wife died six months ago. An apparent suicide—but Chandler insisted it was murder and he had the whole of his department working to prove it. In the end, his captain sent him home on gardening leave until he agreed to see a shrink. So, he's not infallible."

"That poor man," said Juniper.

"He's the enemy now, Avgustin. Neither of us can feel sorry for him. He's the one that found the evidence that could convict you."

"The spot of blood?"

"Yes."

"It was on the balcony. Just one spot. Nothing else."

"I know," Cassandra said. "He could have planted it. We have to sow that seed of doubt."

"*He would do that*?" Juniper said. "I *didn't* kill Annabel."

"I know you didn't," Cassandra said placing her hand on his arm.

Her fingers and palm were warm against his cold skin. Juniper couldn't imagine feeling that warm again. The cold shock of what had happened to Annabel still burned into his heart and soul as clear as the images Chandler had shown him.

It was difficult to believe his world would ever be normal again.

"Is there anything more you can tell me about what happened?"

"I've already told you everything," Juniper said.

"Any detail you recall. Let's look again at when you arrived home."

Juniper closed his eyes. He didn't want to remember but something in her voice soothed him, coaxing his mind to slip back into those last few moments before he discovered Annabel's fate.

"My front door vas open. I thought I had closed it behind me."

He squeezed his eyes shut harder, concentrating on seeing every detail with his mind's eye.

"I went in the bedroom, and then I zaw …"

He stopped. He didn't know what he had seen and it was hard to describe. The only thing he could think of was blackness. A dark stain out on the balcony. It had moved, and he had thought …

"I don't know …" he said. His voice cracked.

Cassandra took his hand and Juniper's mind cleared again. It was as though a thick fog lifted. He had to think. His *salvation* depended on it. Even as he thought these strange words, Juniper couldn't deny that this was exactly how he felt. This meant more to him than mere imprisonment. It was almost as though his very soul was on the line.

"I saw something …" Juniper said. "I think."

Cassandra waited.

"A shape. A figure. I thought it vas Annabel, but now I realize she vas already dead."

Juniper told her every detail. As the words came out of his mouth he thought she would think him totally insane. How would she possibly believe in this dark figure, looming like the shadow of death on his balcony.

"But when I vent out there was no one there," he concluded. "I didn't mention it to the police. I knew they wouldn't believe me. I didn't even think I had really seen anything. Until now."

"Interesting," was all she said.

"You believe me?"

"Yes. But Chandler won't. You did the right thing not telling him. For example, where did this figure you saw go? No. The truth won't help you at all right now. So, we are going to keep this completely to ourselves."

"What do we do then?" Juniper asked.

"In my experience, the way to win this sort of case is to throw doubt on the investigator's handling of evidence. Discredit Chandler for example. We imply he planted the blood sample to make his case against you easier. The defense in the O.J. Simpson trial used evidence to cast doubt on the investigators' honesty for example. A synthetic preservative, known as EDTA, was found in the blood smeared on O.J.'s gate. It couldn't have naturally been in the blood of the victim. We need something like this because reasonable doubt will help you to be found innocent. Or, we find another reason for the blood to have been on the balcony. A nose bleed perhaps."

"Annabel didn't have a nose bleed. At least I didn't zee it."

"We'll talk about this again. But we might have to … elaborate a little on the evening you spent with her. In a way that the police can accept."

"Elaborate?"

"Yes. Sometimes the jury needs to have ideas and information given to them that makes them wonder about the validity of evidence."

Juniper closed his eyes. It was all too much to take in. All he wanted to do was sleep.

"Anyway. Leave all of that to me. For now, you need to go back and prepare for your exhibition. I've been liaising with Joy Awen."

"Zhe gallery owner?" Juniper said as his memory returned.

Yes, there had been a planned life before this tragedy. He opened his eyes and studied Cassandra as though seeing her for the very first time.

"The event is now sold out, but we've put it back a few weeks in order to make the most of the publicity. Everyone who is anyone wants to see your work and I guarantee it's *all* going to sell. So you see, Avgustin, you might just be able to afford to pay me after all. And I can tell you this, I'll be worth every penny."

"Making money on Annabel's death," Juniper said. "That is all so cynical. I don't like it."

"Don't kid yourself that by refusing this opportunity now you will be able to bring her back."

Juniper looked sharply at Cassandra. She was a cold, calculating bitch. But of course! She was an attorney after all. Juniper put his head in his hands to try and dull the ache that had begun again behind his eyes.

"I loved her ..." he murmured.

"Of course you did," Cassandra's voice softened. "I'm doing this for your own good. We're going to get you acquitted, but don't be stupid, Avgustin."

Juniper didn't answer.

"She was your *muse*, right?"

Juniper nodded.

"I know all about muses. My family is Greek you know. I think Annabel would want you to carry on."

"I ... don't know. It was so new, so soon."

The limo came to a halt. Juniper glanced up and saw that they had arrived at his apartment. His stomach churned. He hadn't been here in over a week. The jail had become his asylum. Now he didn't want to open the car door. He didn't want to go outside or inside. He had an overwhelming fear of a world where such evil could exist.

"Come. I need you to show me which pieces are to be moved to the gallery and what you need to take with you to continue your work."

"What do you mean, 'take with me'?"

"I have already sorted out a studio for you in my apartment. You won't be disturbed and there will be security around the clock."

Relief flushed his cheeks, but suspicion soon followed.

"Why?"

"We have to keep you safe, Avgustin. And I want to make sure that you are kept away from the media most of all. They will try to trip you up. Get you to say things or just misquote you."

"I won't speak to anyone."

"Of course you won't. But you can't underestimate the power of the press. Some will champion you. Some will make you look guilty. We can't take the risk that they say anything that we don't control. Plus, there are the death threats to contend with."

"Death threats?" Juniper said.

"Yes. Someone sent an anonymous email to my office threatening to send you where you sent Annabel."

"I did not hurt Annabel!"

"I believe you," Cassandra took his hand.

Juniper allowed it, but his fingers were as numb as his soul.

"These creeps don't care. They get off on it," Cassandra continued. "The only clear future for you is one where you are found completely innocent. That's why I'm taking you to my place."

"I don't want to go inside …" he said.

Cassandra squeezed his hand. "You won't be doing this alone."

Juniper fell quiet.

The door opened and he was hurried outside, flanked by two bodyguards in black suits, before he had time to voice any further concerns. The goons were wearing dark glasses and ear pieces, as though they were involved in national security. A group of paparazzi who had made camp outside the apartment sprang into action in an attempt to get just one clear shot of

Juniper, but the men blocked him from the cameras as he was bustled into the apartment lobby.

The elevator doors were wedged open and two more men in black waited as Juniper was led inside. He couldn't even see Cassandra as the men surrounded him. The doors closed and for once the machinery was in full working order.

Inside his apartment he found a team of men waiting for instruction.

"Who are these people?" Juniper asked.

"They are from the gallery. They are here to safely pack up and take the art for the exhibit. Joy has already been here and has put sticky notes on the ones she's most interested in. You just have to say 'yes' and we let them pack."

Juniper's eyes fell on the portrait of Annabel. "Not that one," he said removing the yellow sticker note from the side of the canvas.

Cassandra looked at the painting. "It's very beautiful, but I'm sure you could improve it still further."

"No. I can't. I just want to destroy it."

"Don't be ridiculous, Avgustin. That painting is going to make you at least one million dollars."

Juniper frowned. He knew that Cassandra was trying to help him, but he didn't like this mercenary side of her. Taking money for this painting was cold, evil.

"I don't want to sell it," he said.

Juniper watched her walk from canvas to canvas. He followed her around agreeing all of the other paintings for the gallery.

"Good," Cassandra said. "Hold out and it will be worth much more in the end. I have to say you have a great deal of talent … but in some of your work …"

"What?"

"Sometimes it lacks … ambition. But then most artists are like that. You paint for the love of it, don't you?"

Juniper didn't know what to respond but then realized that her question was rhetorical.

"Joy will be pleased," Cassandra said finally when the last canvas was packed and the men began to move them out into the service elevator.

"I hope I don't need to tell you that you have to cash in on your notoriety right now. Once you're found innocent, the value of your art will drop."

Juniper focused on the idea of his innocence but her point went home and he began to realize that this might be his only chance at fame and success. Although it wasn't what drove him —she had been right on that—it was still important to sell some of his art so that he could pay his bills. Money in the bank would help him in the future. A man accused of a crime that has no money is rarely found innocent. But a man with money could pay for the right help to prove his innocence. He could see the logic even as he resented it.

As the gallery men left, two more men arrived. They looked more like the other bodyguards than removals professionals but still they wrapped Juniper's canvases, taking great care with the portrait of Annabel, and he told them which of his tools and paints he needed. Then Cassandra led him out of his apartment and to the service elevator.

"The limo's out back now. We wanted the paparazzi to see you come in but not leave."

"A ruse," Juniper said.

Cassandra smiled. "There is always a point to everything I do. You'll learn to trust me eventually."

Cassandra pulled the heavy shutters closed behind them, and the descended into the back storeroom of the building where two more men waited for them.

Outside in the alley Juniper found himself looking over to the still cordoned area where Annabel's body had been found. He was haunted by the memory of their last night together, and his mind juxtaposed images of her in his bed with the photographs of her lying, mutilated in the alley.

"Did you see what that zhat animal did to her? *On zhe chudovishche!*" he murmured. "He is a monster."

"What did you say?" asked Cassandra as she pushed him into the back of the car.

Juniper didn't answer, his mind was elsewhere and he forced it to stay in the happiness of Annabel's smile. What he had felt for her, given time together, could have been something wonderful. Now he would never know where it would have ended. Those dreams, those visions of a blissful future were gone forever. Juniper couldn't imagine ever feeling happy again.

CHAPTER FOUR

Joy Awen put down the phone and stared into space.

The call had been from Cassandra Moúsa and Joy knew exactly who Cassandra was. She had seen enough of her in the papers to know that she would more than likely get Juniper off—even if he was guilty.

What could have been a complete disaster was now working in her favor. Joy couldn't have asked for a better opportunity to launch an unknown artist onto New York's elite collectors.

Joy sighed as she remembered the first time she had met Avgustin Juniper. It was at a party. Juniper was drunk, and somehow they had ended up sharing the same cab. Joy had seen something in him that made her curious enough to go up to his apartment. Of course Juniper hadn't known who she was. She was just a woman he had met that he found vaguely attractive.

"I have wodka," he had said throwing open the door after fumbling drunkenly for several minutes with the lock.

"I think maybe you've had enough to drink." Joy had laughed.

She was about to leave, but then Juniper turned on the lights and she saw the studio. Most of the canvases were covered with old gray sheets and as Juniper went into his small kitchen to fetch them both drinks, Joy gave in to her curiosity and lifted the sheet up from the nearest canvas.

That was when she saw a painting of girl lying semi-clad on a chaise. The art was severely flawed. It was raw, sloppy, but so completely unspoiled that Joy knew immediately that Juniper was something new.

He returned with a glass of vodka, neat—not even any ice—and so she sipped it gingerly. She had found the drink to be surprisingly nice. A revelation because whiskey was her usual tipple.

"Good quality," Juniper said, thick-tongued. "None of dot cheap European crop. Dis is d'genuine article."

Joy looked him over. He was charming in a kind of unkempt way. Eccentric to the point of genius and it was obvious that he really didn't know how good he was. She also found the accent sexy. She knew it would appeal to some of the wealthy frustrated women she often sold to. And it would make some of the business people feel like they were being very cosmopolitan.

She had pulled him to her and kissed him full on the lips. A few weeks later, this was exactly what Annabel Linton would do, in that very same room.

Juniper had responded as any red-blooded male would do and Joy let him lead her to his bedroom.

He stripped her. She was under no illusions about her figure, she was overly skinny, somewhat emaciated, despite the fact that she ate regular high-calorie meals. Her metabolism didn't allow her to put on weight. And her breasts were the size of a twelve-year-old girl's who hadn't quite started puberty. Even so, she was striking and well-groomed. Her mouse-brown hair was nice when she let it down from the severe bun she always wore.

Plus, Joy loved sex, and she gave herself to it with enthusiasm.

Juniper was a rough, clumsy lover but she had enjoyed it. It was, after all, what she had been looking for when she had leaped into the cab with him in the first place. Vigorous sex with no strings: the best kind.

She had stayed the night and in the morning, while Juniper slept off his hangover, Joy looked at more of the canvases, particularly the one that currently stood on the easel. It was of a very young and naturally beautiful girl. She had the figure that Joy had always craved, slender but with curves, and her natural breasts were full and ripe.

Behind the sheets she had found more of the same girl, some portraits, some dressed as a goddess or other renaissance beauty. The poses and situations Juniper had chosen were somewhat clichéd but Joy liked the execution of them. There was a flow in the brush strokes that showed passion.

She had glanced over to the bedroom door, half expecting Juniper to find her looking at his art, but he was sleeping soundly. She wanted to know who the model was—why she inspired Juniper so much. After all, these pictures were clearly his best and contained the most detail as though they somehow deserved more care than all of the others. It was then that she decided to tell Juniper who she was.

Exhibitions in her gallery were coveted. Joy rarely gave space to unknowns because, first and foremost, she wanted to make money, but she had an overwhelming urge to help Juniper. She had taken him coffee and sat down on the edge of the bed and began talking nonstop as he pulled himself up into a sitting position.

"I love your art. You have real talent but it's unfocused."

Then she explained who she was and what she wanted to do for him. "I hope you realize what an honor this is, Avgustin. I don't open my doors to just any artist and I will only do so if you listen to my advice. This makes me your art editor. There are some changes I'd like you to make to some of the paintings. There are too many of the same girl, and so you need to get in some new models, keep the bodies but substitute the faces with someone new. Otherwise there will be too much of the same thing."

Avgustin was shocked, he didn't touch the coffee and instead had demanded more vodka.

"No vodka," Joy had said. "You have work to do."

It hadn't taken Joy long to persuade Juniper to do what she asked. He had, like all artists, wanted recognition, and now he had found it. With her help, he might even make some money too.

Back in the present, Joy blinked and looked down at her desk. It wasn't much to ask but she was a little uncomfortable about promoting Juniper now that he was accused of murder. She was a businesswoman though, and she knew that this terrible tragedy was just the kind of publicity that would ensure a success for the exhibition. Already the private collectors were asking for a painting of the dead girl. It was somewhat distasteful, but Joy had decided to find the altered paintings and have them restored back to their original state. Juniper probably wouldn't like it, but the contract he had signed with her gave her more authority than he realized.

She wondered at her own motives. She had been a little jealous when she had seen Annabel lovingly recreated on canvas. At the time, she hadn't known whether the girl was important to Juniper or if she was even a real model. But it soon became obvious that real or imagined she had been his inspiration. All of the greats had them, and Joy understood that, but she had tried to control Juniper and had, in the process, almost destroyed the art that would make him truly famous. All except one that is. She had seen the new portrait on Juniper's easel and she had known then, that this one was to be Juniper's finest piece.

It brought her back to her conversation with Cassandra Moúsa.

"The portrait is unfinished," Cassandra had said. "But I can persuade Avgustin to complete it."

"He must be in a terrible state," Joy said. "How do you propose to do that?"

"Leave it to me. If you find a private buyer that is willing to pay the price, Avgustin will do it. Money always talks in the end."

"I have buyers. There … could be … an auction?"

"A private one," Cassandra said. "If the press got hold of this, it might seem … offensive."

Joy agreed to complete privacy. She didn't want her reputation sullied any more than Cassandra did, plus she knew the collectors who would want this piece. One of whom she had sold several portraits to. He was particularly fond of Picasso, but Juniper's fine art would appeal to him just the same with this kind of history.

Joy flicked through her contacts book and found the numbers of several potential, and discreet, buyers. Then she picked up her phone and began to dial. This one was a wealthy businessman.

An hour later she had set up an auction date and time with five different, prudent, buyers.

CHAPTER FIVE

Jake Chandler inserted his front door key into the lock and entered the hallway of his house, hesitating before he closed the door behind him. He was bone weary: tired to the point of physical pain.

Chandler lived out of town, on the way to Queens, in a small house, just off the main freeway. It was a quiet neighborhood, occupied by many of his colleagues and therefore had a low crime rate.

He had bought the house for his wife, Jules. They had both loved the layout on the very first viewing, and even though the place needed work, they had the same vision and could see the potential.

"We can't raise kids in an apartment," Jules had said. "But this place is perfect."

Once the house was theirs, Jules had taken pride in painting and decorating it herself while Chandler worked. But their dream turned sour when Jules became sick.

After several consultations and many tests, they learned that Jules had multiple sclerosis; it was destroying her body at an alarming rate. Within a few months of moving into their dream home, Jules couldn't walk without the aid of a walking stick. Then there were the attacks that confined her to bed. She couldn't walk in a straight line during those times, even with the stick.

The memories of their happy plans always flooded Chandler as he entered the hall. It was why he always hesitated just for a fraction of a second every time he came into his home.

He glanced to the right and looked into the darkness of the room there.

"And this … will be the play room," Jules had said. He could still hear the happy giggle she made as she had entered the then empty room for the first time.

Now the room was filled with adult furniture.

Chandler flicked the light switch on and stared into the room without seeing it. He barely noticed the expensive dining table and chairs, or the bureau containing Royal Doulton china. What he saw was how the room should have been. He imagined it full of children's toys, with Jules sitting in a rocking chair, holding the baby they had so desperately wanted. Her beautiful smile would light up her eyes in that girlish excited way she had.

But that was never to be.

His mind flashed a montage of images: bottles of pills, medicines, lumbar punctures with tubes of fluid being drawn from his wife's spine. All he wanted to remember were her smiles, but the suffering he had seen sometimes blighted the good memories.

Chandler turned back to the hallway switching on lights as he went across to the room opposite. He hated the darkness now, and the empty feeling the house had when he returned home. In the living room, he turned on the television. The noise helped—otherwise the house was too still, too quiet, too empty.

In the kitchen, he turned on the radio and opened the fridge, pulling free a TV dinner which he placed in the microwave. Then he poured a large measure of gin into a glass, added ice, lemon and a splash of tonic. He sipped it, grimacing at the strong taste before adding more tonic water.

The microwave pinged and he withdrew the meal, placing the melting plastic quickly down on the breakfast bar. He peeled back the cover, picked up a fork and began to eat the tasteless contents direct from the packet. He hardly ever used the plates that Jules had carefully chosen.

"You want to be ashamed of yourself. In that condition, at this time of the day!" an old woman had said as Jules had staggered down the street, trying to get home after taking ill in the supermarket.

When she told Chandler the story later, she laughed that someone had thought she was drunk, but he could see that she was putting on a brave face. It was a typically New York cruel, unfeeling, judgment based on what this person thought they were seeing, but having no understanding that his wife had a serious illness. It made Chandler angry even though there was no way he could protect Jules from this kind of negativity.

They let it go, moved forward. Tried to keep positive while trying new treatments that seemed to work for a short time, but invariably ended in Jules having a relapse. Chandler was grateful for the medical insurance his job gave him and his wife. Without it he couldn't imagine how they would have coped.

"I want a child," Jules told the specialist one day. "Maybe we should go ahead with that now."

"In your condition that would be inadvisable," replied the doctor. "With MS as severe as yours, pregnancy would only accelerate the disease."

The MS was already advancing faster than the medication could mitigate it. Not that it was very effective to begin with. There was really nothing the doctors could do for this kind of degenerative disease, other than treat the symptoms and pump his wife full of steroids that bloated her lovely features. But for all of this, Jules put on a brave face. She never complained and, if anything, made light of the situation.

As he ate his microwave meal, Chandler remembered how Jules had loved this kitchen. She had been a great cook but as the months following the diagnosis dragged on she had let a lot of things slide. It wasn't that she was too sick to clean or cook, not physically anyway, but she had lost something. Some pride or love for the house. He didn't know which. Chandler just knew that she resented the place as though everything here was bad luck.

I should have known how bad things had become. I should have noticed.

He *had* noticed on some level. As usual he had been working hard. One homicide led to another and he found himself leading a serial murder case. It took up so much of his waking hours. His work days became longer but he didn't think Jules minded because she never complained.

Then the death threats came; supposedly from the killer he was hunting. He began to send Chandler notes and messages, telling him that he would make his wife the next victim. The detective had to take it seriously and report it to his senior. After that an officer began to sit outside their house every day.

By then Jules could barely look after herself. Chandler had hired someone to come in and help every day and take care of the shopping. Jules was bedridden, catheterized. She rallied slower after each relapse. He wasn't sure how long each bout would go on for. But at least it meant that he didn't have to complicate the surveillance. Jules wasn't going out so the monitoring all happened at home.

Chandler didn't tell Jules about the threats. He hadn't wanted to worry her and they were so close to finding the killer that he knew she wouldn't be in any danger.

The real menace of course was already there. It was festering inside her like a poisoned, rotting seed and it had started the day the doctor told her she could never have children. All that time when he was busy, Jules was quietly losing her mind, and Chandler hadn't noticed.

What kind of husband was I? How could I ever have said I loved you when I didn't know what you were going through?

Chandler threw the empty food carton into the trash and tossed his fork into the sink. It wouldn't matter. His cleaning lady took care of his home now and she would be visiting tomorrow. Not that he was ever home enough to really mess the place up.

Chandler climbed the stairs and halted at the top before entering the bathroom. He couldn't go inside without first remembering. This was where he had found her: naked, her head resting on the toilet bowl as though she had accidentally fallen asleep. And he might have thought that but for the blood and vomit and shit that covered the floor.

She had tried to end her life the obvious way at first. Slashed her wrist but didn't realize that once she had cut the tendon in one arm it would become useless and she couldn't cut the other arm. Then she had taken pills. But her body conspired against her and she vomited them up while soiling herself. She had taken her clothes off in an attempt to clean herself up. The slow, but steady, blood loss weakened her so much that she barely had energy. Forensics said that she had tried to clean up the mess from the floor. Chandler could only imagine the effort it would have been for her in her current condition. That was when she thought to use the bleach.

The room had reeked of it.

Chandler couldn't even imagine what must have been going through her mind in order to make her drink the stuff. Maybe she thought it would help her die sooner. The result of course was agony. The pain of dying was on her face, and Chandler would never forget her frozen expression.

Chandler closed his eyes. The memory burned behind his lids and he was overwhelmed by it once more. It was so completely horrible and cruel. His wife had been so beautiful, yet now all he could remember was the awful state he had found her in. The overpowering odor of bleach filled his nostrils, even though Chandler knew there was none in the house.

He covered his mouth and nose, breathed deeply through his fingers. As he calmed, the feelings of loss receded and were replaced by his fury.

He reached out and switched on the light. The bathroom, clean and stain free, lit up and he took a step into the room pushing his rage up until his cheeks flushed and his jaw clenched.

He stared at himself in the cabinet mirror above the sink. He looked crazed. His gray eyes slightly cold, spittle forced itself between his teeth. If anyone deserved to be insane, Chandler knew it was him. But the anger was short-lived no matter how he forced it. He couldn't hate her selfishness, nor blame her for not telling him how unhappy she had been. Deep down he believed he had been the egocentric one, and that his blindness to her grief had made him a failure. He had promised to love and keep her. He had thought they would see old age together. He had failed her in every way he could.

Regret followed and the tears came as they did every night since her death. Chandler felt like a drowning man who constantly gasped in mouthfuls of air to prolong his agony. Sometimes he thought about following her, but therein laid the biggest rub. He was not brave enough to end it all. Despite everything, he would carry on living, and hope, like his shrink said, that one day he would be able to enter the bathroom and not remember.

He turned on the tap, filled the sink and swilled his face in cold water. As he pulled the plug he heard his house phone calling and hurried from the bathroom into his bedroom.

"Jake? How are you this evening?"

It was Lauren Michaels, his shrink. Talk of the devil.

"The same. You know how it is."

"Do you need to talk?" Lauren asked.

"I'll be okay until the session tomorrow."

"That's why I'm calling. I have to go out of town for a few days. I won't be available tomorrow, but I wanted to give you my cell phone number in case you need me."

Chandler wrote down the number on the pad he kept by the phone.

"I'm interested in talking about your new case with you," Lauren said. "How are you coping? I saw the news report, and that Cassandra Moúsa is involved."

"Yes. Moúsa's been a pain, and she loves the media."

"Perhaps you should back out of this one?" Lauren suggested. "Another high-profile case might be the last thing you need right now."

Chandler said nothing for a moment as he thought through her words.

"Is that the captain's wishes or do you really think that?" he asked finally.

"Jake, I don't answer to the force, even though they pay me to see you. Our chats are confidential and they will stay that way. It's my job to take care of *you* and make the best suggestions for you, not your bosses. I'm worried about you, but if you think you can handle this then I will do my best to support you. What I do ask is this: think it over. This is a lot of stress at a very crucial stage of your grieving process. It might be too much for you right now."

"Okay. I'll think on it. But, Dr. … Lauren … I find work helps take my mind off things. Doing nothing is worse."

"All right. I'll trust your instincts on this. But if you need me, call. Night or day."

"Thanks."

Chandler stared at the number on the pad for a moment. He sighed. He couldn't help wondering if Lauren was right, but the case was interesting and he didn't feel as though he could pass it on.

This revelation surprised him. For the past few months he had been "going through the motions" with little or no real interest in the investigations beyond the facts and evidence. His emotions had, strangely, become entangled in this one. Though he couldn't understand why.

He pulled his cell phone from his pocket and began to add Lauren's number to his contacts.

He was aware that he had begun to rely on her. He recognized that sinking feeling when she said she would be away, and that he wouldn't see her tomorrow: disappointment. She kept him grounded and he was glad that she had called that evening, even if he didn't want to do what she suggested. There was something about discussing things with her that made decisions become clearer.

He had, in fact, been toying with passing this case on to someone else until the very moment that she called. Now he knew that he had to see this through for his own sanity. His future mental health depended on it. Win or lose, he would go up against Cassandra Moúsa and provide the evidence and facts for the court to decide Juniper's guilt or innocence. Whatever that was yet, Chandler wasn't sure. Then again, maybe this was the egotistical side of him that had always led him down the wrong path.

INTERLUDE

DIARY OF PABLO PICASSO

I don't know why I am driven to write these words.

I keep recalling Malaga in 1899. I was eighteen at the time. My career in Spain was going nowhere. Despite learning my craft from my father, I felt I still had much to discover about art and the world. I needed to move away, develop now in my own way, and open up to the warm influence of a muse.

That was when I met her. I suppose I was ripe for the picking.

She took me to bed and whispered to me afterwards as I slept. She told me in my dreams of my great future. Explaining all the hardship I must endure first. I didn't think this was anything more than a dream at the time. Even so, a few days later I began to make plans to leave Spain and the urge to move on grew until I couldn't remain in the country of my birth any longer.

In 1900 I found my way to Paris. By then I had almost forgotten this mysterious woman who had told me she was a seer. In Paris I met numerous women and enjoyed many good times. But they all drifted away from me, or I tired of them, because none gave me the inspiration I craved. I worked hard, not always with success, and some of those hardships that had been predicted came to fruition.

I looked always for new models to bring a fresh element to my work. I had live-in lovers, friends – or rather hangers on – who spent time admiring my work, cooing with appreciation and sycophantic expression.

But then I met Marcelle. She had red hair and blue eyes and was all I needed—for a time.

"I want to paint you," I said. I saw her as she loitered in the market place. How could I resist?

"I've heard that line before," she said. She walked away from the market, I followed.

"I'm an artist."

"Of course you are."

My French was imperfect at the time, unlike her own. Yet somehow I knew she hadn't been born there.

"You aren't a local girl," I said. "You have a freeness about you. As though you don't belong anywhere, but belong everywhere all the same."

She laughed. "You're insane."

She cast her eyes around the market place: as though challenging all the other women who stood and watched as we passed by.

"What is your name?" I asked. And when she told me, I frowned. "We've met before, haven't we?" She was so familiar to me. My mind flashed back to Spain and to my muse there.

Marcelle merely said, "How could we?"

I saw her in the market many times before she finally agreed to let me paint her. By then I was having success selling my works to wealthy Americans. I even offered to pay her for her time.

But I had a problem that held my interest in Marcelle at bay. My mistress, Fernande Olivier. Fernande was a jealous lover and never let me paint other women without her supervision. Marcelle offered me a solution: I could set up a studio in her apartment.

"I'm modest and I wouldn't like others to see me," she said. "There are always too many people around at your place. And I wouldn't want your wife to misunderstand…."

"She's not my wife," I said, but accepted her offer and slowly

moved in blank canvases, an easel, and all the paints and brushes I would need.

I painted Marcelle for the first time and posed her wearing nothing but a white sheet. Only one breast was exposed, and part of one leg. But the painting didn't please me, it angered me.

I destroyed the canvas before Marcelle had a chance to see it.

"Picasso, what's wrong?" she asked.

"I must paint what I see. But still it isn't right," I tried to explain.

"I'm sure it was wonderful. Please, start again. And let me see it this time."

I went back to work and Marcelle had stood patiently, posing for me. As was my want, I refused to let her see the painting until I finished it a few days later.

I had drawn her face very much in the style of my earlier Spanish art, but now there were artifacts appearing in the picture. Marcelle had inspired me to draw on something I had seen in the market place: African masks and artwork. The painting was full of these things with her, looking so normal, and so beautiful, in the center of it all.

"You need other models," she suggested to me. "Women willing to pose for you, perhaps some could wear the masks."

I agreed. The fire of stimulation had been ignited behind my eyes.

I took a fresh canvas and my easel and paints and left her for several days.

Eventually I returned with the new painting. Marcelle looked younger than ever, as though she had been renewed somehow, revitalized. I placed it on the easel and Marcelle roused herself from her bed and came to look.

"What do you think?" I asked.

She looked at the painting. Five women, all nude, and two wore African masks as she had suggested. One was in a very provocative pose where she squatted, legs apart.

"What will you call it?" she asked.

"Le Bordel d'Avignon," *I said.*

"The Brothel of Avignon," Marcelle repeated and she laughed loud and hearty, drunk on my art. "I love it."

Looking back, this was the moment my true greatness began.

CHAPTER SIX

Maria Matthews looked back at the imposing structure of the Statue of Liberty as it receded into the distance. The sun was setting over the horizon. It was the time of day she loved the most and she was heading back to Manhattan on the Staten Island ferry to join some of her friends for drinks. They were all meeting up in Madison Square Park at one of their favorite bars. Maria hoped that the boy she liked would also be there that evening.

She was wearing a thigh-length black denim skirt and a white crop top underneath a long, warm coat because the ferry journey was always cold. Even so, she enjoyed sitting outside looking at the bay and the Manhattan skyline as the ferry approached the docking bay. It was so calm and tranquil and the city lights glittered like low-lying stars. It was magical.

I'm such a city girl, she thought.

She smiled as she remembered her awful cousins who lived out in the sticks. Their lack of sophistication and awe as they came to visit one year had been a source of embarrassment and Maria had refused to take the two boys and one girl out to meet her friends. Her parents had been angry, but they had given in when she explained her reasons carefully. "Mom, they just don't fit in here. You want to make me a laughingstock at school?"

Her parents had let it slide. They trusted her fortunately. She was generally a good-natured and reliable girl. It was rare that she would refuse them anything. And Susie, her sister, hadn't minded taking care of the relatives that weekend because she didn't have any particular plans.

Maria turned her head and watched the statue vanish into the distance as the ferry drew closer to the dock. She had thought she was alone outside and so she jumped slightly when she saw someone move at the end of the row of seats. Once aware of the presence, she narrowed her eyes to try to see more. There was a dark shadow near the door and the lights weren't working in that part of the deck.

Vandals, she thought. Her mother's snobbery reared inside her as though she were far older than her twenty-one years. *Goddam street kids have nothing better to do …*

The darkness shimmered and Maria looked harder but couldn't make out the figure. She stood up and went to the rail, looking out over the sea as the sun finally went down. It appeared to be swallowed up, snuffed by the black ocean. Through the corner of her eye she thought she saw the figure mimic her movements at the other end of the deck, but when she looked directly there, all she could see was a dark void. She shrugged. It was probably just her imagination.

She had seen all sorts of things on this ferry over the years and nothing really scared her. Manhattan was her home. She knew all of its dark secrets, and she knew how to protect herself. Even when the city had gone crazy a few years back, with people marauding and violence escalating, she had kept herself safe. As she thought of this, her hand went into her pocket and felt for the pepper spray canister there. It was something her mother had insisted she carried and Maria did so out of habit.

The ferry was approaching the dock and so Maria went back

inside and headed towards the exit gate because it would open as soon as the boat was docked. The ferry rocked as the buffers touched the sides of the dock, but the rocking wasn't much to worry about, she was used to it.

The door to the seating decks opened behind her and she glanced back to see a group of teenage girls coming through. They were giggling and loud and as they approached, Maria could smell beer on them. She observed that none of the girls could be older than sixteen, but it made her smile. She had been just like them, not that many years ago.

The bridge clunked into place and the door opened in front of her, but the five girls pushed their way forward and out before Maria could react.

"Rude!" she said before following.

She glanced over at the station. The big glass partition door that held back the next influx of passengers was lit up from inside like a huge window. Anonymous faces stared through the glass, eager to board the ferry and be on their way out of the City. Maria barely noticed them as she followed the teenagers out towards the exit and onto the main road.

Sometimes she would get a taxi from here to Madison Square Park, but she had spent too much of her salary that month already on buying a watch. It was a special piece, with a large oval mosaic face. The tiny mosaic made up a picture. Susie had said it was based a bust of Picasso. Her sister was studying fine art at NYU and she had been the one to point out the watch in the window of Tiffany's. Maria was really taken with it. She saved up for months and she had been so close to reaching her goal. Then she noticed the watch had been reduced, and even though she knew it would be a tight month, she was afraid that it would be sold. She had bought it on impulse—it seemed too good an opportunity to miss. But it meant that her cash flow was even tighter than usual. So, she had cut down significantly on her social spending to make up the short-fall. That night she really couldn't waste anything on a taxi. Subway it would have to be.

Maria glanced at her watch now. It was seven-thirty. She had plenty of time to get uptown and meet her friends.

She set off, heading towards the subway station and 23rd Street. The park area was quiet but Maria could see that there were still a few tourists around. There always were. This was New York!

She gripped her bag to her as she walked. Too many times she'd seen people on the streets have their belongings snatched by a passing thief.

"Sensible …" said a voice behind her.

Maria looked over her shoulder. She saw a dark silhouette standing on the grass, but the street lamp's light didn't reach the face. The voice was low and she wasn't sure if the speaker was male or female.

She swallowed and picked up her pace. Then, an icy hand fell on the back of her neck.

Maria's stomach lurched with dread. She tried to pull away but the fingers caught hold of her and tightened. She was lifted, feet dangling above the ground: one of her shoes slipped off back down to the grass. A gurgling gasp of terror bubbled from her lips but fear paralyzed her throat: she was incapable of screaming.

The person or thing, because surely no human had such strength, turned her around. A thumb dug into the front of Maria's throat, cutting off her oxygen as it seemed to reposition its hand. She found herself facing a black void. She blinked. There was no one in front of her, yet she couldn't see the park either. Her bulging eyes darted over where the face should have been.

As light shadowed the darkness, she saw the shape of the thing. A tall, dark figure that had no real substance. It was there but unseen. It was as though light repelled the form. Like an old negative in the days when photographs had to be developed. Or maybe she was suddenly struck blind. Maria didn't know. She just knew she was more afraid right then than any moment in her life.

Her body twitched and jerked. Her bladder vented, spoiling the denim mini-skirt as urine dripped down her legs, over her feet, one shod, the other bare. She smelt her own stink, and her already choking throat began to dry heave, while waves of shame washed over her.

The thing began to move, taking her with it, at impossible speed. Branches whipped Maria's face as she was pulled into the nearby brush. She tried to make a sound but the creature tightened its grasp on her throat and her larynx closed. She barely knew she was crying until the tears dampened her cheeks and all she could think about was the indignity of wetting herself.

Maria felt herself slipping away, terror and lack of oxygen making her slither into a blessed unconsciousness. As the stranglehold tightened, and her breath was cut off, it occurred to her that she was dying. Panic shook the dark threads of unconscious away, she struggled properly for the first time, kicking and thrashing in a desperate attempt to live. Her feet connected with something, but it didn't feel solid, or human.

Her whole life did not flash before her eyes, but as she fell into the darkness, she worried about the boy she had been planning to meet. Would he even miss her?

Maria woke.

Cold and damp seeped in her limbs as she realized her back was on wet grass. It took a moment for her thoughts to coalesce. She could see again, albeit through bleary, tear-filled eyes. She tried to move but her body was frozen. It was as if someone had given her a drug that had cut off the parts of her brain that controlled her central nervous system. For a moment, she couldn't remember where she was or how she got there. What had happened? Her throat hurt and she took in a deep rasping breath. She blinked away the tears. She tried to raise her arm, but the strength hadn't returned yet. She turned her head as she glimpsed light peeking through the bushes and then she remembered. She was in Battery Park. Someone, no *something,* had grabbed her, pulled her into the dark.

The dark specter was gone.

Jesus! I've been raped!

And the thought of telling her parents, the look of horror on their faces, consumed the fear that raged inside her. *I'm okay. I'm alive.* She had survived whatever her assailant had done and she had been unconscious. She didn't know, hadn't really experienced it. All was fine. She was alive after all. Wasn't that all that mattered?

Her left arm twitched. Life was returning to her limbs and she found herself able to turn her head to look down the length of it, see her fingers moving. She wriggled them, then slowly raised her hand to her face. She *was* fine. This was an ordeal, but maybe she wouldn't tell anyone about it. Maybe she didn't have to put her folks through that. A rush of guilt colored her cheeks. All her mother's warnings; never leave your drink unattended; never let a stranger give you a lift; stay in lit areas; always get taxis even if it means you have less money for the evening. And the mace … she hadn't even had time to put her hand into her pocket. Hadn't thought to. It had all been so sudden, so horribly quick.

Her mind was in turmoil. She knew this was her fault, but how could anyone imagine this would happen in so public a place as Battery Park? She never walked through Central Park at night. It was obvious that this would not be a good idea, but Battery was usually populated.

Yet, no one had come to her rescue. No one had heard her scream. But then, she hadn't screamed, had she?

She closed her eyes, then opened them immediately when

the darkness reminded her too much of the *thing* that had taken her from the bench.

I have to get up, straighten myself up and go home. I can say I fell, that's why my clothes are messy, that's why I came home early.

She didn't know the time, or how long she had been lying here. Then she remembered her watch, on her right arm. She lifted it. It felt heavier than the other one, but also strangely light, which didn't make any sense at all.

She rolled onto her side, and pushed herself up with her left arm. She put her weight on her right arm, but fell back to the ground again. Something was wrong here.

She raised her right arm and found herself staring at a void where the lower part of her arm should be. It took a moment for her to make sense of the fact that her arm, from the elbow down, was missing. There was no blood. It just wasn't there.

Panic rushed into her ears. Her face flushed. Then she pushed herself up into a sitting position with her left arm and stared at the empty space where her right arm should have been.

I'm losing my mind. This isn't real.

Her arm was gone. Definitely gone. She glanced down at her torso. She expected to see her clothing torn, her panties ripped away. But all was intact. Her coat was the only thing that had been removed and it had been bunched up under her head like a cushion, as though her attacker really didn't want her to be uncomfortable.

Maria shook her head. She was shivering violently and not just from the cold. *I'm in shock!* She needed help. Someone else to look at her arm and tell her it was still there, that she was just in shock after the attack.

"Help!" she croaked. Her throat hurt so much she could barely talk. She was bruised, inside and out. Every part of her body ached from the strain of the assault, or maybe from her resistance to it. And her throat felt like she had tried to swallow something whole and it was stuck there. Panic overwhelmed her again. She imagined she couldn't breathe, and her mouth opened as she gasped in air until she fell back dizzy and nauseated.

Stop it, she told herself. *You're fine. You* can *breathe.* She lay for a moment forcing her chest to slow its desperate gasping, then she forced herself up on her knees, using her left arm to support herself.

She glanced around. Her other shoe had somehow been lost and her handbag was nowhere to be seen. She had to get out of the bushes, find help and tell someone what had happened.

She stumbled to her feet feeling imbalanced as she cradled the stump of her right arm. All she could think about was that her expensive watch was gone. Stolen. Along with her lower arm. The assistant who had sold it to her had said it was a one-of-a-kind. It was irreplaceable.

The tears came again as she focused on the loss of the watch. Anything but think about the arm. The most terrible loss of all!

She pushed her way through the bushes towards the light. Battery Park looked little different from the moments before her assailant had pulled her into the darkness. There was a bench just ahead. It was hard to believe she had been so near to the path. By the bench she found her heeled shoes, one tipped over, the other still upright and her purse underneath.

How long had she been out?

She heard voices as a couple approached, walking arm in arm along the path.

"Help," she gasped.

The woman drew a breath as her eyes fell on Maria's arm. Maria blinked when she saw her reaction. It was true then. She *was* maimed!

"Help, me," she said. "Someone did this … I …"

"Were you attacked?" asked the woman. "What happened?"

"I … my arm …"

"Oh my God, Jarrod. Call the police," said the woman. "Sit down on the bench. We'll get someone. We'll get you an ambulance."

The woman's husband or boyfriend, Jarrod, already had his cell phone to his ear.

Maria moved her left hand through the space where her right arm had been, and the reality sank in at last.

As Jarrod finished his call, Maria began to scream.

She didn't stop until the first police car arrived.

CHAPTER SEVEN

Avgustin Juniper jerked awake.

He was disorientated. Too much good wine and Russian vodka floated in his blood stream and he barely remembered his name, let alone that he was now residing in Cassandra Moúsa's apartment. It was pitch dark and his hand reached out searching for his cell phone on the table beside the bed. The light from it was enough for Juniper to see the room and remind him where he was. He turned on the lamp beside the bed and the room lit up just as he heard raised voices in the hallway outside.

So that was what had disturbed him.

Cassandra Moúsa lived in an exclusive block in a warehouse conversion near Wall Street. She had the top floor all to herself. It was a completely private and quiet place that had large rooms with ceilings higher than Juniper had ever seen in his life. She had given him a suite of rooms all to himself. A studio, with perfect daylight streaming through. A bedroom with an attached bath, and a small lounge area with cable television. He even had a fridge full of cold drinks, beer and vodka. As much as he wanted.

Juniper pushed back the covers, turned his legs out of the bed, stood and reached for his dressing gown. As he tied the robe the door to his room burst open revealing Detective Chandler and a bunch of uniformed cops.

"This is an outrage!" said Cassandra from the corridor beyond.

Juniper noted that she was still dressed and wearing the suit she had worn earlier. He had been alone for the best part of the day, with the exception of the bodyguards who never spoke to him—and all looked so much alike that he couldn't remember any of their names—but he had seen Cassandra leave in the morning for work and had noted her clothing.

"Juniper, you need to come with us. Right now," said Chandler.

"What is it?" Juniper asked.

"Avgustin hasn't left this apartment," Cassandra said. "I can vouch for him. He's had security guards with him all day."

"What has happened?" Juniper asked again.

"Another girl was attacked," Cassandra said.

Juniper blanched. "How horrible. Is it … like Annabel?"

"This one is still alive," Chandler said.

"I'm confused, Detective. Why have you been brought into this? I thought you were homicide," Cassandra said.

"There are some … similarities to Annabel Linton's case," Chandler said. "Which is why we need to establish your client's whereabouts."

Juniper couldn't understand how they would even suspect him of a random attack. Annabel, he understood—on some level. Even though he knew he hadn't hurt her he had at least known her, been involved with her. Also, he had been there when it happened, even though he had been unable to explain to anyone's satisfaction what he had seen.

This whole thing was getting out of hand. It was insane.

"What have you been doing today?" Chandler asked.

"Working. I've been here all zhe time, just as Ms. Moúsa said," Juniper answered.

"Show me," said Chandler and when Juniper frowned and looked confused he continued, "your work. Show me what you've done today."

Juniper met Cassandra's eyes over Chandler's shoulder.

"Do you have a warrant?" Cassandra said.

Chandler turned and looked her in the eye. "Juniper here is on bail under suspicion of a similar crime … we don't actually need one."

Cassandra held Chandler's eye for a moment, and then she shrugged, "Let him see. I can't see any harm in it. Not worth the argument."

The police stepped aside to allow Juniper to pass through the doorway and lead them to his makeshift studio.

This part of the loft had huge windows that looked out onto the street as well as skylight windows above. It was perfect for painting.

"This is your apartment?" Chandler said to Cassandra, but it was rhetorical. "What did you use this room for before?"

Cassandra didn't answer and Chandler forgot his train of thought as Juniper led him to the canvas nearest the big windows.

"This is what I was working on," Juniper said.

Chandler stared at the painting. The girl that Juniper had pictured looked almost exactly like the girl, Maria Matthews, who had been attacked at Battery Park.

"Who is this girl?" Chandler asked.

"Oh, that's Susan Matthews. She's a student at the college. She models for me sometimes," Juniper said.

"*Susan* Matthews? Do you know if she has a sister?"

"No, I don't know much about her. She doesn't talk much and I don't encourage it in the models. It's too much of a distraction."

"When did you see her last?" Chandler asked.

"A few weeks ago. Why?"

"You're coming with us, Juniper, and I want your security men to accompany us to the station for questioning. That's before you get time to talk to them, Ms. Moúsa," Chandler said. "*Maria* Matthews was the name of the girl who was attacked this evening and I'm pretty certain we are going to find out that your model, Susan, is related to her."

"I resent the implication that I might coerce my guards to *lie* to the police, Detective Chandler," said Cassandra. "And Avgustin told you he didn't know anything about his model's private life. This whole thing sounds like an unfortunate coincidence. And I'm sure the DA will agree with me on that."

"I wasn't implying anything, Ms. Moúsa," Chandler said. "Merely that I want to speak to them before you do. And if Mr. Juniper has done nothing wrong then he won't object to it if we confirm his whereabouts."

"This is insane," said Juniper. "Why would I attack my model's sister? Even if what you say is true. I was here the whole day and evening. Why won't you believe me?"

"I have an assault and a murder to investigate, Mr. Juniper. And right now you're coming up as the one thing in common with both of the victims."

"That doesn't mean I did it," said Juniper.

"No. It doesn't," Chandler said, surprising both Juniper and Cassandra, "but you're the only connection we have."

Back at the station, the bodyguards confirmed Juniper's alibi, and Chandler had very little he could use to detain the artist further.

"Maybe it would be best if I am locked up," Juniper said to Cassandra as she bundled the tired artist back into her limousine.

"Why on earth would you think that?"

"At least then, if there are more attacks it would be impossible for me to have done them. Then they might start to believe that I didn't hurt Annabel."

"Believe me, what has happened this evening is for the best. If they had revoked your bail it would have meant the press would condemn you. No way would you ever get a fair trial after that. If there are further attacks we will just keep proving your innocence. Okay?"

"You believe me, don't you? I didn't hurt either of those girls."

"Avgustin, if I didn't already *know* that I wouldn't have brought you into my home."

Juniper sank back into the leather seat. It meant a lot to him that someone believed him. He couldn't understand how, in such a short time, his whole life had taken a turn for the worse. And it had all begun with Annabel. Despite Cassandra's reassurances, he was terrified that he would be found guilty of her murder.

Avgustin had moved to the United States because he believed in their justice system. It was so deeply ironic that he now found himself in this position. It was the most terrible thing in the world to be accused of something that you knew you hadn't done and, somehow, it was even worse that it had happened to him in the land of freedom.

As the car drew closer to Cassandra's apartment Avgustin was overwhelmed with immense gratitude towards her. If anyone would clear his name it would be her, and his career just might be left intact at the end of it too. As much as it still horrified him to be cashing in on someone else's tragedy, he was even coming around to her way of thinking regarding the sale of the paintings.

Back at the apartment, Cassandra poured him a brandy. The security guards were no longer inside. Avgustin wondered briefly if this meant they were still at the police station.

"The guards are outside now. I don't necessarily need my home filled with people all the time. I want some privacy."

"You must be certain, also, that I will not hurt you," Juniper said voicing his suspicions that the men had mostly been there to protect Cassandra from him.

Cassandra laughed. It was three in the morning, yet she still looked fresh. Juniper wondered how she managed to keep going like that. He was exhausted. Frazzled.

"I have no doubt in my mind that you *couldn't* hurt me," Cassandra said.

"You mean, *wouldn't*?"

Cassandra smiled, downed her brandy and wished him goodnight. Then she left the sitting room and went down the corridor to her own rooms.

Juniper stayed in the lounge sipping the brandy until his shaken nerves began to calm down. It was a close call again that night, as though someone was playing a cat and mouse game with him.

Cassandra had learned that the victim was in fact Susan's twin sister. He couldn't deny the connection between Susan Matthews and himself, but why would the killer attack Maria? It was probably just a fluke and nothing to do with him at all, but Juniper couldn't help being paranoid.

"Why would anyone want to do this to me?" he murmured into his glass. "I'm not a bad person. I don't hurt anyone. All I vont to do is paint."

He gazed into space for a while letting his mind wander. He couldn't recall a single moment when he had made any serious enemies. He was a loner for the most part, had few friends, but now he wondered what he had done to make him the target of this person.

He placed the empty brandy glass down on a coffee table near his chair, then stood and made his way to his own bedroom. Outside the small suite he heard running water. He knew Cassandra's room was just down the hallway, but he would never dream of going there. He would never ruin her trust.

Juniper stripped down to his shorts and climbed into the bed once more. His head began to hurt. He was thinking too much, analyzing something that he had no control of. He turned off the lamp and the room returned to the pitch blackness that should help him sleep better, but he lay in the dark unable to switch off his mind.

He heard a noise outside. A strange scraping, like tree branches on glass. It reminded him of the trees on the farm he lived on as a child. Juniper's overactive imagination remembered that sensation, that feeling of helplessness he had as a child when he heard those noises in the night. Part of him knew it was just the wind making the branches move, but another part of him had believed that the trees were crowding round, trying to get inside. Now he had that same irrational fear. A claustrophobic horror pumped adrenaline around his body until Juniper recalled that Cassandra's apartment was several stories above the ground. *No trees could reach the window.*

As he drifted to sleep, barely reassured, his half-conscious psyche shifted into a scenario where he imagined that he stumbled across the room to open the curtains. Outside, his dream conscious could see nothing. No branches, no reason for the ambiguous noise, no lights from the city even. All he could see was a black void, as though some darkness had stretched across the window and now obscured his vision.

He floated deeper into his strange imaginings: he was an artist after all, and much of his inspiration came from his dreams. As the dark fog cleared, he saw another girl, one whose face he *must* paint. A beauty with long dark hair and a cherry red smile. The girl was dancing. A flowing dress falling around her perfect thighs. She was a ballerina then.... That was the picture he must paint; a beautiful dancer, with the most exquisite legs. The shape of them was magical.

Sometime during the night, Juniper heard a scream. In his

dream he saw the dancer tumble. He saw the darkness swoop on her, tearing at those unique limbs until she was left with bloodless stumps.

He tried to run, to get away, but could make no progress.

He looked down and saw that his own legs were no longer there, just stumps waving back and forth.

Juniper jerked upright, a cry of disgust choking in his throat. He sat in the silent darkness, his breath steadying. It was just a dream.

It was still dark out, but the curtains were now open. He *must* have opened them in his sleep after all. The thought that part of his dream was real sent a shiver through him.

On trembling legs, he left the bed and pulled the drapes closed, but not before he glanced out over the illuminated city.

He still felt shaky, but there was nothing wrong with the view outside. *A dream. It was all just a dream.*

He fell back into the bed, not caring what time it was. He was so tired that all he wanted to do was to sleep. And, hopefully, not dream.

CHAPTER EIGHT

Joy Awen dashed from her cab into the entrance of the gallery. Holding a newspaper over her hair to keep the rain off, she pushed the key in the door and turned the lock. A warning beep started inside the gallery as she closed the door behind her, throwing across a small bolt, before hurrying to turn off the alarm.

It was six in the morning but Joy often came into work before her employees, who wouldn't arrive before half past eight. She liked this time alone to work silently without distraction, but most of all it was a time when she could walk around and look at the paintings and sculptures which were on display. It was a time when she thought more about the future, particularly the ongoing success of the gallery. Sometimes she would have moments of complete clarity. Like the time when she moved a sculpture that hadn't sold into a completely different place in the gallery. The piece had stood in the same place for months prior to that. The next day, after she moved it, she had three offers.

It was all merchandising of course. Some things needed to be given more light, turned in a different angle, or even placed in a remote, dimmed corner. Joy had an instinct for it, but it didn't always work when too many people were around to distract her. That was why these moments alone were so important.

She walked to the back of the gallery and into her office. She removed her damp coat and hung it on an old wooden coat stand, then went into her private bathroom. She gazed in the mirror at her somewhat wild hair. It was loose; she had taken to wearing it that way since Juniper had complimented her on it the one night that they had indulged in sex. He said it made her look beautiful. Wanton. Of course it was probably just the vodka talking, but Joy had enjoyed his comments nonetheless. And she had realized that wearing her hair this way made her eyes, which always seemed too large for her small face, appear dramatic and charming instead of just big.

She ran a hand over her hair, smoothing it down a little, before returning to the office. Once there she put fresh coffee into her coffeemaker and walked back out to the gallery while the drink brewed.

She switched on the lights in the main viewing area. Juniper's paintings were mostly in place but Joy still had to decide where the final pieces would go. She walked around the room studying the art, noting again how all of the paintings seemed to revolve around beautiful women. It irritated Joy somewhat how much Juniper loved the female form and she became agitated as she walked around. So perfect. Beautiful, curvy bodies. Some naked, some posed and dressed in classical styles. Goddesses all of them. Except they weren't: these were all very ordinary girls, but something in the brush strokes made them special. A kind of loving admiration that portrayed them all at their best.

Joy stopped. They were so unlike the *other* abomination that she should really revel in them. Her eyes automatically went to the door of her office. And, as though drawn there, she found herself back in the room, gazing at the wall behind her desk.

It held a generic painting. Flowers in a field, not unlike the brush strokes of Van Gogh, but really nowhere near as good. The painting was there as a deliberate distraction. It drew the eye away from the wall where a less casual observer might notice that it jutted out three inches, as though a chimney breast had once been there. Joy walked around her desk then put her hand to her throat, pulling out a thin chain on which hung a key. She pushed the painting askew to reveal a keyhole behind it. She inserted the key in the lock, and a door, little more than a plywood oblong, clicked open to one side of the room.

This was a secret space, one that had been built by an ex-boyfriend as a simple storage cupboard for her office supplies. It was meant to be for fun. A hidden cupboard, and Joy had not thought of its use being applied in any other way. It wasn't even particularly secure. Joy had a bigger vault that her staff knew about. This was where they kept expensive pieces until they were hung or displayed properly in the gallery, with the appropriate security around them. But the space behind her desk was known only to Joy, and she rarely opened it.

A painting hung there. A female form, but not depicted in the usual way.

Joy hated it, but couldn't bring herself to part with it. This painting was an unknown Picasso and she had obtained it by less than legal means from a German immigrant who suddenly needed money.

Joy never asked how he had obtained the painting, but she had a suspicion that the man needed to flee the country. He had hard eyes. The stone, flinty expression of someone who had seen, and perhaps done, terrible things. At the time there was lots of bad press coverage, and an ex-Nazi was being tried for war crimes. A witch hunt ensued to out others. Joy could only imagine, but didn't know for certain, which was why she was able to deal with him, that Mr. Shultz had a reason to be afraid.

He wanted ridiculous money, but fortunately didn't comprehend the real value of the piece. But Joy had, the minute she saw it. And yes, abomination was the best way to describe this awful portrait. But even so it had an allure, a charm that pulled you into its grotesque, distorted world.

"One million in cash," Schultz had said.

Joy laughed. "I couldn't possibly pay that for this. Maybe fifty thousand?"

They had finally settled on seventy-five thousand. Joy gave him cash directly from her safe. As he left, she had wondered what to do with it. The picture wasn't legitimate. Its source unreliable. There would be questions asked. She made all sorts of excuses to herself to hold onto the piece. Joy had stared at her prize and, although it was worth many millions, she knew she could never part with it. Yes, there were collectors that would buy and not ask questions. But she didn't want to sell it. Not at any price.

She had pulled free the shallow shelves in the cupboard and stowed the picture there temporarily. But it had remained there. It was a perfectly innocent hide-away. Potential thieves would be looking for their sturdy metal vault and cash registers. Not a shallow storage cupboard behind an office desk. Plus, she really didn't want her staff to know about it.

She pulled the cupboard door open wide and again the shock of the colors assaulted her. The figure was hideous. Deformed. Similar to, but not the same as, some of Picasso's other works, this woman was made up of odd body parts. The face was different colors and tones, sharp shapes that looked like pieces of broken glass. Her hair was brown, not unlike Joy's in color, but it held a lustrous shine that went around the distorted visage. Its limbs were no better; bent and cut in painful angles. It was as though she were a puzzle that had been wrongly put together. Or had become confused with other puzzle pieces.

The pose should have been nice. The woman lay on a chaise longue, draped in blue satin, one leg crossed over the other. Joy noticed again how peculiar the legs were, one was definitely longer than the other. She closed her eyes. It was horrible. Really horrible. But she couldn't help visiting it, torturing herself with its vile sheen.

She wondered sometimes if this was just a first, and failed, experiment of what had gone on to be Picasso's most successful works. But she thought it unlikely. The brush strokes were too good, too precise. The execution however … *He hated the model!* Why else would Picasso depict someone looking so vile? It wasn't about art, it was about loathing. Pure and simple—the artist was as disgusted by this figure as Joy was by his painting.

Joy's eyes fell on the shadowing. Strange how he had chosen to paint the woman's shoulder dark, ghostlike—as though a piece of the puzzle was missing. Or perhaps … Joy dismissed the thought that came into her head as ridiculous and insane. Then she closed the cupboard again.

She wondered why she tortured herself so much. This despicable travesty was so far removed from Avgustin Juniper's love of the female form, that it reminded her why she had chosen to exhibit his work in the first place.

She locked the cupboard, dropped the key back down under her top, then turned to the coffee machine. She poured her coffee black into a white ceramic mug.

She glanced at her watch. It was half past seven. Had an hour and a half passed already? It was so easy to lose time these days.

Taking the cup with her she returned to the gallery. Juniper's women were now like a breath of fresh air. She no longer felt irritated or jealous of their curves. These paintings were the antidote to the Picasso.

What a strange thought!

She put sticky notes on the frames of the remaining pictures, each with a position number, and as she heard her assistant, Julian, tap lightly on the door, Joy knew she had achieved her goal in finding the ideal position for each painting. She placed the last note and returned to the front of the shop to open the door.

CHAPTER NINE

Take a seat, Jake, I'll be just a second," Lauren Michaels said smiling.

Chandler sank down into a soft, plush beige velour sofa. The sofa was comfortable but he was glad that he wasn't expected to lie back in the clichéd manner.

After the initial panic at being told by the department that he had to see a shrink, over the last few months Chandler had begun to look forward to the sessions. He saw them as his opportunity to say what he felt. And although being *totally* honest and open was still a work-in-progress he was revealing more each time he spoke to Lauren.

The truth was he had expected the experience to be corny somehow, or just embarrassingly formal but his sessions with Lauren were nothing like that. She was natural, relaxed. What's more, he had come to rely on her. A thought he didn't wholly like to admit, even to himself. But knowing he could call her, night or day, gave him a strange comfort. And in the early days he had needed to call her. Often.

Chandler looked around the office. He was so familiar with the layout that he was able to spot the slightest thing that was out of place. Lauren was writing at a huge antique oak desk, which had a red leather panel covering the center. His eyes swept the carved wood, taking in the intricate design around the edges and down the legs. She had a formal brown leather ink-blotter placed before her, but Chandler had never seen her use anything other than a roller ball. He suspected that the blotter had been a present, perhaps from her parents when she graduated but he never asked her about her life or family. It just wasn't done.

The desktop wasn't as tidy as usual. There was a small pile of legal-sized files on the desk in front of her. She had the top one open and was writing notes into it, possibly about her last patient.

"I'm sorry," she apologized as she felt his eyes on her. "Running a bit late today. But you'll still get your full hour."

She looked flustered. Her normally well-groomed brown hair was ruffled, a stray strand had broken away from her neat ponytail. Chandler also noticed a pale pink pimple blooming on her normally flawless skin.

"Don't worry," Chandler replied. "Take your time."

Behind the desk was a large painting; a boring print of flowers in a field. Something generic that reminded him of a famous painting, but not quite. Perhaps the style was like Van Gogh. Chandler's mind barely acknowledged its presence above the cursory glance of expectation to find the familiar piece there as he let his eyes fall on the row of cabinets that lined the wall to Lauren's right. One drawer was left atypically open.

"There," said Lauren closing the file.

She stood up and came around the desk, taking a seat in the chair opposite the sofa, legal pad and pen in hand, even though he was sure she didn't need them with the digital recorder dutifully sat on the coffee table between them.

"Things have been a bit manic. I take a short trip and the world falls apart," she smiled.

Chandler smiled back. "Everyone deserves a break. You should take them more often."

Lauren glanced down at her notepad as though contemplating this advice.

"So how have you been?" she asked. "You didn't call me over the last few days. I'm taking that as a good sign."

"I'm okay. I've been busy—on this new case. I guess it's taken my mind away from my personal issues."

"So you're still on the Juniper case?" Lauren asked.

Chandler looked down at his hands. "I know you advised against it, but I'm enjoying the work. It has … given me … purpose."

"In what way?"

Chandler was thoughtful. Her question was ambiguous. Most of them were. He wondered what part of his answer she was referring to when she asked the question. He struggled for a moment with the thought of giving a generic answer that would tell her nothing. Then realized his thoughts missed the point of his reason for being here.

"The work is challenging. I'm not at all sure that Juniper is guilty. In fact, I suspect he isn't," Chandler said. "Part of me wants to investigate, not only to find the killer, but to clear the artist. He seems harmless. Not like some people I've dealt with before. Plus … the attacks are …"

"*Sick*?" asked Lauren.

"Unusual, but the attacker is warped. They always are, no matter how a murder takes place. Or what their motivation. But I'm curious about this one. I've never seen anything quite like it before."

"Wait a minute, you said … attacks. I thought there had only been one murder?"

Of course the papers knew nothing about Maria Matthews or the fact that the police suspected the same perpetrator. Chandler frowned. He really shouldn't talk about what they had or the other victim with Lauren. But she was bound by strict confidentiality laws. She couldn't reveal this information to anyone.

"There was another victim."

"Another murdered girl?"

"She's still alive."

"Oh my God … but …"

"I'd rather not give you specifics, except to say the injury wasn't bad enough to kill."

"Sorry. I shouldn't have asked," Lauren said. "Tell me how you're feeling? How this is all affecting you?"

Chandler slipped into therapy mode and shared his ongoing anxiety about Jules, his insecurities with his job. But the words felt automatic. He was strangely distant from them.

"I don't think you need me anymore," Lauren said at the end of the session. "I'm going to send an email to the department, explaining that you are fully fit and well."

Panic began to rise in his chest. "You mean, I don't need to come here anymore?"

"Precisely. Jake, you've made excellent progress and your enthusiasm seems to have returned for your job. It's healthy interest. The only thing that still concerns me is your lack of social life. But given the circumstances that may take you a long time to change."

"I don't feel ready to stop the sessions," Chandler admitted. He was so different in Lauren's surgery from the confident professional that his colleagues saw. He felt weak, raw, exposed, and yet it was still okay to be this way around her.

"It's only natural you should feel that way," Lauren said. "I've been your crutch, but now you need to learn to take steps without me."

For a moment Chandler was confused, he wondered if he had spoken his vulnerability aloud, but then realized she was responding to his fear of stopping seeing her.

"In a doctor/patient relationship there is a certain amount of dependency that develops. But Jake, I wouldn't be saying this to you if I felt you couldn't handle it. I think it will be good for you to try being totally independent again."

Chandler shook his head. "I'm not ready.…"

"Of course you are."

Chandler's world was once again spinning out of control, but what frightened him the most was his total fear of not seeing Lauren again. He tried to analyze it. His dependency on her was stronger than he had imagined.

"I'm not saying this is our last session," she said. "But we are going to start spreading them farther apart. Instead of weekly, I'm going to see you every other week this month. Then we will see how things go."

Chandler's heartbeat settled down as the panic receded. He could do that. He could. He didn't always want to come here every week at the same time. Sometimes he would prefer to stay at the station working on his cases. Often it was an unwelcome interruption when he had to go out. But always when he saw Lauren, he became calm. He was welcome here. Reassured by her composed expression and the meter of her voice which was almost hypnotic. The time spent with her always went quickly.

"I think you should try to find a hobby," Lauren was saying. "Didn't you mention you used to paint? Why not take it up again? Creativity gives us a focus for our anxieties and emotions. It could also be something positive. Maybe even take a class at the college. Something that will give you a reason to commit."

Chandler nodded. And a small bell chimed, the timer on her desk, indicating that their hour was up. "*Positive*?"

"Yes. It occurs to me how dark the nature of your job is. It must be hard to feel positive when surrounded by death."

Chandler looked up at her.

"I suppose your job is the same in many ways. You get everyone's troubles, all day long. You must hear some terrible stories. How do you keep optimistic all the time?"

Lauren blinked, then smiled. "I keep positive because that's the only way to stop the horror from drowning me. Pagans believe that we chose to be happy or sad. That if we are unhappy, then negative things happen to us. We draw that bad energy in. Positivity on the other hand repels it. Of course my learned colleagues would tell me that depression is a chemical imbalance, a bad childhood, or because someone has become the victim of bad circumstances. However, some people believe that we create those circumstances by our attitude."

"Interesting philosophy. But you're a psychiatrist, you don't believe that."

"I'm many things, Jake. Psychiatry is my job. What I believe is that *some* people have a chemical imbalance, and that *some* bad things happen that we cannot control. Like the death of your wife. But it has been my observation that not all depression is caused by these things. Sometimes the negativity of a person *does* draw in bad elements or indeed makes them react to a situation in a different way to a happy, upbeat person. Sometimes a person whose, for want of a better word, cup is half-empty, sees the bad in a situation that his opposite will find a silver lining in."

"You've never spoken to me this way before," Chandler said.

"I'm telling you this because I want you to start looking for small joys. Your daily coffee. A polite person opening a door for you. A clue that will lead you to your criminal. Smile instead of frown; the returning smile you will get will inspire a raised feeling of spirit."

"Our time is up," Chandler pointed out as the timer continued to beep on Lauren's desk.

"No. It's never up," said Lauren.

Then she stood and switched off the timer.

"Think on what I've said. Find something that makes you happy. Something that returns some happiness back into your life, no matter how small."

Chandler left her office. His head was reeling. He was enlightened somehow, as though her parting words and advice meant more than the months of psychobabble she had previously given. Maybe this was always her goodbye speech, but somehow he didn't think so. It seemed heartfelt and not rehearsed and maybe that was why she had really struck a chord with him. All of those generic shrink responses she gave to everyone on a daily basis, maybe she was tired of the bullshit, or maybe by analyzing her patients she had realized how diverse their problems were.

Whatever the reason, Lauren's philosophy left him believing that he needed to ponder her words carefully. Perhaps it was just as simple as making a life choice. But how?

How could anyone "choose" to be happy? That wasn't as easy as it sounded.

CHAPTER TEN

Unable to finish, Juniper had put aside Susan Matthew's painting. He was sickened by the thought of what had happened to her sister, and even though he knew he wasn't involved, the urge to complete the painting had completely diminished. Instead, he placed a new, bigger canvas on his easel and began to draw outlines that rapidly filled the space in abstract strokes.

"What's this?" asked Cassandra as she entered the studio.

She was wearing a dark blue, pin-striped trouser suit. Her streaked hair was pulled back in a ponytail. That day it appeared brighter as though the sun had somehow lightened it. Juniper noted the fresh application of red lipstick. That morning she wasn't wearing her glasses, and she had the appearance, despite the business suit, of being much younger than she must have been.

"I woke inzpired," he said returning his eyes to the canvas before she noticed his scrutiny.

Juniper found Cassandra very attractive and he experienced a familiar stirring that he knew was inappropriate in their relationship. It also seemed to be a horrible betrayal of Annabel so soon after the beginning and end of their brief relationship: so soon after her death.

He forced his mind to focus on his work.

Cassandra stared at the rough outline of the figures. Already she could tell the canvas was different from his other works. She detected a female form—as always—but this one was not static, she was moving, dancing. At least that is what she thought was happening.

"Inspired, huh? Can't wait to see the finished product."

Juniper sank deeper into that creative part of his brain as he became engrossed in his work. He forgot his earlier sexual interest in his lawyer as the obsession for painting took over his physical desires. He barely noticed when Cassandra left for the day. At some point in the morning he became aware that the bodyguards had returned to the inside of the apartment because one of them brought him a glass of orange juice and a bowl of cut up fruit.

"What's this?" he asked.

"The boss says you're to have healthy snacks throughout the day. She wants to keep you fit." The bodyguard's voice was flat, and, by not implying anything, it made Juniper speculate what the man really thought about his relationship with Cassandra. He briefly wondered at the level of care she was taking with him, then shrugged. It meant nothing. He was a high-profile case and probably worth millions of dollars to her. That was all. She had to look after him.

He picked up the glass and sipped at the fresh orange juice before continuing his work.

In his mind's eye, he saw a ballerina in a flowing dress. Her arms, legs and torso were magnificently formed. Toned, slender and perfect, she was very different from the women he usually painted.

The legs fascinated him. It was as though he had seen her before somewhere, but he couldn't quite remember where. Maybe she was a Bolshoi ballerina? In his youth, before he left

Russia, he had hung out backstage with a few beauties. The tight leotards hid nothing and it was a great way to study the female form. Perhaps that was where his obsession with it began. He probed his memory for details of this particular girl. All he was clear about was her legs. Her *beautiful* legs, but no more would come. Not even her face. But that didn't matter because Juniper would think of someone else he knew to put there.

Around the dancer, Juniper, drew the shape of a stage, then quickly changed his mind. That was too mundane. He had to put the figure in an environment alien to her movement and beauty. Before he could think more, he began to design a landscape: a rugged, broken down city in ruins. It jarred completely with the image of the girl and so it worked perfectly for his aims. She was the focus, and her magnificence would be even more pronounced in this derelict scene.

Once outlined, he forgot the scene and began to work on the girl herself. He worked oddly. Starting with her dress, he made the fabric flow out as though she were in the middle of a half-turn. He spent most of the morning, painting the pale, sheer fabric, mixing oils until he achieved a pale bluish-white. By midafternoon the dress flared, exposing the sketched legs from thighs downwards. The fabric was accentuated by bursts of light that would eventually be filtering through the cloudy sky, like spotlights.

By evening the dress and legs were perfect and as the natural light faded he stopped working and stepped back from the canvas to review his work.

For some reason, he didn't want anyone to see the painting until it was finished and so he carefully draped a sheet over the canvas. Then he pulled the used brushes out of an old, stained jelly jar and began to clean them in turpentine.

By seven in the evening he was showered, changed and drinking his usual glass of vodka as he sat in the small lounge attached to his rooms. A knock on the door signified the arrival of Cassandra.

"How was your day?" she asked.

Juniper thought the question odd. Surely he should be asking her how the work on his case was going? It was as though they had fallen into some form of domesticity. As if he was a house husband, and she the wife earning their real living.

"My day was good. Productive," he said. "What about you?"

"I ordered food in. There are still reporters outside and, unfortunately some idiot leaked the Maria Matthews story."

"*What*? Who vould *do* such a thing?"

Cassandra didn't look ruffled by the news, she merely shrugged. "Who knows? The police department is full of corruption. Someone probably got a nice payout for the story."

"I need a newspaper," Juniper fretted. "I need to see what zey are saying."

"No. *Absolutely* not. That won't do you any good. But I had to tell you, in case you see anything on the news channels. You mustn't worry about it, Avgustin. This sort of thing happens in high profile cases. Often it will work in our favor. It means that we will get to carefully question all of the jurors when the time comes, and we can reject anyone who we feel are slightly biased."

Juniper switched the television on and began to search the network news channels until Cassandra pried the remote control from his trembling fingers.

"Dinner is getting cold. I had it brought in from my favorite restaurant so let's not let it spoil."

"All right. But you must tell me all that has happened."

In the dining room Juniper found the table set, and one of the bodyguards standing by to help serve the food. He thought it was the one that had brought him food throughout the day but wasn't sure. It occurred to him again how alike they all were. He never heard them call each other by name. It was like being surrounded by clones.

"I took the liberty of ordering you filet mignon," Cassandra said.

Juniper sat down opposite her. He gazed over the plates of

food and the lit candles and thought again how awkward this scenario should be. But Cassandra was so relaxed and comfortable with having a candlelit dinner with a murder suspect, a veritable stranger in her home, that it made him feel even more peculiar.

The bodyguard began to serve them. The steak was already on his plate under a silver cover, which the guard removed, before offering both mashed and roasted potatoes.

"Dis is good," he said taking his first bite.

The meat was cooked perfectly, medium rare, just as he liked it. He wondered how Cassandra knew that, but didn't ponder it too much. Looking down the table he saw she was eating a vegetarian dish. Pasta, feta cheese, and some kind of pesto.

"You don't eat meat?" he asked.

"Yes. But I like this dish too."

The bodyguard poured Chianti into his glass and Juniper swigged the full-bodied wine, washing down another mouthful of meat.

By the third mouthful Juniper began to feel ill.

It wasn't anything specific. More a rolling and discomfort in his stomach. At first he thought it was a reaction to the rich food. He had been unable to afford such good meat for a long time. If indeed he had ever eaten such a fine cut in his life.

"Avgustin? Are you all right?" Cassandra asked.

Juniper sipped from his wine glass once more. The wine caught in his throat and a wracking cough followed, making him splutter wine all over the fine white tablecloth.

Cassandra was on her feet and the bodyguard stepped forward to hit Juniper on the back. They thought he was choking on the food.

Juniper pushed back his chair, and pulled himself up. He swayed against the edge of the table. His stomach hurt with painful cramps.

"Don't feel good," he murmured. He turned and staggered

away, out of the dining room and into the corridor to the nearest bathroom.

"Go with him," Cassandra said and the bodyguard hurried after Juniper just reaching him as the artist stumbled into the bathroom.

Juniper heaved into the toilet bowl, and vile lumps of undigested meat and vegetables poured into the water. There was a strong odor of wine and something else. The smell made Juniper heaved more.

"Oh my God. What's wrong with him?" Cassandra asked from the doorway.

The bodyguard shook his head, "Food poisoning?"

"I'm calling an ambulance."

"Poison," said the doctor. "Most likely arsenic. I'm waiting for the lab to come back with a confirmation, but I've seen these symptoms once before."

"*Arsenic*?" Cassandra said.

"He's lucky we've caught it so quickly," the doctor said. "Acute arsenic poisoning can lead to all sorts of complications. It's fortunate that his body rejected the poison so quickly."

"But how? How was he poisoned?" Cassandra asked. "This was food brought in from a restaurant."

"You should report it to the police. There might be more people coming in from that place this evening."

The doctor walked away.

Cassandra was outside Juniper's room with one of the bodyguards.

"Watch him," she said to the guard. "I'm going to make a phone call."

She walked away to find somewhere quiet to have the conversation she needed to have. Then she dialed 911.

CHAPTER ELEVEN

"I don't know what stunt you are pulling this time," Chandler said, "but you can't have your bodyguards all over this hospital."

"This is not a stunt, Detective. I believe someone tried to kill Avgustin and I want police protection for him," Cassandra said.

They stood outside Juniper's room. The blinds were drawn over the glass window and door so that no one could see inside, but Cassandra knew that two of her men were posted there and they would be checking everyone who came in.

"Your men have no authority to check doctors' and nurses' credentials," Chandler pointed out.

"Then post a detail of *your* men," she said. "We've been receiving letters, death threats. I notified your office but no one pursued it."

"I'll need to take those for evidence and analysis," Chandler said.

Cassandra opened her briefcase. "Here. I got my secretary to bring the file over early."

"I'm going to need the prints of anyone in your office who may have touched these."

"It was just me and my secretary, Jerry Tomas."

Chandler pulled a pair of latex gloves from his pocket before opening the file. On the top of the pile was the most recent one. The letters were carefully written with letters and words cut from newspaper—an archaic form of sending the letters when computer generated prints were just as anonymous. Chandler flicked through the papers. Each one read the same: the sender threatened to kill Juniper.

"He will die slowly and in agony. . . . "

"That might well have happened if we hadn't realized so soon that something was really wrong with Avgustin," said Cassandra. "Has anyone even been to the restaurant?"

"Yes. There was no sign of arsenic on the premises," Chandler answered.

"I believe you," she said. "Someone got to the food though."

Chandler was quiet as he flicked through the letters.

"Perhaps it is an inside job?"

"Detective, if you want permission to come and search my place, you can have it. You won't find anything more hazardous than household *bleach*. We are talking *arsenic*. Surely there are ways of tracing that?"

Chandler blinked. Her reference to bleach sank home, but he quickly covered his sensitivity. Surely she didn't know about his wife? He had done everything he could to keep her death out of the media. Even so, Chandler knew that it was Cassandra's job to find weaknesses in the prosecution. He was her enemy of sorts and it was likely she *did* know. He tried to read her, but she was pacing and focused on her concern for Avgustin. So much so, that Chandler decided her words had not been intentionally chosen to hurt him.

"He needs protection," she said again.

"I will post some officers. I can see you really are concerned about this. And forensics will take a look at these letters. Did you retain the envelopes?"

Cassandra stopped pacing. "Of course, Detective, I'm very

thorough. They're at the back of the folder. So if we're done here?"

Cassandra opened the door to Juniper's room and Chandler glanced in. The artist looked well considering his ordeal. He was sat up in the bed with a tray of food in front of him.

"We're done," said Chandler and he turned to walk away as Cassandra closed the door shutting him out of the room.

Chandler's cell phone rang as he reached the elevator. It was his fellow detective, Gemma Sarasvatī.

"Jake? I have a little bad news."

"What now?"

"Maria Matthews died this morning. She took a massive overdose. In her letter she said she couldn't live without her hand. She also talked about a watch. It was all kind of weird. The family is in pieces because no one realized how depressed she was. I feel a bit bad about this because when I interviewed her sister Susan, she mentioned Maria was taking this pretty hard. Wish I'd done more for the girl …"

As Sarasvatī spoke Chandler felt the floor fall from under him. His mind flashed back to finding Jules. The very idea that a young woman, another one he knew, even vaguely, had committed suicide made his stomach turn. He staggered forward grasping the wall beside the elevator like a drowning man clinging to driftwood. The folder under his arm containing the death threats tumbled to the floor, the papers spilling out.

"The DA will want to talk to you, but this is probably now manslaughter. The girl died because of the direct actions of that freak I guess, even if she did take her own life."

"Detective? Are you all right?" A young nurse ran to help him.

"Don't touch them," he warned as she went to scoop up the papers he had dropped. Chandler slid down the wall. The strange vertigo made the room spin and the floor rock, even when he closed his eyes to steady himself. Nausea churned his stomach and a sickening lump was lodged in his throat. Even so, he knelt down and retrieved the papers himself, stuffing them into the folder.

Then he allowed the young nurse to take his arm and help him up. She led him to a chair in the waiting area.

"Jake? Jake? What's up?" Sarasvatī's voice called with tinny panic down the end of the phone that Chandler still clutched in his trembling fingers.

"I'm fine," said Chandler, half to Sarasvatī and half to the nurse. "I just got a little dizzy. Didn't sleep well last night."

"I'll get you some water," said the nurse. Chandler looked up into kind eyes as she studied him with concern before nodding, satisfied that he really was okay. She left him to walk to the water dispenser and then quickly returned with a plastic cup of cold water.

"Listen. I'll call you back," Chandler said and then closed the call.

His hands were shaking as he took the cup from the nurse.

"Don't move for a while, huh? Dizzy spell like that might take a while to settle down."

"Thank you. I'm fine. Really."

Chandler sipped the water, then he looked up to see Cassandra Moúsa staring at him from the doorway.

"Are you all right, Detective?" she asked.

Chandler nodded.

"You look like you just had some bad news," Cassandra continued.

The intensity of her gaze was not lost on him. It made him feel peculiar. It was as though she knew already what had happened and the implication it could have for her client if he was found guilty. Chandler drank the last of the water and stood cautiously. He was steadier, but still shaken. He didn't know why Maria's death had affected him so much and it was strange the way Cassandra had appeared at that moment. It was almost as though she had been watching him as he received the call. But he knew that was impossible of course. He had seen her enter Juniper's room.

"I need to get back to my office," Chandler said.

He walked towards Cassandra, and for a moment she remained in his way. Chandler was usually good at reading people, but Cassandra's expression was inscrutable. Eventually she stepped back and let him pass.

He passed the nurses' desk, somewhat embarrassed by his momentary swoon. The young nurse wasn't there though, and so he couldn't thank here again anyway. At the elevator, he pressed the call button, then he turned his head to see Cassandra still watching him. His skin crawled. A strangely irrational phobia about being watched surged up in a paranoid wave. It was anomalous. He was relieved when the elevator arrived and he hurried inside, folder and cell phone clutched to his chest.

CHAPTER TWELVE

A few days later Juniper applied the finishing touches to the face of the ballerina. He had returned from the hospital, fingers itching, mind whirling, desperate to return to work.

The painting had beckoned and, as he often did, he imagined a creature that took the shape of a muse, working beside him, hands moving in rapid succession as the strokes appeared on the canvas.

He remembered the ballerina now. A sweet young thing. A new girl at the Bolshoi. He had loved her legs. They were perfect and beautiful. So muscular and developed for her young age. He even remembered her clumsy attempt at seduction when they were alone in the dancers' dressing room. He was not into flat-chested, perfectly toned bodies, despite his study of them. Though he was flattered and he had let her down gently.

"You shouldn't rush into such things," he advised her. "Enjoy your youth. Don't let yourself be spoilt."

He hadn't known how old she was, but knew she was just too young. She barely looked fourteen, and Juniper was twenty-two at the time. A liaison would have been potentially messy.

He preferred instead the less-than-perfect curves of the bartender at his local bar. She was always friendly and flattered by the then-young-man's attention. He was rapidly developing his tolerance to vodka at that time, while admiring her body. At least the barmaid had experience—unlike the ballerina who was probably only trying to get rid of her virginity for a dare anyway.

What was her name? He couldn't remember now—it probably hadn't mattered to him at all at the time and it didn't matter now.

He stepped back to admire the painting. The stark, broken landscape worked so well. At the last minute he had a compulsion to add a broken piano. It was busted open; a tangle of wires fell out like intestines. Grotesque really, inspired perhaps by his love of Salvador Dali's art.

The likeness of the girl was good though. Such a young, innocent face. Such perfect form. Though at the last moment, Juniper added some fine lines, imagining how she might look now. He didn't know why he aged her, it was an impulse, like the painting itself was.

He added a note on the back of the canvas. He called the piece "Last Performance."

He draped a cloth over the picture before removing the canvas from the easel. For some reason he didn't want Cassandra or any of the bodyguards to see it, and so he placed it at the back of the room, hidden behind two others that were earmarked for the viewing.

Tasha Voronov had worked hard to obtain her principal place in the Bolshoi Ballet, and even though she had already passed the age where most ballerinas retired she was still being chosen for starring roles in the productions. This season though, Tasha knew, would be her last. The company manager had told her so.

It hurt, but what could she do? She had gone on longer than most.

Of course there would be opportunities for her to teach now, especially with the fame and experience she had received with Bolshoi. She could take her pick of dance schools—or even set up her own. But what most of the others did, in these circumstances, was they usually found themselves a wealthy husband and had the children that the rigors of their career had so far denied them. It was something Tasha had thought about on occasion but never with any real seriousness. Dance was all that mattered to her. She had worked so hard to maintain her shape that the last thing she wanted was pregnancy.

But then, she had only been in love once. And that had been unrequited.

She was in the rehearsal room, just off Broadway. The rooms were near enough to the theatre for the troop to walk over there when it was time to get ready for the performance. And they were run by a local ballet school, so were adequately equipped with mirrors and bars and a piano in one corner, but otherwise the place was for the most part quite sparse.

Tasha placed her ankle on the bar and stretched down. Her mind flew back to those heady times when she was newly accepted into the Bolshoi as a fledgling dancer. She barely suffered from the enforced starvation. Her mother was ex-Bolshoi-dancer-turned-teacher with a good reputation, and Tasha had not only inherited her skill but had also superseded her. She had a beautiful shape, and never being allowed to overeat meant she had a naturally low appetite.

The early days, as a new and up-and-coming star, Tasha had been courted by many men, but there had only ever been one that truly interested her. His name was Avgustin, an artist.

Her mother had seen trouble immediately. Avgustin wanted to draw the dancers, but she had sent him away. Even so, he returned every night, sneaking backstage when Veronika Voronov was too busy to notice. Somehow he always managed to talk his way into the dancers' changing rooms. But for the most part none of them minded. It bought into their vanity if Avgustin sketched them while he sat quietly in the corner.

One such night he noticed Tasha. Her legs were what interested him, and this became a source of amusement to some of the other dancers.

"You have beautiful legs!" he would say.

"He doesn't like your face, but he wants to draw your legs," said one of the crueler girls, much to the amusement of the rest. But Tasha didn't mind. She enjoyed having Avgustin's eyes on her. It made her feel warm and attractive anyway. It excited her in a way that only ballet had done until then. She pretended to ignore him, sitting down on a chair to tie her pointe shoe laces instead of standing and posing as some of the other girls did. She didn't want to show how interested she was.

Avgustin was attractive, but not handsome or beautiful like the male dancers were. Instead of classical features, his were somewhat rugged and peasant-like. Definitely not a suitable candidate for fatherhood if Tasha wanted to breed her own dancing children as her mother had. Avgustin was like no man she had ever met. And his rough charcoal sketches were good too.

"You inspire me!" he would say to dancers and they would giggle.

Of course if Veronika ever found him there she would order him to leave. "Why do you let that man in here?" she would ask, even though none of the girls would answer. "Foolish girls—you think a man like that will keep you happy?"

Tasha remained remote during these pep talks. She knew what she wanted in life. Her career was all important. Wasn't that what she had always been told? She believed this was a good future and she would never leave for a penniless artist—no matter how intriguing she found him. The pains in her overworked joints and the days when she was *en pointe* so much that her feet bled, skin peeling from her toes, attested to her dedication. That didn't stop her being intrigued by Avgustin anyway.

Tasha heard the girls talk about men all the time. Few remained virgins for long, so many beautiful male dancers around them. It was often a given that dancers would sleep with their partners to increase the intensity of their performances. Rarely, one of them would become pregnant, a situation that was rapidly remedied and the girl in question would take better care next time. Though most were savvy enough to make sure that nothing unwanted happened because of these liaisons.

Tasha, until Avgustin came on the scene, hadn't shown any interest in sex. But she found her one obsession, to become the best dancer at the Bolshoi, wavering as she was distracted by the artist. At night, lying in her single bed, she thought of him while the other girls slept. And she began to listen more intently to the chatter about sexual encounters.

"Did you like it?" she found herself asking one friend, newly deflowered by the company's male lead.

"Oh yes," said the girl. "I can't wait to try it again."

"But did it hurt?" Tasha asked.

"Pah! Just for a second. Like when you prick your thumb when sewing on the ribbons. It was nothing to the pain we all feel every day. And after that it was all very exciting."

Tasha asked no more but she had been left wondering what that level of excitement was. Could it be more exciting than doing turns? Or leaping across the stage? Or being lifted as though weightless by your partner?

Her mind flew back again to the night she lost her virginity. Not to Avgustin, but to one of the male dancers. She'd done it in anger, not passion, because Avgustin had rejected her advances. What was it he had said?

"You're just a child. What is the hurry?"

And it was true that at sixteen, Tasha had looked like a prepubescent instead of a young woman, but all the dancers did.

Even so, she had the emotions of a woman, and so, she was determined to show him she wasn't a child.

The male dancer she picked had been unfeeling as he broke her in. As if he was doing his duty for the ballet. There was no emotion, or respect, just motion. It hurt too. More than the others said it would. Tasha had hated it and she felt dirty afterwards. But she still boasted about her exploits, just as the other girls did, with the same level of enthusiasm. Never admitting that it was the worst decision she had ever made.

Eventually Avgustin stopped coming to draw the ballerinas. Maybe he had all the inspiration and sketches he needed, or maybe Veronika finally managed to block his attempts. Tasha didn't know which but she still regretted her rashness, her hurry to grow up. It was only years later that she finally understood what Avgustin meant when he asked her what the hurry was. There was no hurry really; it was just the nature of things in the ballet. It had been foolish to conform.

Now, some twenty years on, touring in New York with the Bolshoi, she found herself wondering about Avgustin. She had heard he'd moved to America, but didn't know when or where, because they had long since lost touch. Then she had seen the newspaper that had been left in her dressing room at the theatre. The headline condemned an artist of murder and mutilation. Tasha was shocked to realize that it was Avgustin Juniper.

She *couldn't* believe it.

Avgustin had always been so sweet and respectful. After all any other man would have taken advantage of her when she offered herself like that, wouldn't they? It was insane.

Tasha finished stretching and began a series of practice turns. She liked to warm up alone these days, before the other, younger dancers arrived. Her reflexes were every bit as good as theirs but she always thought they were watching her, urging her to pull a muscle, or fall, just so that one of them could step up and take her place. Well that would be happening soon enough: but not before her last performance.

Tasha stopped spinning. She reveled in the breathlessness she experienced from the intensity of the exercise because it was not lack of fitness, but purely the way she pushed herself. She still worked harder than anyone else, and put in longer practice hours too. She had to go out with success, not failure. Nothing else would do to end her otherwise flawless career.

She heard a noise just outside the room that sounded like the brisk beat of a broom as it swept the floor. Tasha often saw the janitor at this time and so she thought nothing more of it until she heard a loud bang.

She stopped working and looked at the door, which she had left slightly ajar when she came into the practice room. It was dark in the corridor, but she was sure she had left the light on. Tasha walked to the door. It was probably a prank. Maybe her male co-star, Vasily, was fooling around. He had a strange sense of humor and Tasha knew he would be glad to work with one of the younger girls instead of her. She never worried about this though because it wasn't personal: just a vanity thing. And Tasha hadn't been interested in developing their relationship sexually because she knew Vasily was steadily working his way through the female soloists.

She pulled the door open. There was no light at all in the corridor. Tasha had never seen it so dark in there.

"Hello?" she said.

She contemplated walking out, trying to find the light switch, but then the dark looked so uninviting that she shrank back into the room. She closed the door. A tremor of fear rippled up her spine. She had travelled the world and never once been afraid of anything. So sure of her own strength and confident in life, Tasha barely recognized the sensation.

She heard that strange noise, an odd shuffling, again outside. She thought of calling out but decided to run the bolt across the door instead. It was an irrational urge but one that she couldn't quash. She felt an immediate relief as the bolt hit home.

She sighed.

She continued with her warm up exercises.

The door rattled. Tasha stopped again and looked at it. It had to be someone fooling around. Otherwise they would have called out by now for her to let them in.

"Who is it?" she asked.

No answer came.

"Go away. I'm working," she said firmly. "I've no time for these pranks."

She walked over to the piano. On top was a CD player. She inserted her practice disc. She turned the volume up trying to ignore the possibility that someone was on the other side of the door.

As she began a series of complicated turns, she chose a point across the room to focus on. Spotting prevented you from becoming dizzy during multiple spins and Tasha did this automatically. The point she chose was a clock above the piano and she turned in a circle on one leg, while extending the other, her arms outstretched.

On the third turn a black fog appeared to be forming over the clock. Tasha slowed down. The clock and indeed the piano had completely disappeared from view. All she could see was blackness. Like a thick miasma floating in front of her. She stumbled mid-turn, then stopped and starred at the spreading darkness.

Something reached for her. Hands stroked her arms, catching her by the forearm as she was yanked forward. But the blackness was a void in front of her eyes. She was pushed down to the floor. It was then that she decided to scream for help. Surely someone was around. What the hell was happening?

The blackness lay over her. Pressing her strong legs down onto the wooden dance floor. She felt a stabbing pain in one hip. Then another pain in her other hip, but the sensation was instantly over. Whiteness spread before her now and she saw legs, a dancer's legs towering over her. The girl was wearing shoes just like hers. Pale pink and worn from frequent practice. Tasha noted that she even sewed the ribbons in the same way she did, with a final sweeping stitch that appeared like an X on each side. Her eyes travelled upwards to see who the girl was, but she was greeted by blackness once more. The only thing she could make out was a strange triangle on the side of her face, one pale blue eye. And one arm. Stark against the black, with a unique watch, a mosaic …

Tasha slipped into darkness as the girl began to spin. The legs were beautiful, just like Tasha's. The spinning continued, until the girl became one with the blackness again. And the whirling dark fog slipped away.

CHAPTER THIRTEEN

Two days to go and Juniper couldn't even begin to feel excited. The fact that this was something he had worked for all of his life was completely drowned by the news about Maria Matthews.

"She killed herself. Stupid bitch!" Cassandra had told him.

"I can't believe how little zympathy you show," Juniper said.

Juniper was already shaken by the news that someone had tried to kill him. This latest information made him feel more afraid of the law than of his attacker.

"My job is to protect *you*," Cassandra said. "I feel a little bit like I failed. Forgive me for sounding heartless. But she was the only person who could have cleared you. And the loss of an arm isn't such a bad thing. It wasn't that life changing. She was weak. She could have lived on and had a happy life."

"You are very passionate about this after all."

"I hate to see waste. I don't have a lot of time for self-pity or for weakness. Suicide is not an option for anyone. It angers me because it is such a shameful waste of life."

Cassandra had hired a chef. All food was being made fresh

inside her apartment from now on. The man was police vetted and all food brought in scrupulously checked.

Juniper had become as much a prisoner here as if he had been kept in jail. Granted the surroundings were nicer. He didn't suffer at all; he was fed well, could drink as much vodka as he wanted, and he was completely safe from the person who tried to poison him. At least he hoped so. If the threats were to be considered serious, Juniper would probably have to have a bodyguard detail with him at all times until after the trial. After that, if he was found guilty then none of it would matter anymore. If he was found innocent though … he didn't know where this left him with the psycho that thought he *was* guilty.

He pulled another fresh canvas from the stack by the window. This one was smaller than the one of the ballerina.

"Hi."

Juniper looked up to see Cassandra at the door. Then he glanced at the clock on the wall. He was surprised to find it was only four. She was home early.

She was wearing a skirt that day. His eyes swept the length of her before he could stop himself. He noted how nice her legs looked in the three-inch heels: well-toned, strong-looking. He looked away.

"Hi," he replied.

"What you working on?"

"I don't know yet. I'm looking at the canvas to see what picture should be there."

"What happened to the other one?"

"It vent … wrong."

Juniper felt a slight flush color his cheeks as he lied to Cassandra. But he couldn't explain, even to himself, why he had to hide the painting from her and everyone else at the moment.

"Oh well. They can't all be winners. I have good news."

"Yes?"

"The charges have been dropped. You're a free man."

"What do you *mean*?"

"Exactly that. Chandler called and said the DA is dropping the charges. There isn't enough evidence, and your alibi is rock solid for Maria and the latest victim."

"There's been another one?"

"Yes. But you needn't worry about it. They can't question you or even accuse you because you couldn't possibly know this girl. In fact, they even had police officers around you all the time."

Juniper felt his heart pounding in his chest. Relief and fear mingled together in inexplicable fashion. He was slightly dizzy, and quite sick.

"When did dis happen?"

"This morning. A dancer. A ballerina in the Bolshoi. This time the attacker took her legs!"

"My God!"

Juniper sank down onto his art stool.

"Yes. Terrible. But not your fault."

"Who vas she? I need to know."

"It doesn't matter. I thought you'd take this news well. You mustn't upset yourself like this, Avgustin." Cassandra came forward and wrapped her arm around his shoulder. "I'm sorry. I can seem a little cold sometimes. Listen this doesn't change anything for the moment. I still want you to stay here. You need to keep working uninterrupted and I think the best place for that is here. Plus, we don't know if this means you're safe from your attacker. And, just because the charges are dropped it doesn't mean public opinion of you will change. Not until they find the *real* killer."

Juniper said nothing but he sank into her arms. She was warm and responsive. It surprised him because she was so very distant and emotionless for the majority of the time. He almost expected that she would be icy to touch.

When her lips found his, it was a revelation.

She pulled him to his feet with surprising strength. Wrapping her arms around his neck as she drew him deeper into the kiss.

Juniper didn't think about the bodyguards as Cassandra led him to his bedroom. Nor did he wonder why she didn't take him to hers. It was the most natural thing in the world that tonight this should happen.

Once in his room though, Juniper became awkward. He stepped away from Cassandra and gazed at her in confusion.

"What do you want?" he asked.

"Make me *feel,* Avgustin," she said.

She lay back on the bed as he peeled off her skirt and opened her blouse. Her body was stunning. White as alabaster, her flat stomach and tiny waist gave way to pert breasts. He pulled away the modest push-up bra and bent to remove the small, boxer briefs. She had very little hair beneath them and Juniper buried his face between her legs and breathed in her scent. Cassandra moaned as he explored her. It occurred to Juniper that maybe this was why she had brought him here in the first place, but he quickly pushed the thought away as ridiculous. They had never met before the day she came to get him out of prison and who could be attracted to a man in chains, brought down as low as he had been?

But he had seen passion in her then: a conviction to free him and win the case. Now that desire had been fulfilled, Cassandra was looking for something different from him.

He slipped over her and her legs opened to receive him. But instead of entering, he merely rubbed against her until she squirmed. She wanted to feel, and Juniper was determined to make that happen. He bent his head; his mouth found her breast, and the nipple hardened immediately as he sucked her. Then his tongue flicked over and over her. Cassandra arched, and Juniper took her nipple into his mouth again.

After a few moments, he slid upwards and found her lips. She opened her mouth, and his tongue met hers. He moved his mouth over her, and plunged his tongue in and out until she got the rhythm and began to respond.

Her arms wrapped around him as she sank into the kiss, enjoying the feel of his invasion. Her beautiful breasts pressed against him, and his cock grew harder. He wanted her. More than any woman he had ever been around. Part of that had been because he always thought she was "off-limits." Even now, doubt leaked into the back of his mind as he realized this would change their relationship significantly.

"We need condom …" he murmured.

He felt her hand reach down between them until she found and grasped his hardness. Then she slid her hand over him until he gasped. The doubts slipped away as the lust surged forward again. Meanwhile she had produced the condom, and slipped it easily over him. She placed him between her legs, opening the soft lips until the head of his cock was lodged between them. Then Cassandra rolled her hips upwards. Juniper pushed back and found himself partially buried in her warmth. She was tight, not quite ready for him, but he pulled back and pushed down and into her once more. His cock went deeper. She was so tight it almost hurt, but the sounds she made beneath him—small gasps of excitement and pure lust—told him she was feeling only pleasure and she wanted more. She rolled back to meet his next thrust and Juniper was all the way in, sheathed inside her as her natural wetness kicked in.

The rhythm picked up between them, Cassandra thrusting back hard until the gasps became cries and she rolled her head in the pillow. Bursts of water leaked from her eyes as she came over him. There was a warm gush and she grasped him as she spasmed against him.

He rested over her, neither moving or pulling away, until her orgasm stopped. Then he began to slowly move again, building the pace until she cried out. This time he followed, letting his orgasm burst into her. It was the best one he could ever remember having, and he didn't know why. Perhaps because she had given herself to him so completely or maybe, after so much stress it was a more intense relief.

Afterwards she snuggled up into his side and he stroked her arm as they lay in silence.

"What was she called?" Juniper asked.

"Who?"

"The girl. The ballerina."

"Tasha Voronov. She's a very famous dancer," Cassandra said.

Juniper didn't answer. *Tasha.* He thought back to the girl with the beautiful legs. Sixteen years old, fresh and innocent. He *knew* it was the girl in his painting. But the Tasha he knew would be close to forty years old now, how then could it be anything more than a coincidence that she was the latest victim?

He fell asleep with Cassandra beside him but his dreams were far from restful. Whoever was doing this somehow had access to his work. In his dream, he saw Cassandra uncovering the painting as it stood on the easel. He saw her eyes widen with something akin to envy as she saw the loving brush strokes on the legs of the dancer. One outstretched, the other *en pointe* as she was captured in the middle of a turn. He saw Cassandra's fingers trace the line of thigh, just below the groin, and in this insane and confused dream, he witnessed the removal of the leg.

He jumped awake, heart pounding, half expecting to find Cassandra gone, but she was there—sleeping like the proverbial baby. Her beautiful face was relaxed and her lips upturned in a half-smile as though her dreams were rich with happy thoughts.

CHAPTER FOURTEEN

Thank you for meeting me," Chandler said as he sat down at the table opposite Lauren.

It was six in the evening. Chandler had only just finished at the latest crime scene when Lauren had called him. It was as though she had some sixth sense that he needed her. The latest attack had left him shaken. Not least because it now meant that Juniper was completely in the clear. They had no leads, no suspect and they had no idea how many more women would be mutilated before the perpetrator was finally caught.

"You sounded upset," Lauren said.

"I was. Sorry. I'm supposed to be standing on my own two feet now, aren't I?"

"I know we aren't working together anymore but I'm glad I called to see how you were doing," she said. "Even happier that I was nearby."

Lauren had suggested this restaurant. It was an intimate Italian with views overlooking the water. From the patio you could see Liberty with her torch held high, regal crown lit up so that low-flying aircraft could see her. Chandler and Lauren had a table overlooking the view. They had never met outside of her office before and Chandler was a little uncomfortable with the intimacy of the chosen surroundings.

The waiter came over with the wine list and Lauren took it. "I don't mind if I do," she said. "Should we share a bottle? I assume you're off duty now?"

Chandler was about to refuse, but then he remembered that his car was back at the station. He had travelled to the crime scene with Sarasvatī. He could get a taxi home tonight. It had been a long time since he had shared a bottle of wine with anyone, and the thought was appealing.

"Okay," he shrugged. "I prefer red."

"Me too," smiled Lauren. Then she ordered something that Chandler couldn't even pronounce.

They ordered steaks, both medium. Chandler was amazed that she liked the same things as he did and he found himself passing the time with trivial conversation as the waiter came back with the wine, which Lauren then tasted and approved. Chandler wasn't much of a connoisseur but the wine was good. The first glass went down quickly while they ate a starter of garlic shrimp.

"So. The case," Lauren said eventually. "A new victim?"

"Yes," Chandler said. He almost didn't want to discuss it with her. He was having fun and didn't want to alter the mood.

"We thought we had our man, but now know we don't. It almost feels like someone is playing with us."

"What do you mean?"

"Juniper looked guilty. The blood splat evidence, the possible lover-argument motive …"

"But you weren't convinced anyway," Lauren stated.

She sipped her wine and looked straight into his eyes while he talked. He was struck by how beautiful she was. Yes—he'd been aware she was attractive, but tonight her hair was loose, down over her shoulders, and she was wearing make-up. The dress she wore was low-cut, purple and flowing. Very feminine and not at all like the formal suits he usually saw her in.

"You're right. I didn't believe he was guilty. It all seemed too convenient from the start," he said looking down.

Chandler was alert, as though this moment was crucial but he couldn't understand why. He wasn't used to talking about work over dinner. It was odd but somehow right, as though this informal environment was the best place to gain clarity.

Lauren nodded. "I always thought so, by the way you talked."

Chandler took a large swig of the wine. He was feeling the effects but he didn't mind at all. It made him relax and sitting with Lauren in this lovely, quiet place was just what he needed. It was such a long time since he had shared female company.

"I wanted to *prove* him innocent. You *know*? Then this latest one … a dancer. I don't even want to tell you the details: it's pretty horrific. Juniper had the best alibi ever. He was surrounded by my men. There was no way he could have done it."

"You said someone tried to kill him?" Lauren prompted.

"Yes. And this all makes me wonder. Is it about *Juniper* really, and not the victims?"

Lauren was quiet. She nodded as though thinking through what he had said.

"You mean … someone wants to frame him for the attacks?" she said finally.

"Yes … No … I don't know. It's just this random thought I keep having. I can't figure it out though. But Juniper is still in this. I just don't know why. Hell. I mean—he still might have killed Annabel Linton. These others could be a coincidence."

"But you don't think so?"

"No. I don't think the man has a mean streak in his entire body. But then most serial killers function as normal people even while they are committing atrocities."

"The mind of a serial killer ..." Lauren mused. "I prefer to work with people who can be helped."

"So, you don't think this killer is salvageable then?"

"Harvesting body parts ... sounds a bit Dr. Frankenstein to me."

"We've been through every scenario you can imagine, from cannibalism to raising the dead. Who knows what motivates this weirdo. Whatever it is, he gets off on mutilation. I mean he has ruined all of these lives. And if he didn't kill them, they go on to finish the job themselves."

"What do you mean?"

"Oh, I didn't tell you. Maria Matthews killed herself."

"Oh my God. That's *terrible*," Lauren said and Chandler noticed she was genuinely upset. Lauren put down her fork and picked up her wine glass. She took a large gulp, not the ladylike sips she had enjoyed previously. "This is all getting out of hand."

"Sorry," Chandler said.

"What for?"

"I've ruined the evening."

"You have nothing to be sorry for, Jake. This isn't your fault at all. I can see now just why you were so upset. I suppose the ballerina will have to be kept on death watch?"

Chandler nodded. "The doctors have her heavily sedated at the moment. She said that the person ..."

"What?"

"It doesn't matter. It was just shock talking anyway."

The main course arrived and they fell silent as the waiter served up their meal and topped up their wine glasses.

"Maria Matthews," Lauren said as the waiter left. "I never would have thought that. Just for an arm. She had so much life left."

"I know. My sentiments exactly. It was horrible but not as bad as ... the dancer."

"Jake, I think you better tell me what this ... person ... did to the ballerina."

"He took her legs," Chandler said bluntly. "Then she said …"

"Tell me. You must know you can't shock me by now."

Chandler paused. He picked up his glass and glanced down at the remains of the full-bodied wine. Then downed the contents in one swallow. "She said that the 'monster'—her words—'took her legs and put them on.' Insane, I know."

Lauren grew very quiet. Then held up her hand to signal the waiter.

"More wine, I think."

Chandler insisted on travelling back to Lauren's apartment in the taxi. As the evening wore on he had become worried about leaving her alone. It seemed an irrational fear, but he believed that anyone could now become a victim of the killer. They hadn't established any connection with Tasha Voronov and Juniper—other than the fact that they were both Russian—and so the latest attack seemed completely random.

At Lauren's doorstep the moment became awkward.

"Coffee?" she said.

"No. Thanks …that would be …"

"Technically we aren't seeing each other anymore on a professional level," Lauren said.

Chandler realized it was true, but her bluntness surprised him. Their sessions had ceased, even though she did still check in on him. Now Chandler wondered if those calls were more for her, than for him. He weighed up the situation while the taxi idled in the street. He wanted to go up to Lauren's apartment, see how she lived. He wondered what he would learn about her personally. Was she just offering coffee or some other form of comfort?

Either way, Chandler couldn't bring himself to go inside. He wasn't ready to cross those boundaries. It would be a betrayal to Jules.

"Thanks for seeing me home," Lauren said as though she could read his mind. She placed a soft kiss on his cheek. "If you need me, you know where I am."

As the door closed behind her, Chandler was left with a tingling sensation where her lips had been. He liked it. He liked it a lot. And a wave of intense guilt blackened the mood of the evening.

As he sank into the rear seat of the cab, heading back to his house for the first time in a week, Chandler knew that their relationship had changed. The thought scared and excited him. He experienced a deep sense of regret and Jules's image came into his head. He saw her on their wedding day. The happiness he had experienced then was like lead in his stomach now, because behind it all he couldn't forget the end.

"One day it won't hurt so much," Lauren had said to him at one of their sessions. Her voice echoed in his head as the cab pulled up outside his home as though she could reach inside him.

He paid. Then, he hesitated on his doorstep.

Lauren, surprisingly, didn't live that far from him.

He could go back.

But no. He had to check his mail—it was a good excuse to focus his mind on leaving the evening where it had ended. Anything else might spoil their friendship. He placed the key in the lock and opened his front door, stepping inside without any thought, and without his usual reluctance.

He closed the door, then, without turning on the lights, walked upstairs. He realized he had a spring in his step by the time he reached the bedroom. Old memories tried to encroach on this new feeling of light-hearted happiness. He pushed them away with thoughts of Lauren. How he had watched her walking with such a graceful tread when she first entered the restaurant to find him waiting.

She had beautiful legs. He had never seen her in a dress before, and this one was only knee length.

The wine was still singing in his veins as he tumbled into bed.

Closing his eyes, he wished for a dreamless sleep.

And for once, his wish came true.

CHAPTER FIFTEEN

Joy Awen was excited. For the first time in years she was actually enjoying her work. It was the evening of the launch for Avgustin Juniper's art, and despite the few protestors outside declaring the viewing as "tasteless" as they called for "justice," Joy knew in advance that the launch was going to be a success.

News had already hit the press that the charges against Juniper had been dropped. This didn't mean, however, that the press weren't going to judge the artist anyway. Besides, as Cassandra said, all it would need was one piece of evidence to point at Juniper again and he would be right back where he started. Unless the killer was found. The press, however, were already calling it a "travesty of justice." Cassandra had leaked the story of the attempted murder of Juniper to gain him sympathy, and the hype had made a whole list of new buyers come out of the woodwork. Joy had already sold the majority of the paintings on display, and had begun to take orders for others. These commissions would guarantee Juniper a lifetime of success, whatever happened.

"Avgustin," Joy said as he and Cassandra Moúsa came into

her office. "It is wonderful to see you. My! Don't you look handsome in that suit?"

"Cassandra chose it for me," Juniper said.

Cassandra Moúsa had chosen well. He was wearing a lightweight navy suit with fine pinstripe, a white shirt, open at the collar—no tie—and smart shiny patent leather shoes. His longish hair was washed and groomed, and combed back from his face it gave him an exotic look which, along with the expensive clothing, made him appear harmless, yet somehow dangerous. Joy flashed back to their brief sexual encounter. She wondered if he would be feeling in the mood to spend a little more time with her in the future. Maybe after the viewing.

Cassandra was wearing a long, pale pink satin dress that clung to her curves in a way that Joy envied. Her hair was swirled up and dressed with small diamantes. Around her throat she wore a very expensive necklace: a choker studded with large oval diamonds. The choker was part of a set, there were earrings, oval droplets that looked like tears, and on her wrist, over long white gloves, was a matching bracelet. Joy observed that the woman looked as though she were dressed for the opera, rather than a gallery viewing, but the event was high profile enough to justify the ostentation. Joy was also dressed in eveningwear. She wore a long dress of dark purple. Less slinky than Cassandra's, the dress was full around the hips and had a ruffle across the bust line, giving Joy the appearance of having more curves than were truly present.

"You look great, Joy," Cassandra said.

Cassandra slipped her gloved hand into Juniper's and the artist raised it to his lips, placing a small, discreet kiss on the back of her hand. Joy blinked. So, the lawyer hadn't wasted any time in sampling the delights of the brusque Russian?

Lucky girl. Ah well.

"You two are an item then?" she asked bluntly.

"It's early days to call it that," Cassandra said. "But we are getting to know each other."

Joy said nothing. She turned and went back to the other side of her desk. "I have something for you, Avgustin."

She sat down, opened a ledger and removed a piece of paper. She held it out and Juniper took the sheet.

"What's this?"

"A spreadsheet of the sales. Minus my commission, of course."

Cassandra glanced over his shoulder. "Ten million dollars in sales so far? That's amazing!"

"It's unprecedented. I have never had pre-viewing sales like these. Some of that is for commissions though."

"Commissions? What do you mean?" Juniper asked.

"I have buyers who have paid deposits for exclusive paintings. Some of them want their wives and daughters painted. I have a list with better instructions for you. But we will worry about that tomorrow."

"I can't paint wives and daughters …" Juniper said.

"Don't be silly. It's just the same as using any model. Only most of these will be provided by photograph, instead of in person. Anyone who wants to pose personally will have to pay more."

"No."

"What's wrong, Avgustin?" Cassandra asked. "This isn't beyond your capabilities. In fact it's easy money."

"It's not that. I don't want to use models, live or otherwise."

"But why?" asked Joy.

Juniper didn't answer but at that moment one of the bodyguards came to the office door. "They are opening the gallery. Any final instructions?" he asked.

"You've swept the premises?" Cassandra asked.

"Yes."

"Caterers and food vetted?"

The man nodded.

"Then let's get this show on the road."

"Wait here," Cassandra said to Juniper. "I'll come and get you when it's time."

He was to make a late and dramatic entrance when the guests were all inside drinking their first glass of champagne.

The event was ticketed and Cassandra stood by the door greeting the arrivals as they passed through the security screening. She recognized several celebrities, a couple of television news anchormen, some sports personalities and many wealthy business people. Once the bulk of the guests were inside, the doors were locked. Only those few late arrivals that had tickets and were on the list would be allowed to enter.

Cassandra made her way around the room, stopping to talk to a senator she recognized and an aging Hollywood movie star, whose face was familiar, but whose name she couldn't remember. The woman didn't know this of course. Cassandra was an expert at endearing herself to people. Every group she spoke to talked about her in warm tones as she moved on. She had a gift for being personable and saying the right thing. After half an hour of circulating she slipped back to Joy's office and found Juniper holding a large glass containing vodka and ice.

"You okay?"

"Yes."

"Joy will be introducing you shortly."

Juniper stood and followed Cassandra out through the storage entrance and to the back of a makeshift stage that had been specifically erected for the occasion.

"We all know why we are here," Joy's voice could be heard from backstage as she spoke concisely down the microphone. There was some brief feedback, quickly adjusted by the technician. Then Joy continued.

"We've already seen the talent of this man. I don't need to remind you of the grave injustice that was almost done to him. His innocence, fortunately, has now been proven."

"Not proven … yet," said a disjointed voice from the cluster of press that had been given entrance to the event.

"The charges," Joy continued, ignoring them. "Were, quite rightly, dropped. But of course we don't need to go over this old ground. What we want is to meet the man behind the talent."

The crowd clapped in the dignified way that the wealthy have.

"And I will welcome Avgustin up here to say hello soon. But first I want to remind everyone of the rules of auction. Envelopes containing your bid and details are to be given to any of my staff. The highest bidder wins the prize. We do however have another surprise for you. A new and previously undisclosed piece, recently completed by Avgustin."

Avgustin and Cassandra were in place to step up onto the stage for the reveal. They both knew that Avgustin's latest piece was a cityscape of New York. The people featured on the canvas were all faceless. Cassandra had thought it eerie and poignant.

In the center of the stage was a large easel on which stood the canvas. It was covered by a thick black cloth. The crowd were clapping and murmuring to each other at the news of a new painting.

"Some of the proceeds for this magnificent artwork will be going to Avgustin's chosen charity. It is a fund to help children suffering from leukemia. A charity close to his heart because he lost a relative to this awful sickness."

The crowd made noises of approval.

"So please bear this in mind when you put in your bids. Be generous. But without further delay, as I can see you are all getting a little impatient, I introduce to you: Avgustin Juniper."

Juniper froze as the burst of enthusiastic clapping signified the interest of the buyers to meet him. He felt queasy and afraid. Every serious artist dreamed of this moment. It was his time to shine. A time for triumph. A burst of adrenaline rushed into his face. He had nothing to worry about. The sales so far already ensured a rich and happy future with no fear of ever going hungry again. He couldn't shake the feeling of tragedy though. It was so awful to him that Annabel's death had led to this.

Cassandra took his arm as the clapping grew louder.

"Come on. You'll be fine."

The applause erupted once more as they stepped out onto the stage. Cassandra knew they looked like a couple. It was her intention that the press should realize a romance had blossomed between them. She clung to his arm, feigning being led, not leading, as camera flashes exploded in their faces, temporarily blinding them.

Joy held out a microphone to Juniper. He starred at it uncomprehendingly. "Say a few words," she prompted.

Juniper took the microphone, took a deep breath and began the speech that Cassandra had helped him rehearse.

"It has been a very difficult time. Not so much for me but the family of the victims. My heart goes out to Annabel's family. She was a beautiful talented girl, and it waz my privilege to know her. She was a brief candle snuffed too soon. A shining light in a wildernezz of night.

"I did not know Maria Matthews. It broke my heart to learn of her attack and the awful way this turned out must have been such torture for her family. I can only say that I hope my familiarity with her sister was not somehow a cause. I believe the police are doing everything they can. I do not regret that they have questioned me, or even mistakenly thought I was involved. They must do everything in their power to find this evil person and put him to justice and I will continue to help wherever I can."

After the speech, the reporters in the group rushed forward, throwing questions out. Cassandra took the microphone from Juniper.

"Ladies and gentlemen. This is not the time for questions. Avgustin has said all that he can this evening. I ask you respect that. It's time now to reveal the new painting. This is a personal favorite of mine. And I believe it may well be Avgustin's best work to date.

Two of Joy's employees appeared on stage. A man and a woman, both young and smartly dressed. They stood either side of the easel, carefully taking the top and the bottom corner of the cloth in each hand.

Joy nodded and the cloth was pulled away. The crowd stared dumbfounded at the painting and started to speak in hushed tones to each other once more.

Juniper cast his eyes out over the crowd. This was not the reaction he expected to his New York cityscape. He frowned, then stepped forward so that he too could see the front of the canvas on the stage.

It was a ballerina standing, poised, in a wasteland.

"No!" cried Juniper. "That's the wrong one!"

After that all hell broke loose.

CHAPTER SIXTEEN

There was no mistaking the fact that it was Tasha Voronov, albeit some twenty years younger. One of Chandler's officers had been present in plain clothes when the painting was revealed and now Chandler had been called in to take stock of the situation.

"I need to interview Juniper," he said to Cassandra.

"Not now. I had the bodyguards take him back to my place. He was *very* upset. I will bring him into your office tomorrow."

"Then I have some questions for you. You knew that Voronov was the latest victim and yet it never occurred to you that to sell this painting would be distasteful?"

"I never saw this painting before tonight, Detective. Avgustin never showed it me. This isn't the artwork that I had sent to the gallery."

"Then how did it get here?"

Cassandra spread her arms in a shrug of confusion. "I just don't know."

Joy stood below the stage.

"There's something strange going on here, Detective," she said. "I can vouch for the fact that this wasn't the painting I saw earlier today. It wasn't even remotely like it. In fact, I have a picture of it on my camera I can show you."

Chandler turned to look at Joy. "I'd like to see it. Perhaps you can email it to my office. I suppose this ruined your sales too?"

"The evening was ruined. Avgustin was too upset to carry on. It didn't help that your plain clothes officer pulled a gun and started yelling that he was under arrest," Joy snapped.

"The officer in question did what he thought was right. You didn't answer the question, Miss Awen," Chandler said.

"I don't know what you are asking me, Detective. But if you mean did we make money then that is between me and IRS."

"I'm confiscating this painting for evidence," Chandler said.

"You can't do that! That piece is extremely valuable," Joy said.

"Unfortunately, he can," Cassandra sighed. "But I must insist that the utmost care is given in transporting it to the station. Let Joy's people pack it properly at least."

"I'm afraid I can't have anyone other than my team touching this. It will need to be fingerprinted."

Detective Gemma Sarasvatī and Sergeant Steve Kristian climbed up onto the stage. Kristian took several photographs of the canvas, then began the careful work of fingerprinting the frame.

"It's the same frame," Cassandra observed.

Chandler turned his head to look at her while he waited for her to explain.

"The painting we were showing was the same size as this, and had the same frame. I assume whoever did this, switched the canvas somehow. Joy, where might someone hide the other painting? Any ideas? That will at least help us prove we didn't know of this one's existence."

Joy didn't answer.

"And who had access other than you today?" Chandler interjected.

"All of my staff. Some of the bodyguards," Joy said.

"My guards were thoroughly vetted!" Cassandra said, her voice sharp and impatient.

"That may be the case, but they do have access to the studio. Only someone on the *inside* could have switched this canvas for the one you say should have been there. I need to search these premises. Am I going to need another warrant, Ms. Moúsa?"

Cassandra looked at Joy; she saw the frown of concern crossing the brow of the gallery owner. "You know the drill, Detective. No warrant, no search," she said automatically.

Joy appeared relieved.

They let the police take the painting and as Joy closed the gallery door, only she and Cassandra remained on the premises.

"Drink?" said Joy.

"Why not?"

Cassandra followed Joy into her office. Joy opened a drawer in the filing cabinet and retrieved a bottle of whiskey and two tumblers. She opened the bottle and poured a large shot into each glass. Then she passed one to Cassandra.

Cassandra sat down in the chair that Avgustin had occupied earlier. She was facing Joy's desk as Joy sat down in her chair and kicked off her uncharacteristically high heels.

"Glad you said he couldn't search the place. Bad enough having him trample in like that, scaring away my customers. I really couldn't have coped with that tonight."

"The shit's going to hit the fan tomorrow as it is. Big mistake letting reporters in. That was a very bad call on my part. Sorry."

Joy took a swig of her drink. "We both did what we thought was best."

She placed the glass down on her desk.

"You looked a bit worried in there. Anything I should know?"

Joy rolled her eyes. "Off the record?"

"Of course."

"I have something that isn't quite … legal. I'm not sure if Chandler's detectives would notice but …"

"You mean the hidey hole behind that boring painting?"

Joy frowned. "You spotted it, huh?"

"You know … I have that same picture in my bedroom. I've always disliked it. But somehow I can't throw it away. Know what I mean?"

"Yes. I do." said Joy.

"So … what're you hiding?"

Joy stood, she pulled the key from around her neck and pushed aside the fake Van Gogh. When she opened the cupboard, Cassandra gasped.

"That's *horrible.*"

"I know," Joy answered. "Hideous."

"It screams of … hate."

"I agree."

"How did you find it?" Cassandra said.

"A few years ago someone brought it in. I knew right away it was valuable. I hated it but *had* to own it. Now I can't bring myself to … *sell* it."

Cassandra sipped the last drop of whiskey from her tumbler.

"More?" Joy asked.

Cassandra considered for a moment. "Okay … I understand what you mean, though. About that painting. It feels like … bad *karma*. You almost don't want to pass it on to anyone else."

Cassandra held out her glass and accepted another shot of whiskey."

Then Joy turned and closed the cupboard. It was a relief for both of them.

"It's like the picture of Dorian Gray," Cassandra mused. "That's what it reminds me of. Except it's a woman."

Joy shrugged and frowned. "Mmm. I know what you mean."

Cassandra finished her drink and stood. "I'd better get back to Avgustin. I'm sure he will be in a terrible state tonight."

"Artists," Joy said. "They really are hard work."

"If I were you I'd get that out of here before Chandler comes back with his search warrant. He's very astute."

"I will. Thanks for putting him off. It'll give me time to shift it."

Joy didn't say it but she was relieved to have an excuse to move the picture. Whenever she was in her office she was aware of it. As though the distorted cubistic eyes could see her through the wooden panel.

CHAPTER SEVENTEEN

Back at the station Chandler looked over the painting of Tasha Voronov. He really wanted to talk to Juniper. Despite the obvious evidence, Chandler was still convinced that Juniper was innocent. He couldn't have committed the crime. He was nowhere near Broadway and he had been under the watchful eye of his own officers. It was impossible.

There was always the possibility that Juniper had an accomplice though.

But why Tasha? Why now? The youth of the ballerina made him think that Juniper hadn't seen the woman recently. He already knew she must be someone from his past. It was obvious. It also meant that someone else knew that Tasha was part of Juniper's history.

Chandler glanced at his watch. It was midnight. Too late to pay another call to the hospital to talk to Tasha, plus the last report he had told him the woman was still under sedation. The Bolshoi insisted she be treated this way, they feared her waking, feared her learning that her once beautiful limbs had been taken from her in a mindless, cruel attack.

"Hi," said a female voice behind him.

Chandler turned to find Lauren standing at the door.

"Hi. What are you doing here?" he asked.

"I was called in to give a psych evaluation on a prisoner."

"Not usual …" Chandler said.

"No. They were desperate as they couldn't get hold of their normal doctor and because I'm on the payroll my name came up. Hard to refuse."

Chandler smiled. Lauren looked gorgeous. Unlike the other night she was dressed formally again. A black trouser suit, with a high neck blouse.

"Come in," he said.

Lauren walked into the incident room and began to follow Chandler towards his office when she saw the canvas of the ballerina. "My God. That's beautiful."

"Juniper," Chandler said glancing over his shoulder.

"Really? What's it doing here?"

"Long story."

"Why not tell me over a drink?" Lauren said.

"That's the best offer I've had all night."

A cab ride later they were sitting in an intimate booth at the local club.

"It's the first time I've been here," Lauren said. "Don't make a habit of going to bars alone."

Chandler was intrigued. The club was in walking distance of Lauren's apartment and she had recommended it. He couldn't understand why someone as lovely as her would ever be alone. He considered her for a moment. Early thirties, professional. Incredibly attractive. She could have anyone she wanted.

"So no one special in your life at the moment?" he asked finally.

"No. I broke up with my long-term boyfriend a few months ago. Haven't quite had the heart to try the dating circuit yet."

The waitress came over and Chandler ordered a gin and tonic. Lauren asked for wine.

Chandler wasn't sure what to say. Anything he could think of was clichéd, so he paid the waitress and they sipped their drinks in silence. It occurred to him that Lauren's ex must be some kind of jerk to let a woman like her go.

"That painting …" Lauren said.

Relieved, Chandler was glad to tell Lauren about the night's escapades and the painting.

"Sounds strange," she said. "If I was a criminal psychologist, which I'm not, I'd say the perpetrator is attention-seeking. They want you to keep looking at Juniper for some reason I can't fathom. But yet it's perfectly obvious that it isn't him. Unless he has an accomplice of course."

Chandler nodded. "It's what I've been thinking too. Whoever it is must be close to home. I suspect they were the person who sent the death threats, and probably poisoned Juniper too."

"Could he have poisoned himself?" Lauren said.

Chandler grimaced. "I can't imagine it. The guy is … nice. Kinda naive. You know? I think he's as much a victim of this fucked up thing as anyone is."

Lauren grew thoughtful. "Look. I'd like to see some more of his work. Maybe I'll take a trip down to the gallery myself tomorrow. I might be able to throw some light on his mental state. Although I can't guarantee anything."

"I can't see any harm in that. The gallery can't object to me taking you there."

"Wouldn't you rather I went as like … a customer? They might reveal more if I did."

Chandler thought about it. "I don't want to put you in any danger, Lauren. Whoever is doing this is connected somehow to Juniper. I think it best I come with you."

"Okay."

Chandler noticed that Lauren's wine glass was almost empty. "Another?"

"It's late. I have something much nicer at home. Want a nightcap?"

Chandler followed Lauren inside to find a pleasant open-plan lounge, dinette and kitchen just off a wide corridor that led in from the hallway.

"Take a seat," she said pointing to an expensive-looking white sofa. "I'll go and get us a drink."

Sitting down, Chandler glanced around. Lauren's apartment was nothing like the plain and serious environment of her office. There were several pieces of art on her wall. All much nicer than the generic painting he had seen above her desk. The room was painted in shades of mauve and cream. The sofa he sat on was plush and comfortable, made of a silky velour that he couldn't resist running his fingers over. On the floor was a long, shaggy, rug of mauve and silver, which subtly matched the walls without being too much. Against the wall he saw a bureau that was polished chrome in color. On top was a decanter set. One port, one whiskey and one possibly brandy. Lauren liked her spirits.

The room was separated from the kitchen by a marble-topped breakfast bar and work surface, under which were three cupboards. Lauren went behind them into the kitchen space to fetch glasses from a cupboard on the back wall. Chandler noticed two doors down a short corridor past the kitchen. The oddest thing about the room was the lack of a television. Chandler always switched his on when he was home: the noise made the place less empty. Lauren was used to living alone: silence didn't bother her at all. There was also no sign of anything left over from the "long-term boyfriend."

Lauren returned with two crystal glasses and ice, and then she went over to the decanters. “Brandy?”

“Great,” Chandler said.

She poured a heavy measure of amber colored liquid into both glasses. Then she came over to the sofa. She held out one glass which Chandler took, then she sipped from the other.

As Chandler lowered his glass, resting it on his thigh, Lauren bent down. She placed a small kiss on his lips. The drink he had taken earlier hadn’t dulled his senses enough for him not to be taken by surprise by her direct approach. He swigged his own brandy as she pulled away.

“I won’t be long,” she said. Then she walked over to the breakfast bar and left her glass there.

She carried on down the short corridor and opened the second door. Then she disappeared inside the room.

A few minutes later she returned wearing a lightweight robe which parted to show her beautiful legs as she walked towards him.

“What’s going on?” he said.

“Jake, you aren’t that naive. I’m seducing you.”

“We can’t …” he said.

“Yes, we can. You’re no longer my patient.”

She took his hand and with surprising strength pulled him to his feet. She wrapped her arms around his neck drawing his head down until his mouth reached her half-opened lips.

Her kiss was warm and Chandler immediately lost himself in it. He crushed her slender body to him, tongue searching her mouth as lust coursed into his loins. The sensation was so intense it hurt. He had cut himself off from his sexuality the day Jules died, now he didn’t think about her at all.

Lauren backed away and for a moment Chandler’s sanity returned as she released him.

What am I doing? This shouldn’t be happening.

She took his hand, and he felt powerless to resist as she led him down the corridor and into the room she had just come from.

It was a bedroom, deceptively large for the size of the apartment, and the bed in the center was a super king size. Chandler didn't resist as Lauren pulled away his jacket, tossing it casually over a chest seat at the foot of the bed. She undid the buttons on his shirt one by one, and then peeled it away. He was sweating a little now. Partly from excitement, partly nervousness.

When she kneeled down at his feet and unzipped his trousers, Chandler stopped her hand. He sat down on the edge of the bed and pulled Lauren to him, kissing her lips, then he let his hands roam over her arms, as his mouth lightly kissed her neck.

He didn't remember removing his trousers after that but suddenly he and Lauren were lying close on the bed. He pushed away the robe to find she was wearing matching bra and panties in blue satin.

The robe fell to the floor at the side of the bed and Chandler reached around her to unclip the bra, only to find it was a front fastener.

Lauren giggled as he struggled with the clip, and then she helped his trembling fingers.

"It's okay," she said, kissing him again as the bra fell away.

She took one of his hands and placed it on her breast; they were incredible. Pert, not too small or large, just perfect.

Lauren rolled him onto his back, then she reached down and removed her panties. Lying down half beside him, half across his chest, she ran her hand over his smooth hairless body, and down towards his boxers.

Chandler was so hard that her touch almost hurt, but her gentle fingers only briefly lingered on him as she pulled away the boxers and cast them down to the floor the same side as her robe and underwear.

She slid over him, eyes meeting his, beautiful smile in place.

It wasn't smug, just loving, and Chandler trusted her as she straddled him.

His cock pressed against her stomach, Lauren made no move to place it closer to her center. Instead she leaned forward, stroking his chest, running light fingers over his nipples until she drew small gasps of pleasure from him.

Chandler's excitement grew to painful proportions. He couldn't remember ever being so aroused and so, growing a little impatient he rolled her onto her back and positioned himself between her legs.

"Not yet," she said.

They kissed again. Chandler stroked Lauren's body, hands and mouth searched and explored until he thought he had tasted every part of her. Then he parted her legs, mouth descending into her soft folds.

She gasped beneath him.

"It's time," she said.

He slid over her again, this time Lauren opened her legs to him, and reaching between them as she helped his cock find her opening.

Chandler was so excited he couldn't wait to feel her. He pushed in hard, and Lauren rolled her head back into the pillows moaning with pleasure as he filled her for the first time.

They made love. It was sensual, passionate, and fierce. And it was like nothing Chandler had ever experienced before.

When they had both reached climax, Chandler rolled away and then pulled Lauren into his arms. He was still shaking from exertion and nerves as he held her. But he felt completely satisfied.

She snuggled into him. Chandler was surprised by how comfortably she fit under his arm and against his chest. It was as though she belonged there.

He closed his eyes, consciousness drifting until he fell into a deep—and for the first time in months—dreamless sleep.

CHAPTER EIGHTEEN

"You've taken your time," said Joy. "I called in at six thirty this morning."

"What d'you mean?" said Chandler.

Waiting for Lauren, Chandler was surprised to find Joy Awen opening the gallery door to him.

"We had a break-in last night. Two of Avgustin's paintings have been vandalized."

"What?"

"Do you want to see?"

"Yes. I was … waiting for someone. She may turn up any moment."

Chandler's phone vibrated in his pocket. He withdrew it and looked at the message that had just arrived from Lauren.

Sorry! Patient emergency! I'll call into the gallery later anonymously and check out the paintings.

Chandler stowed his phone and followed Joy inside. Joy locked the door behind him.

"Obviously I can't open until your forensic people have been and we can clean up."

"Show me," Chandler said.

Joy led him into the main gallery. There he looked around the room. Juniper's pictures hung on the walls, and one, that of Annabel Linton, stood on an easel in the center. The picture would normally have been roped off from the room so that viewers could look, but not touch. However the thick red rope was pulled away, and the heavy metal stands it had been threaded through were knocked over. The painting itself was scored and ripped over the face. The canvas looked as though it had been attacked in a frenzy with a knife.

"That painting was worth a million dollars," Joy said. "The other one is around the corner."

Chandler followed Joy through the arch that led into the second part of the gallery. On the wall, lit by a down tilted spotlight, the painting of Susan Matthews was also ripped and torn. Again, the girl's face was spoiled.

"Another valuable piece," Joy remarked.

"How did they get in?"

Joy took Chandler out of the gallery and into the staff kitchen. At the back of the room they passed through another door that led to a giant loading area. This led out into an alley at the back of the building. The loading bay had huge doors that rolled up and down by a well-maintained mechanism inside. The large shutters were closed and secure. There was also a small, reinforced door at the side of the loading bay: this was open and had been busted off its hinges.

"What the hell could do that?" said Chandler.

"Exactly," said Joy. "That door is better than security standards recommended by my insurance company and they are strict. It's extra thick. Steel reinforced."

"You say you rang this in?"

"Yes."

Chandler retrieved his phone from his pocket again then he called the station. Within half an hour the forensic team was on the premises.

"Do I need a warrant now, Miss Awen?" Chandler said.

"Of course not, Detective, your people can go anywhere they wish. I have nothing to hide."

Chandler left the team to do their work and then he went outside into the back alley. He looked around for any evidence that the burglar could have left. There was nothing that could explain how the door had been damaged.

Then he remembered Lauren. He hadn't replied to her text, and so he thought it best to call her.

He found her details in his contact list and pressed dial. She answered on the third ring.

"Hi. Sorry I had to duck out this morning."

"That's okay. Just wanted to let you know the gallery is closed today anyway."

"Really? Why?"

"Break-in last night. Two of Juniper's paintings were defaced."

"Good God. Which ones?"

"One of Annabel, the other Susan Matthews."

"Tell me about the defacing."

"It was a violent attack as though the person doing it hated the subject not the art. If the ballerina picture hadn't been in police custody I suspect it would have been destroyed too. The frenzy was focused on their faces."

"It's like … the killer is crossing these women off a list."

"My God. I hadn't thought of that," said Chandler. "They may still try to get to the other painting. I'll have to put some security on it, though you'd think it would be safe in a police station manned twenty-four seven."

"Hopefully this person isn't stupid enough to try anything there," Lauren said. "On a happier note, I had a great time last night. Come round for dinner later? Say around seven, if you're free?"

"I'm free," Chandler said. "I'll be there."

Chandler realized he was smiling.

"For fucksake," said Gemma Sarasvatī. "I've been waiting out here for half an hour, while Cassandra Moúsa gives us the run around."

Chandler was taken aback by Sarasvatī's uncharacteristic fury as he exited the elevator at Cassandra's apartment.

"You've told them we want to speak to Juniper?" Chandler said.

"Yes. But he's asleep. Then in the shower. Not quite dressed yet … Probably eating a luxury breakfast while we hang around out here."

Chandler knocked hard on Cassandra's door. The bodyguard on security detail outside the door looked at him and frowned.

"You want to stop justice being done?" Chandler said. "Then we can take this up at the station."

The bodyguard pressed the button on the microphone on his radio, "Detective Chandler is outside."

The apartment door opened and Chandler found another guard on the other side.

"Come in Detective," he said. "Ms. Moúsa is waiting for you."

Chandler glanced at Sarasvatī, who was looking decidedly pissed that she had been refused access when the door was opened for him immediately.

"After you," Chandler said.

Sarasvatī hurried in through the door as though she feared it would be slammed in her face. Chandler followed.

They were led into Cassandra's lounge. It was a huge room, with a grand piano in one corner, a large open fireplace in another, and impressive antique-looking furniture that wouldn't have been out of place in an English country house. Cassandra was sitting by the fire like the Lady of the Manor reading a newspaper. Juniper was next to her.

Juniper looked out of place: like a puppy who feared punishment when allowed on the furniture for the first time.

Cassandra put the newspaper down, but not before Chandler noticed the photograph of Juniper standing next to his painting of Tasha Voronov. In the photograph, Juniper hadn't noticed the error and he was smiling. It must have been taken seconds before he realized. He looked excited, pleased and the headline took his expression completely out of context.

SMUG ARTIST REVEALS PAINTING OF LATEST VICTIM

Chandler had already seen this particular tabloid, and he hadn't been very impressed with the condemning story that was bound to prejudice future jurors. Now Cassandra placed the paper face down on top of a pile of others at her feet on the floor. All of them had a different angle, but most of them implied that Juniper was guilty.

"Ah, Detective. If only you were as effective at finding the real killer as you are at hassling my client."

"Ms. Moúsa," said Sarasvatī. "You know we needed to speak to Mr. Juniper about the painting. This is an ongoing murder investigation."

"Detective Chandler," Cassandra said ignoring Sarasvatī. "Do take a seat; my client is obviously willing to help however he can."

Sarasvatī crossed her arms in fury but said nothing more as Chandler sat down. Chandler was confused by the open hostility between the two women. He didn't know why Sarasvatī had been refused entrance until he arrived, or why Cassandra wouldn't address her. He glanced at Sarasvatī again. He would have to ask her what had happened before he arrived. She must have done something to piss Cassandra off.

"Mr. Juniper, can you tell me about your relationship with Tasha Voronov," Chandler asked.

"Tasha was a dancer at Bolshoi."

"We know that," snapped Sarasvatī. "When did you first meet her? How well did you know her?"

Juniper frowned, glancing at Cassandra for direction.

"You may answer the Detective," Cassandra said coldly.

"I went to draw them. Years ago, when I lived in Moscow."

"When did you last see her?"

"I don't know. Twenty years I think."

"Yet you drew a picture of her. Older than she would have been twenty years ago," Chandler said. "Which implies you've seen her since."

"Maybe I saw her on the television sometime. I don't remember. I have photographic memory. Images just come out sometimes onto zhe canvas."

"When did you paint this one?" Sarasvatī asked.

"A few days ago. When I came out of zhe hospital. I had dream about her dancing. Zhen I remember her face."

"I see," said Chandler. "Who saw the painting when you finished it?"

"No one. I put it at the back of my canvases. Next I know it's in gallery."

"You didn't see the painting before then either, Ms. Moúsa?" asked Chandler.

"As I said last night, I didn't even know it existed until it turned up at the viewing," Cassandra said. "If I had, I would have wanted it displayed anyway."

"Even knowing the girl had been attacked?" Sarasvatī said. She was still bristly.

"Not because of that, Detective Sarasvatī. Because it is a *magnificent* piece of art. Detective, where is this line of questioning going?" Cassandra said, once more addressing Chandler. "You know my client couldn't have been involved."

"Someone close to your client *is* involved, Ms. Moúsa. This same person had access to a studio in your apartment that is surrounded by security. More than likely that person swapped the paintings, and tried to kill your client. So if you don't want our protection, then continue to be difficult. If you do, then start to be a little more cooperative."

"I suspect that the painting reached the gallery completely by mistake. It's obvious to me that it was carried in with other artwork, and when I told them to put the one of the derelict city up, one of Joy's employees thought it was this one. A completely genuine error, but this person is afraid to admit it. There is no way that my security men are involved and so it is the only logical explanation."

"What about the break-in at the gallery? Was that an accident too?" Chandler said.

"What break-in?" Cassandra said.

"Miss Awen hasn't told you yet? Two of Juniper's pieces were damaged. Sorry to be the bearer of bad news."

"That's terrible! We had another private viewing booked for this evening. Joy should have told me it was cancelled." Cassandra stood up. "I need to call her. Please don't ask my client anything while I'm gone."

She left the room for a few moments. Chandler sat in silence and Juniper looked around the room uncomfortably while he waited for Cassandra's return.

He's completely dependent on her, Chandler thought, realizing that Juniper wouldn't or couldn't meet his eyes.

Cassandra returned. "Thank goodness. Everything is still okay for this evening. Joy's people have the place cleared up, the door fixed and strengthened. I've said I'll post some of my men there overnight too. We can't let this happen again. Fortunately, the insurance company are likely to pay out on the paintings, so you won't lose out, Avgustin."

"This viewing tonight," Chandler said.

"Yes?"

"A private affair. No press I assume?"

"Not after yesterday's fiasco, no," Cassandra said.

"I'd like to be there. I'll be bringing a friend."

"Of course, Detective. A police presence would be welcome.

I'll make sure you're on the guest list. Detective Chandler and Detective Sarasvatī."

"No, not Detective Sarasvatī. I'll have Dr. Lauren Michaels with me," Chandler said.

"Very well," Cassandra said. "Now if you have no more questions, Avgustin and I both have work to do."

CHAPTER NINETEEN

Chandler collected Lauren from her apartment. She was wearing a plain black dress and high heels—showing off her lovely long and perfect legs. There was a brief awkwardness after the intimacy of the previous night, but as she wrapped her arms around him and kissed him, Chandler's embarrassment disappeared. He held her hand as he led her back to his car, and as they drove to the Gallery, Lauren placed her hand on his thigh.

"Thanks for letting me change our plans," he said.

"That's okay. This is important, isn't it?" Lauren said.

A red carpet lay in front of the Joy Awen Gallery and a stream of limousines were lined up to drop off their celebrity cargoes. Chandler drove past and found a parking space a few blocks away. Then he and Lauren walked back, hand in hand.

The exterior was swarming with security. Chandler had to show his badge before the men let them approach. The paparazzi had got wind of the "private viewing" and were being held at a distance by the mob of security men. That didn't stop them from using telephoto lenses, and Chandler and Lauren were caught in a round of flash bulbs as they walked up the carpet.

"So much for Cassandra Moúsa not having the press here ..." Chandler murmured to Lauren as they reached the door.

"You think she leaked it?"

"Of course. That's her MO."

The door was opened by a tall brunette with a clip-board. Chandler gave their names. The girl ticked the list and then stepped back to let them in. They entered, leaving the madness behind.

A young waiter offered canapés which were beautifully displayed on a silver tray, while another one brought around flute glasses filled with champagne. Lauren took a glass, but Chandler was technically on duty and so he opted for orange juice instead.

"Sorry," Chandler said as the waiter moved away.

"What for?"

"We were supposed to be on a date and I bring you out on a work thing instead."

"That's all right. I like working and I'm interested in Juniper's art. Besides, we can spend time together just as well here, and later."

Chandler smiled at her. Lauren noticed how much younger he looked when he smiled. She squeezed his hand.

"Come and see the paintings then," Chandler said. "I'd like to know what you think."

The gallery was heaving with the rich and famous once more. Chandler and Lauren walked through the throng then traversed the first art-covered wall. The room was cramped and so Lauren could only view the artwork up-close.

"His work is incredible," she said. "I'm not an art expert, but I'm struck by the realism of what he does. It's as though he sees everything, captures it all like a photograph, then translates that into paint."

"Today he told me he has a photographic memory. It was

why he was able to paint Tasha Voronov so well, even though he hadn't seen her for years."

"It stands to reason," Lauren says. "I expect that even when the models move he would still be focusing on them in their original positions. What talent."

Chandler nodded.

"There's definitely a connection between Juniper and our killer. Though I fail to see it," he said. "Other than some of his models have been attacked."

"I know what you mean. This girl for example …"

Chandler looked closely at the young model. She was blonde, petite, wearing a white Greek-style toga and posed in a classical "Greek goddess" manner. Chandler knew that all of the women Juniper had previously remembered using as models were now under police surveillance. Oddly, none of them had been approached. It was as though it were only Juniper's newest artwork that was attracting the attentions of the killer. This girl he remembered was called Tiffany Redman, and he had interviewed her about Juniper at the beginning of his investigation. Tiffany didn't live in New York, she had gone back home after finishing her degree, and she was in Indianapolis. Even so, the local police still had her on their watch list. Possibly that would cease if no further attacks occurred.

"She's fairly safe. She's not even living in New York now," Chandler said.

"Who is she?" Lauren said.

He said her name, and then immediately regretted it. He looked around but thought they were unobserved, and hadn't been overheard.

"Are you okay?" Lauren said.

"Yes. Just a little paranoid. I don't want to bring any press attention to the other models. We've managed to keep their names and locations completely secret so far. After all, you don't want to make it easy for the killer to seek them out."

"I understand. I shouldn't have asked."

"Lauren, you can ask me anything." He leaned closer with the intention of kissing her.

"Detective Chandler. You made it then."

Chandler and Lauren parted and they turned to see Cassandra and Joy behind them. He was surprised to find Gemma Sarasvatī there too.

"This must be Dr. Michaels," Cassandra said holding out her hand.

Lauren hesitated for a moment before responding then she took Cassandra's hand and shook it firmly. Chandler noticed that the women exchanged a look that said how curious they were about each other. Lauren gave Joy the same expression as she too introduced herself, and then she avoided contact with Gemma Sarasvatī completely. But Gemma didn't offer her hand and Lauren shrank from her, taking hold of Chandler's hand in a way that not only staked her claim but also sought, he thought, comfort.

"So, you work with Jake," she said to Sarasvatī in an attempt to cover the awkwardness.

"Yes," Sarasvatī said. "You work for NYPD too, don't you?"

Lauren nodded.

"Well, how nice that we've all met," said Cassandra.

Joy frowned at her side. "Yes. *Nice*."

"Absolutely. I'm admiring the artwork, though I'm no expert," Lauren said.

"Oh, I'm sure you have a valid opinion," Sarasvatī said. "Even I have one."

"I need to see more of them I think," said Lauren. "Excuse us."

Chandler found his hand being pulled and they turned away from the other women and came face to face with Juniper.

A look of total shock fell on the features of the artist.

"Avgustin? What's wrong?" said Cassandra.

Juniper looked from Lauren, to Cassandra, then to Sarasvatī and Joy. He backed away. Fear blanched his features.

"What's wrong Mr. Juniper?" asked Sarasvatī stepping forward.

Juniper turned and pushed his way through the crowd and rushed towards the kitchen Chandler had seen on his way to the loading bay.

"Go after him!" Joy said to Cassandra who rapidly followed her client.

"He looked like he'd seen a ghost," Chandler said.

Lauren was pale beside him, so was Joy, but Sarasvatī watched with predatory interest as Juniper hurried away.

"Excuse me a moment," Chandler said to Lauren. "Sarasvatī. A word."

He led Sarasvatī away from Joy and Lauren. He found a corner in the gallery, not empty, but less occupied than the rest of the room.

"What are you doing here?" Chandler asked.

"I thought it might help to have more police presence. There's a few other plain clothes in the room too."

"I said I was coming. That was overkill, Sarasvatī."

"After the murders, the break-in, and defacing of the art, I thought it necessary."

Though Chandler and Sarasvatī were both equal rank as detectives, Chandler was Sarasvatī's superior on the case. He didn't like the fact that she had gone behind his back, and against his instruction. More so that she hadn't told him.

"What did you do to piss off Cassandra Moúsa this morning?" he asked.

"Nothing. She came to the door and wouldn't let me in. I don't know what her deal was."

"Well, it was obvious that she had a problem with you, and for that reason alone you should have stayed away."

"I didn't see it, so it wasn't obvious."

Earlier that day Chandler had received a complaint about Sarasvatī via Moúsa's law firm. They had accused Sarasvatī of being unnecessarily rude to Juniper and Cassandra. Chandler hadn't seen it as a big deal and so he hadn't escalated the complaint, merely sent Cassandra's office a formal apology that he hoped would smooth things over. Her appearance at the gallery now might well mean that, despite Chandler's efforts, the complaint would reach their superiors.

"Go home," he said after explaining the issue clearly. "Let's hope a verbal apology now will stop this going further."

Sarasvatī left, but she wasn't pleased. Chandler, however, was happy to see that arrogant expression leave her face, even for a short time. Her behavior concerned him and he wondered how much of it was alpha females butting heads. Sure, Cassandra was annoying, but not so much that deserved this obvious and intense dislike from Sarasvatī. He decided that he would recommend her removal in the morning and would get her assigned elsewhere as soon as possible.

He returned to where he had left Lauren only to find she wasn't there. So he worked the room, observing who of the elite were present and keen to see Juniper's work so badly that they would come out on short notice. Had many of these people staked a claim on one painting or another? Or were they just voyeurs?

He saw Lauren and Joy talking just outside Joy's office. The two women appeared to be having a very intense, somewhat intimate discussion. They looked like old friends, not new acquaintances.

They stopped talking and turned in his direction as though they both felt his observation at the same moment. It was somewhat unnerving how they looked at him with a similar expression: curiosity.

"There you are," he said to hide his discomfort.

"Joy was just telling me all about Mr. Juniper's work ethic," Lauren said. "Fascinating."

"Really? In what way?" Chandler said.

"Well, Avgustin works incredibly fast. I've known other oil artists who take months on one piece. But Avgustin takes days, sometimes only hours, depending on the piece. Landscapes are effortless for him. He does take more time on portraits obviously. And yet all of this is still photo-realistic. Once, Cassandra witnessed him painting two pieces at once. Both completely different pieces of art."

"Two at once?" Chandler said. "How is that even possible? Is he ambidextrous?"

Joy laughed. "Oh no. He had two canvases side by side. One moment he worked on one, the next the other. It was very inspiring," Cassandra said.

As though hearing her name Cassandra came out of the kitchen. "I'm going to have to go. Avgustin has *run away*. I don't know what's upset him but I'm going to try and find him. Detective Chandler, if that Sarasvatī woman has said anything …"

"Ms. Moúsa, I doubt Detective Sarasvatī, who has an exemplary record, has said anything at all. I don't know what your problem is with her but …"

"I haven't time for this, Chandler," Cassandra said. "Ladies, do excuse me."

Cassandra left by the way she had come. Joy followed.

"I think we might have outstayed our welcome," Lauren said.

CHAPTER TWENTY

Juniper was in a state of severe agitation. He had roamed the streets for a while until he found a bar off the beaten track. Hoping no one would recognize him he ordered neat vodka and found the darkest corner of the bar to sit in. Then he considered what he had seen that evening. His heart was still pounding at the shock of it and he wished he could just erase it completely from his mind. But once seen, never forgotten.

He swigged down a shot of vodka in one gulp. Then topped it up from the bottle he had purchased from the bar. The alcohol didn't help: he couldn't get drunk, no matter how much he consumed or how quickly. In fact, he just got more and more sober as the evening wore on.

He looked around the bar but saw nothing as his mind tried to make sense of the last few weeks. He had hardly been outside during that time, and rarely had any moment alone except in his studio, and that was always subject to someone coming in to check on him.

There was something very freeing now about being away from Cassandra and the bodyguards. Even though technically his life was still in jeopardy. He realized he had needed breathing space. Everything was moving too quickly. His career, his affair —if that was what it was—with Cassandra. Now he also needed time to think about that *thing* he had seen at the viewing. Like a *Rusalka*—a mermaid—from Russian myth. He shuddered twice, as though a cold breeze had rushed through the bar to find him. But he wasn't cold. He couldn't stop thinking. What was it he had seen?

There was a group of women together, he vaguely remembered Cassandra was among them, but not who else. And one of them …

Juniper closed his eyes. It was the stuff of nightmares. Was his mind playing tricks on him?

The bartender flashed the light over the bar signifying last orders. Juniper glanced at his watch. It had been around eight thirty when he left the gallery and it was three thirty in the morning now. He had been there for hours.

Feeling guilty he decided the only thing he could do was return to Cassandra's apartment. He knew she would be worried, but hadn't been able to bring himself to turn on his cell phone to call her. Probably there would be messages, missed calls. It had been selfish of him to run away like that.

Look at me, I'm thinking like a married man, he thought. Then chuckled at himself because the thought of being tied to Cassandra wasn't that unpleasant.

He paid his bar tab and left. Outside the streets were deserted. Not even a car or taxi passing by. He would have to walk to one of the main avenues if he wanted to hail one.

He looked around for a minute trying to get his bearings. He was on 10th Avenue. Not too far from Madison Square Garden and the gallery. He took a right on West 30th Street.

At the next junction, he saw a cab coming his way. He hailed it but the driver ignored him.

"You bastard!" Juniper said.

"Need a ride?" said a voice behind him.

Juniper turned to see a female shape standing at the street corner. She was under a street light that didn't seem to be working. All he could make out was a black void that moved occasionally.

"No, thank you," he said. He wasn't in the mood to be bothered by some cheap street girl.

Another cab approached. Juniper waved his hands frantically and stepped out onto the street. The driver pulled over. Juniper quickly scrambled into the back and gave Cassandra's address. He glanced out of the rear window, back at the street girl, but all he saw was darkness. He shrugged. She had obviously moved on when she realized he wasn't customer material. The taxi pulled away and he sank back into the seats with relief.

A short time later the cab pulled to the curb outside Cassandra's loft. Juniper paid, then climbed out. He was tired now, and it occurred to him that he didn't have a key to get back in.

He doubted that Cassandra would be still out, and there were always guards around, so he rang the buzzer to her apartment.

"Yes?" said a voice he didn't recognize.

"It's me. Avgustin."

There was a burst of ear piercing noise as the door released. Juniper entered. Then closed the outer door behind him.

He glanced at the reception desk. No one was around and so he made his way over to the elevators.

He pressed the call button. Then, as he watched the numbers on the display going down, he heard movement behind him. He turned to look over his shoulder. The reception area was darker around the doorway than the rest of the space. Juniper frowned at the blot, which appeared like a black hole by the door. Then he glanced around. The marble floor was polished to a high sheen and it reflected the light from all of the lamps and spotlights that were turned on. Yet not in the area nearest the door.

The elevator arrived. Juniper stepped in but quickly turned to face the shadowed area. The doorway no longer looked dark and the floor glowed with reflected light. He shrugged, maybe a bulb in that area was on the blink, intermittently working. He would report it to the guards so that the janitor could fix it.

The elevator doors closed and Juniper relaxed as it started to move upwards. It came to a halt on the next floor. Sighing he waited while the doors opened.

No one was there.

Juniper frowned into the dark corridor, then pressed the button to close the doors. The same thing happened on the next floor, and the next. In fact, the elevator stopped at every floor. Each time Juniper gazed out into a black void. Juniper's nerves became more and more frayed. Finally the elevator arrived at the top level. But as the doors opened Juniper felt a compulsion to remain inside the elevator. The dark corridor was unappealing. And the lights on this level didn't seem to be working either.

He stared out into the blackness. A prickle of anxiety brought the hairs up on the back of his neck.

The darkness was staring back.

Juniper was frozen to the spot. His heart pounded in his chest with a primeval urge to flee, but there was nowhere to run to. Then the door to Cassandra's apartment opened and light flooded out into the corridor. A flurry of blackness swirled and disappeared, as though a breeze followed the light as it opened up the corridor once more.

Juniper knew that he had seen something inside that void but not what it was. He crossed himself quickly, something he had not done for many years. It seemed the right thing to do.

"Avgustin? My God, where have you been? I was so worried."

Cassandra threw her arms around him. The elevator door closed on them. Cassandra released him and pressed the open button. She took his hand and led him out into the corridor and towards her apartment.

Juniper looked up and down the corridor. It was now fully lit, with no dark corners. He ran his free hand over his brow.

"You scared me. I don't mind telling you."

"I'm zorry," he said.

Inside the apartment, the hallway was well lit. Juniper couldn't remember a time when it wasn't. Even at night, when he had ventured out looking for a snack, lights were on in hallway, bathroom and kitchen. He hadn't been aware of it until now. The darkness had never scared him before that night. Maybe the vodka he had consumed had made him paranoid.

He glanced at the door as Cassandra closed it behind them. She hadn't been concerned about the darkened corridor, but he still wondered, *what is out there*?

"Let me get you a drink," she said noticing he was trembling. "Something really upset you, didn't it?"

"I don't need one. I need to paint."

"Why?"

"Because I saw something tonight. I can't describe it. But I can show you."

"Okay," Cassandra said. "Do you want me to watch you paint?"

"No," he said.

He walked down the corridor and into the room set aside as his studio. Cassandra stood by the living room door watching him. Juniper entered the studio, switching on the light as he did so. The room lit up as bright as day, because Cassandra had installed extra lighting to ensure that Juniper could work at any time he pleased.

Juniper looked around and noticed a dark patch in one corner. He halted and stared at it, almost willing it to move.

Nothing happened.

"Cassandra!" he called from the doorway.

She came to him immediately and when Juniper looked back into the room, the peculiar patch of darkness was gone.

"Come in. Sit over there while I work," he said. "I need you to be my muse."

She came in with uncharacteristic meekness and sat in the chair Juniper had indicated underneath the skylight windows that gave Juniper the best light in the daytime and showed him the stars at night. Once he had thought only his own apartment made the best studio, but Cassandra's place appeared to have been created for him. This realization terrified Juniper now. The hairs stood up on the back of his neck once more and he shuddered again.

"Are you okay?" Cassandra asked.

Juniper didn't answer. Instead he obtained a fresh canvas from a stack by his easel. Then he removed the half-finished painting that was there, placing it down on the opposite side.

With the new canvas in place, he picked up a brush and began to paint.

From her place in the corner Cassandra watched him work for a while, her eyes narrowed as though she were looking for something around him. Then she grew tired. She looked around the room and followed stray shadows as they moved in time with Juniper's movements. It was as though he was conducting an orchestra of shadow, and the light and dark danced to his tune. Eventually her eyes closed and she fell asleep in the chair.

Cassandra opened her eyes and blinked. Juniper had stopped moving and was standing, staring at the canvas.

"Avgustin?"

She checked her watch. Two hours had passed. Surely he couldn't have finished already.

Cassandra uncurled herself from the chair and walked over to where Juniper was standing. His eyes were fixed on the painting.

It was hideous.

CHAPTER TWENTY-ONE

"I hoped you would come back," said Joy Awen as she gazed out into the dark alley behind the gallery.

Lauren Michaels stepped out of the shadows. Joy moved aside and the psychiatrist entered.

Joy secured the door. Then she led Lauren through the loading bay and kitchen and into the gallery. Her office door was open and she walked inside. Lauren followed.

"I haven't seen another of our kind for over fifty years," Joy said. "Then four of us meet in a matter of weeks."

The gallery had been closed for a few hours. Joy had remained, and the whiskey decanter on the desk, with the half-filled glass, was evidence that she had been there for the duration.

"Avgustin has a lot of talent," said Lauren. "Does it surprise you that so many of us have been attracted to it?"

"It shouldn't. But it does. I thought I was the last."

"The last time there was a calling like this it was Pablo Picasso," Lauren said.

"I remember. I was called."

"Me too," said Lauren.

"I don't remember you. Perhaps you wore a different face?"

Lauren smiled. She sat down and Joy poured another shot of whiskey into a clean glass. She held it out and Lauren took it without hesitation.

"Who's the fourth?" Lauren asked. "I obviously recognized the third."

Joy shrugged. "She'll come out of the woodwork, when she's ready. She's very good at hiding who she is. I think she may even believe she's human."

"So you knew Picasso too?" Lauren said.

"I was his muse, for a while. And then he found inspiration elsewhere."

"That's the thing with artists. Fickle." Lauren sipped her drink. "Good whiskey."

"Only the best for us," Joy said.

"I have that picture. In my office," Lauren remarked, looking at the fake Van Gogh above Joy's desk. "Isn't that odd? It's an awful knockoff too."

Joy laughed, "A joke. That's why I have it. So, you're a shrink?"

"We help people where we can, don't we?"

"I stayed with artists. Normal people don't inspire me."

"There's nothing normal about the people I deal with," Lauren said.

"I suppose there isn't …" Joy said.

"I gave up on artists after Picasso. He disheartened me. And the times were changing. You see, I was his muse for a while too."

Joy nodded her understanding. "So, you and Chandler …"

"Lovers. But it's a new thing. He needs me right now. He's been through a lot."

Joy nodded. "And we go where we are called."

Lauren downed her drink in one gulp. "So who is killing the girls? Any insight?"

Joy shook her head. "Not Avgustin, obviously. He's just … the truth is I don't know."

"A rogue then?"

"What do you mean?"

"I remember something like this happening before. In France. Don't you remember that? The missing girls?" said Lauren. "All around the area where Picasso lived?"

"No," said Joy. "I wasn't around for long."

"Funny. You seem so informed I thought you'd know more. But I'm glad we had this talk," said Lauren. "If you find out who is doing this perhaps I can help?"

"I'll call on you."

Lauren stood; she walked to the office door, then turned and smiled at Joy. "Don't get up, I'll see myself out."

She faded into a pale mist which hung in the still air for a few moments. Then a breeze picked up inside Joy's office. The mist turned like a miniature whirlwind. It swirled out towards the front door of the gallery in a fine line until it was narrow enough to slip through the key hole and away.

Joy was left alone in her office. She reached for the whiskey decanter and poured another shot.

"Show off," she muttered.

INTERLUDE

THE DIARY OF PABLO PICASSO

I don't know why I am driven to write these words.

My life is changing. I am surrounded by people who love me, need me, adore me. Everything in life that I have worked for is coming to fruition. And now the strangest thing.

A muse—I know this is what she is—has come into my life and is leading me down a path I had never considered.

CHAPTER TWENTY-TWO

"What the hell is that?" said Cassandra as she stared at the canvas. "That's horrible."

"It's what I saw. At the gallery," Juniper explained.

"You saw … *that?*"

Juniper nodded. "It was why I ran away. I was scared."

Cassandra stared long and hard at the painting. It was an outline mostly. A female shape. But parts of it were inky black, while other parts were … parts. *Human* parts. The head was dark but for a triangular shape in the face. This thing had one ebony arm, but the other was fully painted from below the elbow with a thin and expensive-looking women's watch on the wrist. Then there were the legs. Beautiful, toned, long and slender. Dancer's legs.

"Avgustin this is … it's the parts of the women you knew. Don't you see you're hallucinating? I probably need to get someone for you to talk to. It's no wonder you're disturbed after all that's happened."

"No. I saw it."

"You can't have. Nothing like this exists. It couldn't."

Avgustin sat down on chair that Cassandra had vacated. His head fell into his hands.

"I'm losing my mind."

"No. You're not. It's stress."

Cassandra looked back at the painting. There was an area around the stomach that Avgustin had painted gray. It was over the abdomen. Otherwise the whole of the torso was black.

"What were you thinking when you did this bit?" she asked.

Juniper looked up. "I don't know. It was just how it appeared to me. Not all black like the rest, just different."

"Come on. You need to rest," she took his hands and helped him stand. "Off to bed for some sleep. For both of us. I'm exhausted too."

Juniper's room was closer but Cassandra led him along the corridor into her own bedroom. The curtains were drawn in there, and Cassandra turned on a small lamp by the bed. Juniper was too tired to be curious and so he did not look around other than to note the two doors off the room. One, he assumed, would be the bathroom.

Cassandra sat him down on the edge of her bed. It was a super king size, plush and comfortable. She helped him remove the designer clothing he had worn for gallery viewing the night before, laying the items carefully over her dressing table stool. Then she slipped out of her own clothing. She turned down the covers and pulled Juniper into the bed beside her.

She wrapped her arms around him.

Despite his tiredness Juniper grew hard at her touch. She ran her hands over him, bringing him to full attention while her lips pressed kisses, interspersed with her tongue licking a line, down his body. She took him in her mouth, deeper than he could have thought possible. Then she sucked, drawing back.

Juniper's breath caught in his throat. It was ecstasy: so good it hurt. Cassandra worked him like a porn star. When he thought he couldn't hold back any longer, she slid over his body. Kneeling astride him, she placed his cock in position and then she lowered herself onto him. It was slow, gentle torture, and Juniper was completely at her mercy. But it wasn't all about his contentment, Cassandra worked him, and herself, until she shuddered in pleasure, flopping down onto his chest as the orgasm wracked her body.

Then Juniper rolled her onto her back, and pulled her knees up, wrapping her legs around his waist as he entered and moved inside her.

She moaned and came again and Juniper soon followed. Only then did he realize his mistake.

"We didn't use a condom," he said pulling away from her even though it was already too late. He had been diligent about that last time. What was wrong with him?

"I can't get pregnant."

"You sure?"

"I don't take chances. Come here."

Cassandra pulled him into her arms again, holding him tightly against her breast as exhaustion finally caught up with him.

Juniper fell down into sleep. But it wasn't untroubled. The image he had drawn, the thing he thought he had seen in the midst of the crowded gallery, followed him into his dreams.

Tiffany Redman climbed into her car. It was four in the morning, and her shift had just ended at the all-night store where she worked. Of course this wasn't her ultimate goal. It was only a pit stop, something to help pay back her student loan until she became a famous artist, like Avgustin Juniper.

In her first year at college, Tiffany had posed for Juniper. Like some of the other girls, she had even done some nude work for him. She didn't have an issue with this at the time, but later, when she had met Chris and they had started a serious relationship, she had asked Juniper to amend the paintings, adding clothing. This was because Chris was from a family with staunch religious beliefs and it was looking certain that they would get married.

As she started the engine she thought of Chris now: he wanted lots of kids. The thought made her smile because she knew he was planning to propose that weekend. Even though he had sworn her best friend to secrecy, Rebekah had been unable to keep silent. Naturally she would feign surprise. But the warning meant she had bought a special dress to wear, just for the night. She imagined the photographs being posted to social media: she would look her absolute best.

Chris had a lot going for him, and of course she loved him. But he also had a great job which meant that Tiffany would be able to pursue her art career, while bringing up the children of course, and never have to worry about doing a crappy job again. It was a thought that appealed to her more and more as she stacked shelves and ran items through the check-out. All that back-breaking work that took no passion and no imagination. Someone had to do it, but why *her*?

She glanced in her rear-view mirror and realized that it wasn't in the correct position. All she could see was darkness: not even the lights in the car park that she knew lay behind her. She adjusted the mirror but it seemed to be broken. All she could see in it was blackness. *How could a mirror be broken?* she wondered to herself. It's not possible.

She twisted in her seat and glanced over her shoulder. Nothing. The mirror was working, it was just that everything in the back seat and beyond was in darkness.

Maybe the lights are out, she thought, stifling a yawn as she put the car into drive. *It will all be okay on the main road.*

Tiffany pulled out of the car park, turned left onto the road and then drove home, but rear visibility remained poor all the way back, as though her mirror had a cast over it.

She was relieved when she finally reached home. She activated the garage doors and was pleased to see them smoothly slide open for her.

She drove in and killed the engine.

A gentle breeze blew across her face as she slammed the door shut and pressed the key fob to lock it. The car lights blinked and then went out, plunging the garage into pitch darkness. Her mom had forgotten to leave the lights on for her again. Tiffany hated it when that happened. She rested one hand on the car, and made her way around to where the entrance door to the house should be.

There was no sound, but Tiffany thought she sensed movement in the darkness. She paused, listening.

Nothing.

After a moment, she guessed that she was in around the right position to get to the door, so she moved away from the car and took tiny steps into the darkness. The last thing she wanted to do was stumble and fall.

Two strong arms abruptly grabbed her from behind. Tiffany had no time to cry out before she was pulled back and down. Her head smacked into the concrete floor and she lay there dazed.

She felt her clothing being torn away. She tried to scream as her panties were ripped off but no sound came from her paralyzed throat.

She felt cool air brush her skin as the last of her clothing fell away. She was naked now. And the thought of her nudity brought a flush to her cheeks, even though it hadn't bothered her at all to remove her clothing for Juniper.

She tried to move but her limbs were frozen and not just by the cold. Something was controlling her. She had no power to resist.

She stared into the darkness, her eyes straining to see something, anything, but the blackness was absolute.

A searing pain ran across her abdomen. *A knife*, she thought.

I'm being murdered. Her mind screamed, but still no sound came from her throat.

She felt a sickly pulling sensation as her stomach opened up. There was no pain now, just a dull numbness and the memory of the knife. Her neck hurt from the strain as she tried to turn her head, to see who was attacking her, and what they were doing to her. But she couldn't move and there was nothing to see anyway but blackness.

Then a cold murkiness trickled inside her. Her numbed limbs felt as though they were turning to stone, with prickles of pins and needles shooting through them, and then, by some mercy, Tiffany fell into unconsciousness.

CHAPTER TWENTY-THREE

Juniper awoke. Cassandra was no longer in the bed and he was anxious again. The room was dark but he saw the clock illuminated at the side of the bed. It was eleven AM. He pushed back the covers, disoriented. He forgot momentarily that he was in Cassandra's room and not his own. He stumbled along the room, searching the wall for a light switch, eventually finding one outside the master bathroom. He turned it on and the bathroom lit up, spilling light into the bedroom through the partially open door.

It was a relief for him. The darkness had begun to generate a paranoid fear that was growing in intensity.

He went in the bathroom, relieved himself and then looked at his reflection in the mirror.

Despite having shaved only the evening before he was already sprouting bristle over his chin and above his lip. He ran water into the sink, then swilled his face, washing the sleep from his eyes.

What had he been dreaming? Yes. Tiffany. He hadn't thought of her for years.

He wanted to wash away the memory of Tiffany, naked, as

he had once drawn, then painted, her onto a canvas capturing her alluring curves.

Why had he dreamt of her? They had never been lovers. Juniper had desired her, though his style had always been to remain indifferent to the women. He didn't want to be seen as a letch and needed them to trust him. When Annabel came into his life, she was the one who baited his other passion beyond his control. Had she not made a move on him, Juniper doubted he would ever have made one on her.

Now he couldn't shake the image of Tiffany from his mind. How she had come to him, begging that he spoil his beautiful art. And he had done it too, he couldn't see her so worried, so upset. But there was still one piece remaining. He just couldn't destroy it. He didn't know why. It was a nude of her draped over a chair: one leg over the arm, the other down on the floor. Her legs casually apart, her womanhood displayed. So natural, so beautiful, and so pure because, despite her willingness to show her body, Juniper knew that Tiffany was a virgin. The chastity ring she wore was a giveaway.

Juniper liked women and he understood girls like Tiffany. Over time others like her had landed on his doorstep. They wouldn't sleep around, but they wanted the thrill of being found sexy. Some of them asked him to disguise their faces, wearing a mask while completely naked. Some had regretted their decision after the paintings were done, just as Tiffany had. He was always a gentleman about it. Even though it hurt to alter or paint over those special canvases completely. He often didn't do them all: it wasn't possible, even when he had intended to keep his promise. There was always one painting which he'd already sold, or which he couldn't bear to deface.

He left the bathroom and switched on the bedroom light. Last night he had hardly noticed the plush surroundings. Cassandra liked her comfort, and this room was certainly that. The only surprise was the lack of a four-poster bed, but maybe that was just too ostentatious, even for her.

He was naked and so he looked around for his clothes. He recalled that Cassandra had placed them on the dressing table stool. Now he found his robe there instead. He pulled it on and left her room, making his way down the hall towards his own suite.

The apartment was completely quiet and he wondered briefly where the security detail was. Cassandra, he knew, would be at work.

Juniper entered his room and then went into the bathroom. He showered, shaved and found his casual working clothes, cleaned and put away in the wardrobe. He had never been in a position where he was looked after, but now Cassandra's staff took care of everything and he barely saw any of them coming and going.

Once dressed Juniper left his room and went in search of food in the kitchen. There he found a platter of cheese and cooked meats left in the fridge. In the bread bin were fresh croissants and so he served himself while making a pot of coffee. It was actually a relief to be alone, and he enjoyed pottering around the kitchen without any formality to observe.

Now he was up and dressed he felt surprisingly fresh, and after eating a croissant and some cheese, he refilled his coffee mug and took it with him down to the studio.

When he opened the door, he saw the canvas he had painted the night before. It still shocked him but in the light of day, his vision seemed ridiculous and all a figment of his imagination.

He looked upon it with new eyes; he could make a better piece of art out of it. Yes, the triangle part in the face did resemble Annabel's face and the part of her eye that was cut away, and the legs were certainly similar to those of the dancer Tasha, but the arm he had no idea about, because Maria Matthews had never set foot in his studio. He assumed though, that because she was the twin sister of Susan, who he had painted, that her arm would have had the same proportions.

I made all of this up in my mind, he thought. *Those awful pictures the detective showed me. The attacks on these poor women. My imagination was fed by it. Well, let's take this focus away from them. I will add a bit. Here.*

Juniper picked up the paintbrush.

It's already grotesque. I shall make it more so!

And then, as though he were cutting a caesarean line, he drew a thin red scar on the lower abdomen of the female shape, rapidly covering the dark gray stain with flesh tone paint until the figure now had a smooth, flat beautiful stomach. Then, like a ghost over the flesh, he painted the interior of the woman's stomach, drawing in the uterus and womb, and adding one ovary. By the time he had finished it looked like a scan superimposed over a real image to show the inside of the human body.

He paused to sip his coffee and then glanced over his shoulder to see Cassandra standing in the doorway. She was holding a plate of cookies. As Juniper turned around and stepped away from the canvas, Cassandra saw the full picture.

The plate fell from her hand and clattered on the floor. Cookies and crumbs everywhere.

"Oh God!" she said.

"What is it? What's wrong?"

Cassandra bent to pick up the cookies, throwing them and the broken plate into the bin beside Juniper's door.

"Sorry. It's nothing. It's just. You've added more …"

"I know it's hideous but I'm exorcising my demons. I'm sorry I was so silly last night. The pressure just got to me. You were wonderful though," he said.

He put down his paintbrush, forgetting the painting, and came to her.

"You all right?"

"Yes. Avgustin … let's go somewhere today. A trip."

"Where to?"

"A friend of mine has a place in the Hamptons. We could go there. A few days out of the city would be good for us both."

"What about your work? What about mine?"

"All work and no play isn't good for anyone. I already cancelled my meetings anyway."

Juniper glanced over his shoulder at the painting.

"Don't show that one to Joy, okay?" said Cassandra.

"Why?"

"It's not your usual style. I don't want her to think you're going off the rails."

Juniper laughed. "I'm an artist. I'm already 'off the rails.'"

Cassandra picked up a sheet and threw it over the painting. "Even so, let's keep this one under wraps."

She took his hand.

"I've sent one of the maids to pack up what you need."

"Okay," he said, even though he realized how easy it was becoming to accept everyone doing everything for him when he had spent his whole life being totally independent.

Cassandra led him from the room. Then she inserted a key in the door and locked the studio. Juniper had never noticed the keyhole until that moment.

"I don't want anyone going in there while we're away," she said. "Not even the cleaner."

CHAPTER TWENTY-FOUR

Detective Chandler?" said a uniformed police officer. "I'm Deputy Wright, and I'm here to take you straight to Dr. Phillips."

"How is the victim?" asked Chandler.

"She's very distressed. The doctor is keeping her under sedation for the time being."

"Probably wise," Chandler said. "But we will need to talk to her."

"Do you think this is the same guy?" asked Wright.

"I don't know, but it's a hell of a coincidence if not. After all Tiffany was one of Juniper's models," Sarasvatī said.

"Sick bastard, whoever it is," said Chandler. Sarasvatī said nothing. They walked down the hospital corridor to Phillips' office.

"Knock on. He's waiting for you," said Wright, then he turned and walked back down the corridor.

Sarasvatī knocked.

"Come in," said Phillips.

They found Phillips alone, typing notes onto a desktop computer.

"Detective Chandler?"

"Yes? And this is Detective Gemma Sarasvatī," Chandler said.

"Take a seat. I won't be a moment. I'm just finishing something."

Chandler and Sarasvatī sat down and waited as Phillips saved his work.

"Tiffany Redman," Phillips began, "was given a hysterectomy. Her attacker took everything: uterus, cervix, and one ovary."

"Jesus, she was only twenty-three years old!" said Chandler.

"I know," said Phillips. "Whoever did this had medical knowledge. It wasn't a butcher job, and they cauterized all the wounds which is the only reason she's still alive and didn't bleed to death while she was lying on her garage floor. I had to sew her up properly afterwards."

"Let me get this straight. The wounds were cauterized, but she was left open?" Chandler said.

"Yes. Which is odd in itself as the parts were removed with great care," Phillips said. "And since this person knew enough to staunch blood flow, why not sew her up too?"

"They may have been interrupted," Sarasvatī said.

"Apparently she was lying there for some time before her mother found her. The woman is beside herself and I had to treat her for shock too. Imagine finding your daughter like that?"

"Is there anything else you can tell us?" Chandler asked.

"Not really, other than she is somewhat lucky to still have one working ovary," Phillips said.

"Why?" asked Chandler.

"We can harvest eggs. She may not be able to carry a child but she could at least still have one in the future with the aid of a surrogate."

"I see," said Sarasvatī. "Will you tell her that? Because when she wakes, she's going to be devastated and I don't think we want another suicide."

Chandler glanced at Sarasvatī with surprise that she was showing uncharacteristic humanity but her face was as neutral as usual. Chandler didn't know what to make of it.

"I have every intention of telling her and her boyfriend this. A terrible start for a young couple about to embark on marriage."

"She was getting married?" Sarasvatī asked.

"Well, he was about to propose, or so the mother said. She was really concerned about how he would take the news."

Sarasvatī was quiet for the rest of the interview while Chandler gathered as much information from the doctor as possible.

"This will all be in my report, of course," Phillips said. "But if you think of anything else I can help you with, please don't hesitate to ask. I've never seen anything like this in my life and I'd like to see the perpetrator caught."

"Thanks," said Chandler.

They left Phillips' office and made their way to the ward.

"You were pretty quiet in there," Chandler asked Sarasvatī.

"I'm just a little … shocked," Sarasvatī said.

"And there's no crime in admitting that, Gemma."

"What d'you mean?"

"I've been working with you for three years and you never show any emotion. I've seen men lose their lunch over road kill, but you are indifferent to everything we see."

"There's nothing wrong with having a strong stomach in this job," Sarasvatī said. "And when I joined the force I promised myself I'd be strong."

"And you are. This isn't a criticism, more an observation. But it's nice to see a reaction from a colleague once in a while. It reminds us that what we do isn't normal. That it should affect us. That we are human."

Sarasvatī shrugged. "I suppose."

"Now, what do you think is going on here? What's this person doing?"

"They are collecting body parts. Isn't that obvious?" Sarasvatī said.

"But why? What's their agenda?"

Sarasvatī shrugged again.

"You see," Chandler continued, "when we know the answer to that question, we will find this guy."

"Or girl," Sarasvatī said.

"*What*?"

"It might not be a man."

Chandler was quiet for a moment and then he said, "Whoever this is has serious mental issues. Or they just get their jollies out of ruining the lives of women. If it is a woman, is this out of jealousy? Perhaps this person loves to destroy the one thing that each of them really cared about in their lives? I mean, that makes sense, doesn't it?"

Sarasvatī said nothing and Chandler wasn't expecting a response. All he wanted was to rant a little, get this whole sordid business off his chest.

"Annabel Linton's head and face were so damaged she couldn't have survived—but maybe she was vain about her looks. Why did Maria Matthews care so much about losing her arm that she wanted to die? There was mention of an expensive watch she had recently bought. This watch had been taken along with her arm. Tasha Voronov's loss was far more severe, her whole life had been about dance, and now she'll be wheelchair bound for the rest of her days. Tiffany's injury—God, how can I even call it that? As if it was an accident? The girl was going to get married, probably desperately wanted kids. Now she'll only ever be able to experience that through a surrogate. What kind of sick mind plans this? It's obviously all been thought through. So vicious and calculated. Wouldn't you say?"

Sarasvatī paused in the hospital corridor. "Looks like she's awake. So you can ask her."

"Who?"

"Tiffany. This is her room."

Chandler looked through the pane of glass and into the room. Tiffany had visitors and it looked like they were her future husband and possibly her mother.

"Okay. I will," said Chandler.

"Mind if I sit this one out?" said Sarasvatī. "I've had all I can stomach today."

Chandler glanced at her again. She wasn't acting in character at all.

"Sure. Perhaps you can chat to Deputy Wright and see if he can get us a copy of the police report. He's over there at the coffee machine."

Sarasvatī looked down the corridor. "Will do."

She walked away. For the first time Chandler noted how light her step was. She moved like a dancer. He wondered what she did in her spare time and was surprised to realize he knew nothing about her private life at all.

He shrugged. Maybe that was why he found her so cold, so distant. She never shared anything, not with anyone.

He turned back to Tiffany's room, took a deep breath and opened the door.

"How are you feeling?" asked Lauren later as she gave Chandler a glass of merlot.

"A little shocked. I thought Redman and the other women were safe. Now we have to up the detail on them all."

"Are there many more women Juniper has painted?"

Chandler nodded. "We know of a few, but not all. I went over to Mousá's house to ask if we could have a comprehensive list. Now that Juniper is completely in the clear I thought his lawyer might be more cooperative."

"And was she?"

"Not really. Her goons said she and Juniper had gone away on a trip. They wouldn't let us in without a search warrant and no judge is going to give us that the way things are. Juniper isn't a suspect and we've been warned to leave him alone."

"That stinks," said Lauren. "Surely this is for the greater good, to help the victims get justice and of course to make sure no one else is hurt."

"The law doesn't care about that, only following the right procedure. Did you give anymore thought to helping us establish our perp's motive?"

"Yes. And I'd like to help. You know I'm not a criminal psychologist though?"

"Yes. But we have those. What I need is a fresh perspective." He sipped his drink.

"All right. I looked at all the files. What I say may raise more questions than answers though. It seems to me, though it might be fanciful, that your perpetrator might be trying to … build a woman from the parts. Like a Frankenstein's monster. And I know that's ridiculous, but the mind of this person can't see that this is impossible."

"But why are they doing that?"

"An element of jealousy is involved. These women all have something the killer doesn't have. And these parts, sick as it is, represent that. Obviously there's a connection with Juniper and the killer. Otherwise why not randomly choose anyone? This connection will be the thing that leads you ultimately in the right direction. For example, is this someone from Juniper's past who has reason to hate him? So you need to ask him now about enemies. Or is it someone currently in his life that has another motive. Making Juniper look like a murderer in the first place for example brought him a certain amount of infamy. And success for his art."

"I hadn't even considered where Juniper would be right now without his connection to the murderer. Not selling his artwork for a million dollars a canvas, that's for sure."

Lauren sat down beside him on the sofa. "Who else benefits from his fame?"

"Awen. As his agent she'll be earning twenty percent from all sales of the paintings. If not more. It depends on what deal she got him to sign I suppose."

"I can't see Joy Awen being involved though," Lauren said. "It isn't her style."

"What about Cassandra Mousá then? She has goons and money coming out of her ears. She could pay someone and she wouldn't even get her hands dirty. She's also perfectly placed to know who the girls are that Juniper has painted."

Lauren shook her head. "Unlikely. From what you told me Mousá only met Juniper *after* the first murder. How could she have known him before? Why pick him anyway? And she doesn't need any money or fame, she has plenty of that already."

Chandler leaned back into the cushions. His head hurt. He didn't want to spend the whole evening with Lauren talking about work. But she had such a logical brain, and saw things differently to others in her profession.

"That's enough for now," she said as though she could read his thoughts. "I'll bring the wine bottle in and we can cuddle up and watch a movie if you like?"

"I do like," said Chandler but as she went to get up, he pulled her into his arms and kissed her. "I know this is all so sudden and I don't want to scare you off. But you make me incredibly happy."

"That doesn't scare me. It's great to know I'm doing a good job," Lauren kissed him then she pulled away and went to fetch the wine.

Chandler closed his eyes and thought through her words. *Doing a good job.* It made him feel a little uncomfortable, as though their relationship had evolved as part of his therapy, and not a progression of the friendship they had built.

It's just a turn of phrase, he thought. *And typical of her sense of humor.*

The explanation felt as though it had come from elsewhere and not from his own mind. But he shook the idea away: it was a ridiculous thought. Lauren was his girlfriend now. And he knew in his heart that she wouldn't be spending all of this time with him unless she wanted to.

Lauren sat down next to him, but he didn't open his eyes. Instead he listened to the sound of the bottle being opened and wine pouring into the glasses.

He opened his eyes as she held out a glass to him.

"You okay?" she asked.

"Yes. A little tired. Wrung out too after speaking to Tiffany. There's a young woman whose whole future has been altered, put in jeopardy even. All because of this … sicko."

"It is awful," Lauren said. "I really feel for the girl. Wish I could do more to help you find whoever is doing this."

"Sorry," he said. "We're supposed to be relaxing."

"I am relaxed. And so will you be, soon."

Lauren sat down and nuzzled into his arms. After they exchanged a few kisses, Chandler did indeed begin to relax. Lauren was like a drug that changed usage automatically as his needs altered. One minute she was an aphrodisiac, the next she was diazepam.

CHAPTER TWENTY-FIVE

Gemma Sarasvatī had never been ill. Now nausea was swirling around in the pit of her stomach. It wasn't like her to feel so weak. The sensation was disconcerting; along with the new play of emotions that made her more sympathetic to crime victims and people in general.

When she joined the force, she was in perfect physical fitness and she could keep herself free of emotional engagement. Recently though this had become harder. She couldn't seem to disengage herself from work, even when she arrived home.

As she entered her apartment she immediately began to peel off her clothing. She lived alone; didn't want anyone permanently in her life because relationships made things too complicated in her line of work. She had learned the hard way that regular isolation led to less pain. Loneliness could be briefly relieved by a one-night stand. Only recently, she hadn't been interested in that either.

She was falling apart. And although deep down Sarasvatī had always suspected that this moment would come, she wasn't ready for it. Not at all.

Once the world had been a beautiful place: she had held so

much enthusiasm for it. Relished her job! Helping people gave her such a rush of excitement. A barrage of self-worth! That was the reward she got for all of her hard work.

But the last one hundred years had been difficult for one reason or another. Humanity was not easy to encourage; people were growing ever more selfish and draining. She was tired all the time these days. And keeping her emotions in check was a constant challenge.

Seeing Tiffany Redman had exhausted her remaining resources. She was aging with it.

Sarasvatī had never been able to have children. She had been created with no urge to procreate, even though she could, and did, enjoy sex. Her only goal was to help others. Now she experienced Tiffany's pain and it was all consuming. Worse was her inability to help.

She stood naked in her hallway. Hand pressed on her abdomen. What would it be like to not just influence life, but to create it?

Blasphemy!

The dull echo in her head came from the thousands of years of her indoctrination, not from the celestial plane. No: that kingdom was silent now.

The world had changed too much. And her present deterioration was a by-product. No one really believed in the gods anymore—even though some fanatical groups said they did. Their faith was not real; it was used as a way of controlling the behavior of others. Human hypocrisy had made a mockery of the reality of the supernatural. Their lack of belief had killed it.

Sarasvatī had no way of going back to Olympus. The memory of its location was lost to her. She was abandoned. Left on this cold planet of unbelievers. And why? Because now creativity inspired itself, or humans inspired each other.

Until recently Sarasvatī had believed she was the last of her kind.

For most of her existence she had inspired others to do

more. Moving around the world, going where needed, she took on new and normal roles and became part of the communities she inhabited. When her job was done, she moved on, discretely disappearing into the night.

She had been drawn to Paris at the end of the 19th Century. Then in 1902 she became the inspiration for Picasso's painting "Blue Nude." He had been depressed at the time, having lost a close friend, and Sarasvatī had done her best to raise his spirits. They had been lovers too, for a while, but she soon realized she was not the muse he needed. There were so many others there, loitering, wanting to be involved in his rise to fame. And so, despite being drawn to his superior talent, she left Paris and searched for a new and less somber creative to inspire. She watched his career from afar though, and when he made his break into cubism, mourned the days of his blue period. Picasso, the way she saw it, was a far better artist when he was suffering from depression and financial desolation.

Sarasvatī had often seen the change in people when fame found them. And Picasso was no different. Eventually she turned her vision completely away from him, refusing even to acknowledge any of his future successes, and aided instead the smaller, and less dramatic, rise of another artist.

Art lost something for her eventually and so she moved into the more abstract world of fighting crime. Being able to take on the appearance of anyone she liked, she passed herself off as a man when she first joined the force. When that excitement paled, she resigned and rejoined as Gemma Sarasvatī. She wanted to be a strong female influence, to inspire other women in the force. It worked for a while. She became empowered. Energized. And then—the women began to motivate themselves.

It was time. Sarasvatī wanted a change, but only that morning, after several failed attempts to alter her appearance and try on a new face, she realized that the decay had robbed her of her ability to camouflage. She was stuck in this body. This image would be hers now until the final end came.

She glanced at herself in the mirror in the hallway now. The body had been a good one. Tall, attractive—when she wanted to be—and stronger than a normal woman would have been. There had been nothing wrong with it, except her urge to move on. An urge that was difficult to resist when there was nothing left for her to do in a current location. But with the realization that she couldn't transform, came a different kind of sickness.

If she had lost the ability to change form, what other skills had she lost?

"I'm becoming human," she said to her reflection. "Which means aging. And human death."

The thought didn't thrill her at all.

What was it she had been promised all those years ago? She had been told at her birth that she would live forever as long as she inspired. But who the fuck could she inspire these days?

Sarasvatī sighed and walked away from the mirror. It was just as well she had chosen a form she liked now that she was stuck with it.

She laughed: crazed and cynical.

If only Chandler knew what she really was. Would he freak out? *Probably*. Or he would think she was crazy, refer her to the shrink.

Sarasvatī laughed again.

Why had she picked this form? Oh yes to inspire ethnic women to achieve success in the police force. It was a hare-brained scheme and a total failure.

She entered the bathroom. The sink was coated with shed skin and the plug hole filled with molted hair. She cleared up the mess.

It was all happening too fast now. How long did she have left?

Sarasvatī smiled when she realized she was asking herself a typically human question about her mortality. But the smile fell when she stubbed her toe on the sharp edge of a floor tile. Looking down she saw the blood pouring into the grouting.

The toe would heal but at human pace. How could anyone put up with such weakness?

She opened the bathroom cabinet and took out a pack of Band-Aids. Then she washed and cleaned her foot, covering the pierced skin. It throbbed.

Sarasvatī left the bathroom and walked naked into the bedroom. The blinds were closed day and night and so she didn't fear she would be observed by a neighbor in an opposite apartment block. Her privacy meant everything to her. Especially now. She couldn't allow anyone to see her until she learnt what to do to about her current deterioration.

She peeled off the wig that looked almost exactly like her own hair. It was expensive and she used a strong glue to ensure that she couldn't lose it if forced to give chase to a criminal. Underneath her scalp was completely bald. Her hair had all fallen out.

She removed the rubber band that held the wig in a ponytail then placed it onto a wig stand on her dressing table. She brushed the hair with the same care she would have given her own, but her image in the tabletop mirror distracted her once more.

I look like a cancer victim, she thought. *Chemotherapy has taken its toll.*

She quashed the thought. *I'm not dying. It's impossible.*

But she knew in her heart that she was.

Sarasvatī lay down on her bed. Perhaps a good night's sleep would help her renew? It had worked in the past. Especially when she had dreamed of Olympus. That time the gods had reached out and helped her.

Where are you now?

No answer came and yet she said her prayer.

I am the wave that controls the tide

I am the breath that propels the wind

I am the nutrient that feeds the soil
I am the heat that fuels the fire
I renew with the dawn, rise with the sun
Inspire with the moon, sleep when it's done

Sarasvatī closed her eyes. Hot tears slipped from the corners and rolled down her cheeks. The salt made tracks on her skin but it was a relief to let the tension out. *A human release,* she thought. *Is there nothing that can be done?*

A voice echoed back to her from far away.

Save yourself, sister.

"I can't. I don't know how."

I do....

CHAPTER TWENTY-SIX

Returning to New York made Cassandra tense. She had spent five wonderful days in the Hamptons, escaping the phone, refusing to look at the newspapers, and avoiding anything that would show Juniper the latest news. They had spent lazy mornings in bed, making love whenever the mood struck. Then reality hit, and one of her bodyguards, left behind to watch over her apartment, had turned up and said that Detective Chandler wanted to speak to her. Probably about the Redman girl, even though Juniper was in the clear.

She couldn't protect Juniper any longer and so she decided to return and face what was happening.

"I have something to tell you," she said on the drive back.

Juniper was relaxing at her side in the back of the limousine, and Cassandra took his hand in the hope that she could comfort him. He was now very comfortable with their affluent surroundings.

"Yes?" he said.

"Tiffany Redman is the latest victim."

"I know," Juniper said.

"What do you mean you know?"

"I saw it. In a dream. I painted it," Juniper said.

"No Avgustin. That was just your imagination."

"What did zis monster do to her?"

Cassandra took a deep breath. "Took her womb."

"My painting showed it. I knew."

He didn't speak for the rest of the journey but he was quietly reflective rather than stressed.

As they drew closer to Cassandra's building Juniper said, "I am linked to it. I am capturing its crimes on canvas."

"Yes," Cassandra said. She was starting to believe it was true now, that this thing was reading or manipulating Juniper somehow.

"I can help the police catch zis monster."

"Can you?"

"Yes."

"How?"

"I paint and it happens. All we have to do is figure out where it vill happen before the … *I don't know what to call 'it'* … does the next crime."

"Monster is good enough," Cassandra said. Her voice was flat. Unemotional.

"So. I will paint when we return?"

"Yes. And I'll ring Detective Chandler and see what he wants."

"He wants to know the names of all of the women. All I ever painted."

"That shouldn't be too difficult," Cassandra said. "We have the paintings to remind you."

"I told him some, but not all of them. Some I sold. I had bills to pay."

"But you remember them, don't you?"

Juniper didn't reply.

The limo door opened and Juniper climbed out. They were in the underground parking lot of Cassandra's apartment block. The bodyguards were more relaxed now, only glancing around casually to see that no one was there. The second guard had opened Cassandra's door and she stepped out.

The elevator had been called and Juniper approached. He watched the numbers illuminate. He remembered the last time he had stood by an elevator alone.

He glanced back as Cassandra walked up.

"Glad to be home?" she asked.

Juniper smiled and nodded. Then he turned his attention back to the elevator. He wondered if there would be a black void inside it, just like the one that had waited for him when he had been inside.

"I remember them all," he said. "I will repaint the ones I zold."

Cassandra was only half listening as she turned back to the first bodyguard. "Don't forget our bags."

The man returned to the limo, the driver had already opened the trunk and the two medium sized suitcases were lifted out. The first bodyguard picked them up and as the elevator doors opened he approached Cassandra and Juniper.

Cassandra wrapped her arm through Juniper's and she nuzzled into him. She was amazed at how calmly he was taking this new revelation and how he accepted that he had some link to the killer. This plan of his was so simple, but it might just work. How would she explain it to Chandler though? She was sure the Detective would think her completely insane. She was working out the conversation she needed to have with him when the doors of the elevator opened.

A figure in black stood inside. "Avgustin Juniper, you murderer!" said the man, and then he raised his hand.

"He's got a gun!" Cassandra said.

The bodyguard dropped the two cases and reached inside his jacket.

The man in the elevator fired two shots as Cassandra threw Juniper aside. The two of them rolled on the floor as the limo driver, and both bodyguards fired into the elevator. The doors closed on them, but the first bodyguard pressed the button.

The would-be assassin was prone inside. His body was riddled with bullets.

Cassandra stood up and then pulled Juniper to his feet.

"That was lucky!"

"You're injured," said Juniper.

A spot of blood blossomed on the side of Cassandra's white satin blouse.

"A scratch," she said.

"Let me see," he said.

"It's nothing. Really."

The first bodyguard bent down and checked the body. The attacker was wearing a thick balaclava. He pulled it off revealing a man of around fifty underneath. He had salt and pepper hair and a few days' stubble on his chin.

"He's dead," said the bodyguard.

"You'd better call the police. We'll use the stairs to the lobby and go up in the elevator from there. I think you'd better wedge this one open." Cassandra said.

She took Juniper's hand again and led him out of the parking area and up the stairs. The second bodyguard followed, hand inside his coat, just in case he had to draw his weapon again.

"Who was that man?" asked Juniper. "Why did he want to kill me? Everyone knows I didn't hurt the girls."

"The police will find out," Cassandra said.

Juniper's fingers were trembling, but he noted that Cassandra's hand was steady when she took his. Once again, he was stunned by Cassandra's lack of emotional response. Even a male criminal defense lawyer of her standing would be shaken by an armed assassin trying to kill their client. She did not react or behave like any female he had ever known. In fact, she had shown superior strength when she threw him out of the line of fire. And what of her injury? He would make every effort to examine that at the first opportunity.

They reached the lobby elevators without further incident. The bodyguard checked the first one to arrive and hurried them both inside. On Cassandra's floor he blocked them both until he was sure that no one was waiting to take advantage of them as they left the elevator.

"Oh, this is silly," Cassandra said, pushing past the guard. "The guy is dead. I doubt he had an accomplice. He was just your average nut job. Come on, Avgustin."

She opened her front door and walked in ahead of both of the men. The bodyguard swept the hallway after closing the door behind them, and went through the apartment checking every room.

"He's just doing his job," she said. "You've nothing to fear. The man who's been after you is dead."

Juniper sank down into the couch his trembling hands pushed back his hair. Cassandra sat beside him. She took his hands in hers and held them until the trembling stopped. A strange calm overcame him. A sense of safety as long as he was with her.

"You really think that's the man who poisoned me?"

"Very likely. But the police will get to the bottom of it and find out his deal."

Cassandra released his hands and then stood up. There was a sideboard in the room, antique in a rich mahogany. She opened the door on the left side and extracted a bottle of brandy.

"I know you prefer vodka. But I think this might be better for the shock. I don't mind telling you I could do with one myself."

She poured two shots into crystal brandy glasses.

"These glasses are English crystal," she said. "I always think booze tastes better out of crystal."

Juniper took the glass. His hands were steady now.

"Drink up," she said. "Then you need to go into the studio and call up this muse of yours."

"Muse?" Juniper said.

"The thing that's riding you. Let it inspire, and we'll pass on the info to Chandler when he arrives."

"I can't paint that fast."

"Yes, you can."

CHAPTER TWENTY-SEVEN

Juniper was in the zone when Cassandra brought Detective Chandler into the studio. He was painting what looked like a row of statues on a large canvas. Chandler saw female shapes and outlines, but only one of the figures was filled in and almost complete.

Cassandra pressed a finger to her lips to warn Chandler to remain silent. Juniper's right hand flopped down by his sides as though he were a marionette that had just been released from its strings.

"Zhe first one," he said.

He walked away from the canvas and took a seat in the chair under the skylight.

"You look tired," Cassandra said. "And you haven't eaten the food I brought you."

Chandler walked up to the canvas. He could see clearly now that each of the figures, were being depicted as Grecian statues reminiscent of the renaissance period. And the women, these frozen, poised figures, each had their own plinth. The finished girl was standing one arm held upwards. There was a plaque painted onto the plinth as though the name should be there, but Juniper hadn't finished it.

"Who is she?" Chandler asked.

"A foreign exchange student who came to the university to study for a year. I painted her as Venus," Juniper said.

"What about this patch here?" Chandler said, pointing to a grayed-out area around the girl's head.

"Zhe monster vill take her hair," said Juniper. "If you don't find her first and look after her."

"Her hair?" Chandler said. "And her name?"

"Maya Nilsson. She is Swedish."

"You don't happen to know where she is right now?"

Juniper shook his head. "I didn't see that. But maybe if I am left alone the muse will come back and show me."

"*Muse*?" Chandler said not realizing that he was repeating the word in the same puzzled way that Juniper had done just a few short hours earlier.

"Inspiration ..." said Cassandra. "All great artists have something that inspires them."

"We need to talk," Chandler said to Cassandra.

"You go back to work, Avgustin," Cassandra said. Then she bent down and kissed his forehead. "But eat something first, okay?"

Juniper nodded as though he were a psychiatric patient on lithium.

"Detective, if you'll follow me?"

She led Chandler out of the studio, closing the door as Juniper stood and returned to the canvas.

"He won't eat," she said. "I'm worried about him. About this thing that has a hold of him."

"What thing?"

"The person who's doing all of these atrocities. It might kill him with exhaustion before he manages to give it another face."

"I think you'd better explain," Chandler said.

"Come with me." She led him down the hallway and into the kitchen. "Take a seat," she said indicating the breakfast bar.

Chandler sat down.

"Coffee?"

"No thanks."

"Tea then?"

"Nothing. Why are you stalling?"

"Because I'm not sure how to tell you this, but I feel I have to if we are going to save the lives of any future women that Juniper had contact with and painted."

"Just tell me."

"I'm not given to flights of fancy…."

"I believe you."

"Avgustin is being manipulated by something," Cassandra said. "Or at least he believes he is. When he paints a real person, something happens to them."

"Someone is getting access to his work then?"

"No."

"Then how is it possible? How does the perpetrator know who he's painting? There has to be a mole in your household."

"No. There is no mole." Cassandra sighed. "I knew this would be difficult. Detective Chandler, I have a feeling that you can be quite open-minded. I know you were the first person to realize that Avgustin was innocent."

Chandler said nothing.

"Even though you think that some of the stuff that's happened has been by my contrivance."

"I've never said that," Chandler said.

"You didn't have to. The point is, Juniper does have a connection with the … perpetrator. It's controlling him."

"How?"

"I've seen things that a few weeks ago I wouldn't have thought possible. Juniper painted something else and I think it is the … creature," Cassandra said. "I'll show you soon. But first I want to tell you about what I've seen, and Avgustin's visions."

Chandler listened as Cassandra told him of her observations.

"He told me about this dark thing that followed him. After he was spooked at the gallery. He said it was there. And later painted what he saw. I tried to dismiss it, but sometimes I *feel* it."

"What are saying? That Juniper is being haunted by something."

"I guess you could call it that but this creature is no ghost. It's real. As real as you or I, but it needs Avgustin for some reason that I don't understand. Maybe it has to have a focus for its fury. It lurks in shadows. Hides from light in case it can be identified. I know this all sounds insane but ..." Cassandra's cell phone rang. "Excuse me one minute, Detective, I have to take this."

She left the room and as Chandler waited, the clock ticking for fifteen minutes or more, he began to wish he had accepted her offer of coffee. He mulled over her words. It did sound insane, but yet, he believed her. There was something going on that might not have a logical explanation.

At that moment the door opened to the kitchen and Juniper entered. He pulled at his hair and his face was a mask of terror.

"It's too late!" he said.

"Avgustin, what is it?" Cassandra said coming back into the kitchen.

She went to him and for the first time Chandler saw her genuine concern. Maybe he wasn't just a pawn to her after all. Perhaps she genuinely loved him.

Juniper fell into Cassandra's arms, sobbing and hysterical.

"What's happened?" she asked.

"It got her already. Look!"

He pulled away from her and hurried from the room. Chandler and Cassandra followed.

Back in the studio the goddess statue canvas had been replaced by the painting Juniper had done the night of the gallery viewing. Only this time the picture was painted in a little more. The figure now had a full head of long blonde hair.

Chandler stared at the painting, knowing immediately what it represented. Then his cell phone began to ring in his pocket. He reached for it blindly, unable to take his eyes from the monstrous painting.

"Chandler," he said as he answered.

"Detective Chandler, we need you to come to Newark Airport right away," said a male voice he didn't recognize.

"What's happened?"

"A young woman was attacked."

"Can you tell me more?"

"Yeah. Swedish visitor. She was … scalped. Awful business."

Chandler completed the call. He met Cassandra's eyes.

"You see?" she said.

He shook his head in denial. "I have to go. The forensics team is still downstairs, but I need to hurry them along to … something else."

"Detective?" Cassandra said as he turned to leave. "Who was the man that tried to kill Avgustin? You didn't tell me."

"Ken Matthews. Maria Matthews' father. He worked part time as a deliveryman at the restaurant that delivered the poisoned food. He was off the books, which is why we didn't pick up on him when we looked into it earlier."

"He really thought Avgustin attacked his daughter, caused her suicide?"

"Apparently. Though I haven't interviewed his wife yet. My colleague is there now."

"I'm sorry for him," Cassandra said. "And his family."

Somehow Chandler didn't believe her.

"Hey? Chandler! Over here," called Sarasvatī. She was standing with a group of uniformed police outside a ladies' bathroom in the airport.

"Surprised to see you here, Gemma," he said. "Thought you were with Mrs. Matthews."

"I was on my way there when I got the call for this. Seemed more urgent. I sent McCullock over to take Mrs. Matthews' statement instead."

"Right. What do you know about this one then?"

"Maya Nilsson, that's the vic's name. She was here to catch her return flight home to Oslo. She'd been over for a couple of weeks visiting old college friends."

"Was she travelling alone?" Chandler asked.

"She was with two other girls. Her companions were waiting for her in the bar at the gate. When she didn't return and they started boarding, one of them came looking for her."

"She was found slumped in one of the cubicles," one of the uniformed cops interjected. It was Dan Shallit, who worked a lot in homicide. Chandler realized it was Shallit who had called him.

"Walk me through it," Chandler said.

Shallit led Chandler under the cordon tape and into the bathroom. The room looked fairly normal. A little water splashed on the floors, as well as soap stains on a couple of the basins. Otherwise it was a lot tidier than most men's rooms.

"Her friend found her in the end cubicle. She knocked on it. It was locked. She bent down. Looked under. Saw Nilsson slumped over the toilet bowl and thought she must have collapsed. She went for help. The bathroom attendant had a key that opens the cubicles from the outside. They opened it. Found Nilsson in a terrible state. Our guys and the medical team got here and discovered she'd had her entire scalp removed in what appeared to be one piece. In fact, not just scalp. All of the hairline. Like the sicko was making himself a wig out of her hair."

"The wound was cauterized?" Chandler said.

"Yeah," said Shallit. "Same MO as the others."

"Okay, I want forensics in here as soon as possible and a full report on my desk by tomorrow morning."

Chandler left the bathroom and then he saw Lauren talking to Sarasvatī.

"Hey, what are *you* doing here?" he said.

"Jake. Is this …?" Lauren asked.

"Yes. Can't say more though, obviously."

"I was passing through and saw your colleague here. Thought I might be able to help."

Chandler blinked at Lauren's casual expression of "passing through" the airport.

"I was called in to do an evaluation on someone who had some kind of breakdown prior to getting on their plane," Lauren explained. "He was in such a state they couldn't risk letting him board. I had to have the guy sectioned pending further evaluation."

"God. What a day," said Chandler.

"Yeah. If there is anything …"

"Not at this stage," Chandler said.

"Okay. See you later?"

"You going home?"

"Yes."

"Let me get someone to escort you to your car. The perp could still be around."

"That's okay," Lauren said. "I have a lift, so I'm not leaving alone."

"You sure?"

"Yes. There she is now," Lauren said.

Chandler turned to see Joy Awen waiting on the other side of the security gate.

"I was at the gallery when I got the call to come over. My car wouldn't start and so Joy offered to drive me."

"That's good of her," Chandler said but he was confused by Lauren's new-found friendship with Joy.

Lauren said goodbye and he watched her as she showed her

ID to the security guard who let her pass back through and out into the main concourse.

"I didn't know they were friends," Sarasvatī said.

"I want the names of anyone who passed through security today. Where they were going, and where they came from," Chandler said ignoring Sarasvatī's observation.

"On it," said Sarasvatī.

CHAPTER TWENTY-EIGHT

I've called this meeting because we need to think about what we are going to do," said Joy.

"I told you. I'm letting Avgustin finish his painting. We'll pass any clues onto Chandler," Cassandra said.

"And in the meantime, more girls are going to be attacked," Lauren said. "Don't you want to *prevent* that?"

The three women were sitting around Joy's desk in the gallery office.

"Why can't he just give you a list of their names, and maybe not paint their images this time?" Joy said.

"He says he doesn't know until their face appears on the canvas. Then he sees who they are and where they will be attacked," Cassandra said.

"He's being ridden," said Joy. "But by whom?"

"The other one you mentioned," Lauren said. "Could it be her?"

Joy shook her head. "I think I'd know if she was harvesting. I'd *see* it. Like Avgustin can. We'd all see it. Wouldn't we?"

"I don't know, Joy. I just don't. I'm so tired and most of the time I can't think straight," said Cassandra. "We're all coming to the end. Aren't we?"

Joy said nothing.

"Perhaps," said Lauren. "But we aren't as close to it as this one is. I can still evaporate. And change form if I want to. What about you?"

"Yes. I can. But I *need* to inspire soon. I thought Avgustin was going to be my next big thing," Cassandra said.

"Mine too," said Joy. "Is he why you came here, Lauren? Like Picasso."

Lauren shrugged, "Maybe. But we can't all inspire him. Only one of us can be the muse. Have you let him paint you yet?" she said to Cassandra.

"No."

"Then he's still open game. Which is why our rogue can do what she's doing," said Joy.

"You think I should encourage him to paint me then?" Cassandra said. "It might bring the rogue out. *After me*. And then we'll see who is the strongest."

"No. At the moment it would be best to stay on the side-lines," Lauren said. "None of us want to be exposed."

"I agree with Lauren. But I have something to show you both. Something I've held onto for a long time," Joy said. She opened the top drawer in her desk and extracted an old leather-bound book. "I haven't told you both everything I know. In fact, I had forgotten about this until Lauren mentioned something to me about the Picasso years."

"What is it?" Lauren said.

Joy noticed how nervous it made Lauren to see the journal. She placed it down on the desk. "It is Picasso's diary. And in it he talks of a muse that came into his life. Picasso *knew* what she was."

"I didn't know he kept a diary. Where did you get that?" asked Cassandra.

"It came with the painting," Joy said.

"What painting?" asked Lauren.

"I'll show you some time. It's an unknown Picasso. I don't have it here right now." Joy explained.

"Okay," said Lauren.

"In the interests of disclosure, I tried him out," said Cassandra.

"I don't doubt it," said Joy. "We *all* did. As did some others."

Joy pulled out two piles of photocopies from the drawer, then she placed the original journal back inside.

"I took these for you. So that you can both read them and consider the clues in the journal," Joy explained. "It makes interesting reading. It's in Spanish, naturally. I'd like to discuss it with you when you read his notes."

"Not a problem. Thanks," said Cassandra taking one of the piles.

Lauren stared at the sheets for a moment, then she reluctantly pulled the second pile over to herself. "Can I take this with me? I have to go and meet with Jake. He's already a little suspicious of my friendship with you, and there are only so many 'a client needed me' excuses I can give."

"Of course," said Joy. "But make sure he doesn't see it."

"Naturally," said Lauren.

"You know," said Cassandra. "I was pretty shocked to realize you were one of us."

"Why?" asked Lauren.

"Well, your surname. It's like you've gone truly native."

"Moúsa and Awen aren't as obvious as my version. Which is just Muse," said Lauren. "It brought me too much attention in the early part of the 20th century and so I went for something different."

Cassandra shrugged. "In this day and age you could be as blatant as you like. None of them will see it. They are so tuned out to the supernatural. It's why we are all failing."

"I don't see what I'm doing as a failure," Lauren said. "I diversified."

"I tried writers for a while," Cassandra said. "But they are all batshit. Too hard to control and some of the random crap that came out onto the page when I inspired, I wouldn't wish on any generation of readers. Besides, everyone these days thinks they can write."

"You don't need inspiration when any old rubbish you type up can be put up onto ebook platforms with little effort," said Joy. "The art is being watered down. Just as cynical opportunism is confused with talent. The age we are in is not kind to us."

"Which is why I started working with people with mental problems. Helping them fed me, but didn't drive me crazy along with them. Unlike artists who can be … difficult," Lauren said.

"Tell me about it," Joy said. She laughed but the sound lacked mirth. "We'll talk again when you've read the diary."

The two women left the gallery and Joy was alone once more. She found herself staring at the cheap painting hanging over the hidden cupboard behind her desk. Behind it the Picasso painting glared at her. She had lied when Lauren asked about the painting. It was there. It was always there. But at that moment she hadn't wanted to reveal it. She couldn't face seeing it. *I really should sell it*, she thought. *Or better still destroy it.*

CHAPTER TWENTY-NINE

"*No sé por qué me siento impulsado a escribir estas palabras . . .*"

"I don't know why I am driven to write these words." Cassandra translated as she read the diary.

Juniper was in the studio again working on his painting of the seven women and so she was alone in her lounge. She sat on the sofa by the unlit fire, and even though it was warm inside the apartment she shivered. A tremor of fear made her feel vaguely nauseous. Joy had thought it important. How much would she learn about the rogue muse from the writings of this famous man?

Her mind flashed back to when she had first met him. It was in Malaga in 1899.

She seduced him and bedded him and insinuated herself in his dreams as she told him of the greatness yet to come.

In 1900 he left Spain and eventually found his way to Paris.

Cassandra lost sight of Picasso for a while, not knowing that he had met and now shared an apartment with a journalist and poet called Max Jacobs. Cassandra knew he was in Paris, could feel his presence, but had to stay away and let him suffer before her true inspiration could take root. He was hers, she was sure of it, but she began to doubt her influence when several other muses descended on the city, all following Picasso's trail. All she could do was step back and watch each of them try him. Hoping that ultimately he would reject them all.

It was torture. She needed to inspire—had to renew in the next ten years or so. Otherwise it would all end for her.

One by one the muses tried to influence Picasso, and for a short time some of them did, but it was never lasting and, disheartened, they would invariably drift away looking for their next big thing. Cassandra knew why. *She* was his muse. She got there first. No one else could take her place no matter how hard they tried.

She stayed in the background though, always watching as Picasso's muses took him through various periods of his development. Then, the time came, and she stepped in. Her foresight always let her know the right time for everything. All life stories were already written, she knew this, and she could read those invisible pages. But some things could be changed if the influences were removed. The power in question this time was her. And she wouldn't fail to do the job she had been sent to do.

Of course, he wouldn't recognize her: she was not wearing the same face as she had in Spain. No, she was different now. Leaner, with red hair and sky-blue eyes—later she preferred to be blonde and remained with similar coloring to the present day, but at that time she liked a dramatic change. And she acted like her fiery hair suggested she might.

She made sure he saw her as she waited in the market place. She spotted another of her kind, one with dark hair, sultry good looks, who was hiding in the shadows watching him. She didn't get a good look at the other muse and Picasso was unaware of her and the others, lurking behind, in front, over his shoulder, always there. They watched with envious eyes as Cassandra, calling herself Marcelle, took him over completely.

He painted but was unhappy with his work. She inspired

and he started again. Eventually he disappeared for days, working on something, and she felt herself grow and renew as her inspiration worked its magic on both him and her.

When he returned, he had a new piece for her to look at.

"Le Bordel d'Avignon."

As she read those words in the diary, Cassandra remembered the piece. Five women, some in African masks, one of whom was Fernande Olivier … but it was magnificent.

Under Cassandra's influence, Picasso's true talent and vision had started to emerge. Back in the 21st century, Cassandra looked up from the photocopy of the flowing Spanish penmanship. She had been mentioned. Of course she had.

She was almost afraid to read on.

I don't know why I am driven to write these words. My life is changing. I am surrounded by people who love me, need me, adore me. Everything in life that I have worked for is coming to fruition. And now the strangest thing.

A muse—I know this is what she is—has come into my life and is leading me down a path I had never considered.

Cassandra halted. Oh, the pain of the memory.

He had told Fernande to leave. There were tears, arguments with bitter recrimination. All of it meant nothing to him, Picasso was an endearing lover but he could also be very cruel. He was finished with Fernande now and nothing she said would change that. When his muse went cold, Picasso always moved on to the next one that inspired him.

Cassandra took Fernande's place.

She had no guilt that she had displaced the other woman, and that a life of struggle would follow Fernande, as Picasso had no legal obligation to give her anything. They weren't married. In fact, Fernande had never divorced her last husband.

Cassandra moved in with Picasso. The name that Picasso

gave her was Eva Gouel, even though she had originally told him her name was Marcelle.

She was his muse and so much of her appeared now in his work. His obsession grew. He painted her over and over, all in different guises and styles. Some of the paintings barely even resembled the title he gave them. But he was inspired and Cassandra fed and renewed. It was a feast like none she had ever had. The reward was that her beauty grew, her powerful influence expanded, rubbed off on others around Picasso, who believed that the artist was their inspiration, not a real-life muse who regularly brushed shoulders with them. It was a heady time for Cassandra; she burned with her own flame.

And then the unthinkable happened: her influence stopped working.

A day came when Picasso had grown in ego, as well as in talent and fame, and he no longer saw Cassandra as a muse, more someone to use in his art. She realized that, as she had supplanted Olivier as his mistress, so someone else was now replacing her.

She learnt that the woman's name was Gaby Lespinasse.

Unlike Olivier, Cassandra realized quickly that her time with Picasso was drawing to an end. She never revealed herself as his muse. She had inspired him and his friends so much that she would live well for years while she searched for another to help.

Meanwhile Picasso grew ever more distant, and so Cassandra decided to end it, before the negative impact of his indifference began to drain the power she had earned. One rule of her life, and that of all muses, was, what you reap, so shall you sow. She had given to Picasso and gained longevity and the power to continue inspiring from him. Now that was ending she had to get away from him as soon as possible.

There was only one way out. Cassandra took to her bed with a fever. Feigning death soon afterwards.

She had the satisfaction of watching Picasso's devastation

from afar. But she did not go back to him; it was time to move on. She had done all she could for him.

"Away from Avignon," Cassandra said to the empty room.

She looked at the fire in the sitting room, wishing it was lit as she shuddered again. Did she really want to read Picasso's journal?

Her eyes scanned the pages without reading. There were no dates. He could have been talking about anyone. She wondered if, somehow, the muse would be revealed in the pages. Joy had thought the content important, but Cassandra didn't have the stomach for it. Those days were still raw. Failure. A major failure. It was always so hard to accept.

But no.

I inspired his greatest era, she thought. *All the art critics said so. Cubism. But then, what of that other monstrosity? Did I inspire* that *too?*

She stood up, walked to the bureau and poured a large shot of brandy. It wasn't even lunchtime and already she had the urge. Hard liquor eased the pain of muses, just as much as it did humans. Though being drunk was not an experience she could have. It soothed, but did not intoxicate.

The memory of Joy's mysterious painting burned behind her eyes even as Cassandra squeezed them shut. She had been horrified when Joy revealed it. Cassandra thought that it looked like herself. Vaguely. But then who could tell with Crystal Cubism?

No. Not that. Never that. It's not me *in that picture. He couldn't have* hated *me like that.*

She gulped down the brandy then refilled her glass. Her heart hurt. Yet she was forced to return to the chair and pick up the photocopy.

If the fire had been lit she would have thrown the papers into the flames, never to be read. But she couldn't do that. She had to read. Had to know what was in Picasso's mind all those years ago. Who was it that he had bonded with after she left? Who had taken away her glory in the moments before she achieved it? Was it Gaby? Or some other muse? And, if it was a muse, a real one, and not one of the women Picasso played with, then why draw her like that, with so much despair? So much anguish? So much pain?

CHAPTER THIRTY

Avignon 1915-1916

"The love of my life is dead. How will I ever again be inspired?"

"Oh Pablo!" said Gertrude Stein. "Work your way through this. Muses were never meant to last forever, only to start a talent on its right path."

Picasso buried his head in his hands. Eva! Eva! All he wanted to do was cry and tear out his hair. Maybe he would never paint again. Was this the end of all of it for him? Why had she left him? Dying so cruelly when she had been so vital and young.

He was surrounded by all of his influential friends. Oh, and they had all meant so much to him. He had barely noticed when Eva had taken to her bed. A chill the doctor had said: a fever that had rapidly become something else.

She was gone now. Even her body had left the house and the funeral had taken place so quickly. Eva had left instructions of how it should be. Almost as though she knew she would never live beyond the age of thirty. Too cruel!

"It is my punishment," he said. He had watched his friends go to war, feared they would never return, but had carried on with his art regardless. Pretending as always that the world did not affect him; only his art was important. Nothing else. And Eva, she had been a casualty of his selfishness. That and so many other things in his life.

How would he go on now?

Gertrude comforted him. She helped him to bed and shooed the rest of the hangers on from the house. Picasso needed his rest. The love of his life was gone.

"Do you think he'll be all right?" asked Max Jacobs.

"He's Picasso. He'll pull through. And there is Gaby to keep him warm at night. It's just as well that Eva never learnt of that dalliance."

As it turned out, Gertrude was right. Picasso recovered with Gaby's help, but his art changed again. Every upheaval, every tragedy reflected in his work.

"What shall we call this?" he said to Gertrude when he unveiled his latest piece.

They named the style Crystal Cubism.

Gaby fell by the wayside and another woman took her place. Picasso was never alone, his spirit and passion for art and his love of women remained indomitable. And then *she* came back into his life. It was a miracle. A woman he once knew, had thought long lost. True she had changed, but he could see it was her, shining through the façade.

He was alone in his studio, adding the finishing touches to a painting when she appeared.

He felt eyes on him first. Fierce eyes, a lot like his own, and they burned with an irrepressible fire.

He stopped painting, placed down his brush and turned.

It was daylight and the sun streamed in through the windows, all the natural light he could hope for filled the room with the exception of one corner. Now that part of the room appeared to be darker still.

Even so, he could see a shape emerging in the shadows, as though it were made from the darkness itself.

The studio door was locked, no one came in while he was working, unless that person was the subject matter he cared to paint.

"Pablo," said the woman. Then she stepped out from the dispersing shadows: an image of light and perfection. "Pablo Picasso?"

"Yes." He was stunned by her materialization and almost fell to his knees before her. Surely she was a goddess?

"Picasso …" the creature said again. "Would you care to paint me?"

"Y … yes," he said. He felt incapable of speech, and his usual charming and flamboyant vocabulary eluded him.

She looked at the artwork on his easel and laughed.

"Surely you can do better than this?"

"I can," he said. "I can paint any way I wish."

"Then paint me. As you see me," she said.

She stood before him, naked now. A woman of outstanding beauty. He pushed aside the previous canvas and started fresh on another.

Her shape, curved and sensual, emerged before him. He was working with lightning speed, faster than he had ever done before, and only a few hours later her image was captured. It was outstanding and perfect. Inspiration burned in his chest. This new style, almost as realistic as a black and white photograph, and yet in color, was as good as he would ever achieve.

"Realistic," she said. "So much better than this awful defacing of the women in your life."

She looked around the studio as she spoke, and the Cubism and Crystal Cubism paintings began to look ugly to him. All this experimental art, and what he really wanted now was precision. His beautiful pieces appeared to be repulsive in comparison with this one striking piece. For the first time he had achieved the dream of truly painting as he saw.

"Don't show this to anyone," she said. "I will return to give you more inspiration, but only if this remains a secret—between us."

Picasso agreed. How could he not?

To have such a muse as her made his whole world change. The colors he saw around him reflected into the work he was commissioned to do. He was bursting to talk of her, desperate to show the piece to his long-standing friend Gertrude Stein, who would, he knew, come up with something to call this new direction he was taking.

"Gertrude …" he began, and then he felt those eyes on him again, and he glanced over his shoulder, knowing that he couldn't tell anyone. Not even his closest friends.

"What are you working on?" asked Gertrude, as though she knew this was what he wanted to talk about.

"More Crystal Cubism …" he said. "You know I'm fascinated with it." He revealed the last piece he had finished before the muse had appeared to him.

"It's fabulous!" Gertrude said.

Picasso didn't agree but he pretended to follow her diagnoses of the meaning of the painting, nodding as she spoke.

"You always understand me," he said. "Now, I need to work."

Gertrude left the studio and Picasso locked the door behind her. He placed a fresh canvas on the easel and then lifted his brush.

The woman emerged again and came to stand before him. She was different this time, shorter, younger, her features flowed and changed until he saw Eva in them.

He was stunned but didn't say anything, but he began to paint, this time showing that flow and change, the features of a woman becoming a girl, a girl becoming something else.

Picasso stepped back from the canvas. His mind returned to the present. Looking around the studio he found he was alone again. His muse had gone, merged once more with the shadow in the corner of the room. He was empty, hungry, confused by the painting that was now in front of him because he couldn't remember what he had seen.

The painting combined the collective faces of all the women he had ever had an affair with. It held elements of all the periods his art had passed through. It was a veritable confusion. A monstrosity. A tribute to them all and to his life's work so far. But it was so confused, that he thought he must be losing his mind.

He hid the painting behind a stack of others, promising himself that if he lost time again he would talk to Gertrude, or Max Jacobs, or any other of his friends and ask them to watch over him in these frenetic moments.

"Tell no one," the muse's musical voice echoed around the studio. "Eat now. Rest."

He did as she told him, leaving the studio to go in search of food and drink and then he went to bed and slept for thirteen hours.

The next morning, feeling refreshed, he returned to his studio. A blank canvas waited for him on the easel. His paints were lined up, brushes clean and ready to use. There was no reason to procrastinate, but still he found one. He sorted through his latest works. Some of these would go to a gallery. Some were already reserved for sale and could now go to their new homes. Picasso could also then be paid in full, not that money was much of an issue by then. His days of poverty were far behind him.

He came across the confused painting from the day before. It hadn't been dry when he had hidden it in the stack and so some of the oil was smeared, but the smudges added to the chaos of the piece. He looked at the painting, enjoying it more now than yesterday, but a chill of fear rippled down his spine when he couldn't recall the idea behind it all. It was just what it seemed to be: a massive outpouring that reflected his life.

He placed it by the wall at the far end of the room, face turned into the wall.

Now that his canvases were organized he could no longer avoid the task of returning to the blank one that waited for him on the easel.

He stared at it for a while, then blinked. He was tired despite all of the sleep he'd had. He blinked again. Yawned and stretched.

In his hand was a brush, covered in brown toned paint. He blinked once more.

The canvas was no longer blank. It was now filled with an image. It was of an aged and deteriorating woman.

He stared. *Who was she?* He did not recognize the face, the rotted teeth that showed between the lips of a Mona Lisa smile. The woman's hair was missing in clumps and *he* had painted bare scalp, dotted with liver spots.

He closed his eyes. The memory of painting it flowed behind his lids. And he knew it was completely his work. That he had fallen back into that trancelike state from which he had only just emerged.

He glanced at the windows. The day had grown long. His legs ached as though he had stood for hours.

I did, he told himself. *I stood and I painted this. And before me was the woman it represents.*

Picasso staggered away from the painting. It was horrific. The hag appeared to be deteriorating on the canvas. Even her eyes were white and dull as though already in death. And yet—she had something left in her appearance that reminded him of the goddess who had emerged from the shadows. But how could that be, in only a matter of days!

"What is happening to me?" he said.

I need you, she had spoken directly into his mind even as he had painted her still lips.

He hid this new canvas, placing it facing the wall with the previous one, and he left his studio. In his drawing room, several friends had arrived and were sitting, talking and drinking wine together. Picasso joined them. He was somber and quiet, but because the artist was often distant, no one noticed this more intense mood he was in.

"A present for you," said Gertrude sitting down beside him. She held out a leather-bound book.

Picasso took the book and opened it, realizing it was a small sketch book, thick with blank pages for him to fill.

"Thank you," he said.

"It's small enough to carry around, for when you become inspired when away from home," Gertrude explained.

Picasso's expression remained serious, but the thought of turning this book into a journal began to relieve some of the pressure from his mind. He doubted his sanity, and if he wasn't insane, then a real muse was visiting him. She was driving him to create new things. But these new images weren't what he wanted to paint.

He took the book out of the room, leaving Gertrude and his other friends, and he went into his bedroom. There he began to write the strange tale of the muse. When he finished writing he hid the book in a place under the floorboards in his room, directly underneath the rug beside his bed. No one, not even any of his lovers, knew about the hideaway. He kept emergency money in a box there too. There was the constant threat that Germany would move across France now that they had taken Belgium and Luxemburg. Should they break through the Western Front they would gain control of Paris.

If Paris fell, Picasso knew that the whole of France was in danger and he might have to flee the country, perhaps even return to his Spanish homeland. Therefore, as well as a wad of francs, Picasso held pesetas and expensive jewelry that he could sell for currency depending on where he ended up. He would of course take as many of his canvases as he could carry.

Fortunately, the Allies were holding the Central Powers back for the time being, and Picasso, and his friends, were as safe in

Avignon as they would be anywhere else in the world. But he still made sure he had an escape plan.

As he replaced the wooden panel in the floor, and once again covered it with the rug Picasso wondered if leaving Avignon might be for the best sooner, rather than later. Could he escape this muse that held onto him, using his art for some devious plan of her own? Or would she follow him, wherever he went. He hated that he could not control their peculiar relationship. He had always been the person in charge, always led rather than followed, and it was not a natural state to feel such insecurity.

He left his bedroom and went out into the lounge and rejoined his friends. He decided that he would throw himself into their decadent party, finding and choosing, from one of the many single females, a young woman to share his bed. He did not want to be alone, or to return to his studio any time soon.

What followed was three heady days of drinking and lovemaking. The girl reminded him of one of his previous loves, Fernande, though she was not as volatile and appeared to be taking his attention in her stride. She did not expect anything, merely went along with their bohemian fun. Her name was Alice and her fair hair was cut in a boyish style, her body juvenile in shape, and Picasso enjoyed her particularly androgynous appearance. He loved women of all shapes and sizes, but Alice was so different from the muse, that he used her to take his mind completely away from the new paintings.

On the fourth morning, he woke to find Alice gone from his bed, and Gertrude sitting in the chair beside him.

"Pablo," she said. And it was rare for her, or anyone else, to call him by his first name: he was usually referred to as Picasso by everyone that knew him well. "This isn't like you."

"What?" said Picasso.

"Forgetting everything for a girl. She's not that good, surely?"

"I haven't forgotten anything, Gertrude," he said. "I'm

merely taking a holiday. Alice may yet become my next source of inspiration."

"Good," said Gertrude. "Because I have sent her to your studio. You can start using her for more practical purposes today. At night you can do as you please."

Picasso laughed. He always found it amusing when Gertrude resorted to her maternal tone with him; as she had on a few occasions in the past. She was always the voice of reason, but perpetually his biggest supporter.

So the debauched days had to end. Gertrude was right. It was a waste of his life and talent.

He pushed the covers aside and climbed out of his bed naked. Gertrude was not fazed. She watched him dress and only left the room when she was sure that he would soon follow.

The mental break from work, and the distance he had put between himself and the eccentric artwork he had created, now helped Picasso put some perspective on what had occurred. He began to consider that he had imagined the whole thing and that the muse did not exist at all. In fact, he was sure that the whole episode had been brought on by exhaustion. It was his mind and body telling him that he needed to take a break.

He had been sexually dry for a few weeks prior, a thing that had rarely occurred throughout his adulthood. He often had an affair with one or even several women at a time. Alice therefore had broken this pattern of abstinence, and Picasso was definitely feeling more like himself as a result.

He entered his studio to find Alice sitting with a bowl of fruit. He took a new canvas and began to paint as the girl peeled an orange and ate it.

The piece would be called "Girl with a Fruit Bowl," an obvious title but then he knew that the piece would need it once he had finished. It would be Crystal Cubism, and the girl, Alice, would not resemble much of herself in the end anyway.

The brush swirled on his palette and Alice's boyish form began to take shape. She was wearing a silk robe and she sat on a chaise with the bowl on her knees. Picasso stopped painting and walked up to her. He pulled open the robe and exposed her small breasts. Alice said nothing; she continued to eat the orange, dropping the peel onto the floor beside her bare feet.

Picasso returned to the canvas and began to outline the fruit before Alice ate it all. He did this in Crystal style, with sharp angular shapes representing the food. Then he moved onto Alice's hands and that was when he noticed the first anomaly. Alice had a scar around her wrist: a bright red line as though her hand had been caught in a wire mantrap and the skin had been marred.

He frowned but drew what he saw. He noticed other parts of her were oddly shaded. One breast had a weird angular mark around it. The other breast was—different. Normal. They did not match in color tone or size, although the difference was so slight that only someone looking very closely would notice it. He painted it nonetheless and then focused on her lower body. Surely he was imagining that one of her legs was a fraction shorter than the other, and didn't the shortest one have the faintest hue that suggested the skin of someone born of color?

He stopped painting when he reached the detail of her face. Her eyes were different colors. One had the whitish tinge to the blue iris that suggested old age, and myopic vision. The other was rounder with a brown iris. The white of her brown eye was clear and fresh and exactly how a young woman's eyes might look.

She was smiling as he drew her lips. One piece of orange was held up. He saw the tongue flick over her mouth, and she suckled on the juicy fruit for a moment before opening up to take the piece completely inside her mouth.

Her tongue was odd.

"What's wrong?" said Alice when she noticed he had stopped working.

"I'm trying to capture the real you."

"Good," she said.

He went back to work, highlighting and accentuating all of her flaws. There were so many. When he finished the piece, he tweaked it for a while longer. He didn't want to show Alice what he had observed about her and so he threw a sheet over the canvas and sent her away.

Alice left dutifully.

Picasso took the canvas and placed it with the other monstrosities, facing the wall at the back of the room. He didn't look again at the other paintings.

That night Picasso chose to sleep alone. He dreamt of a black cat leading him away from a dark forest. The cat led him to a white-washed building.

The next morning Picasso painted white over all three canvases completely eradicating all of the weird images. The dream had shown him that this was the only way he could cleanse his mind.

He put a fresh canvas on the easel and began to paint a simple bowl of fruit. He spent hours perfecting it, fixing the light and shade to such perfection that the fruit looked realistic. He didn't finish the rest of the canvas, just the bowl of fruit. Then he put it aside and began another piece.

Picasso's hands moved and swirled and his brush remembered the contours of Alice as he painted her lying, now, not sitting on the chaise. She was still wearing his robe, and her bare legs were visible as the fabric parted. He saw the dark triangle of her pubic hair and painted it. It came out gray, and no amount of effort would fix the shade.

He stopped painting and pressed his fingers against his closed eyelids. He rubbed gently. He was tired and the light was fading. When he opened his eyes again the painting was complete.

Alice, or someone who looked like her, was an abomination.

He stepped back from the easel. Why had he drawn this? All those imperfections? All of those scars? Yes, they were scars as though parts of her had been joined together from different body parts, and different women.

Picasso picked up his white paint and moved to white-wash the canvas.

At that moment. the shadows in the corner moved. Picasso felt tremendous pain burst behind his eyeballs at the start of a headache. Some instinct told him that he mustn't let the muse see this painting. He picked it up and deposited it in the back of the room, face towards the wall. Then he returned to his easel and began to clean his brushes.

"Picasso?" said the woman's voice.

"Yes?" he said.

The muse was before him and her face was a jumble of parts. Scars new, as well as old, held her patchwork body together. Now that he had become aware of her real condition, he couldn't unsee it. Try as he might.

"Do I inspire you?" she said. Her face was part Alice, part Eva, and then he knew. She was all of these women because parts of them were in her.

"Yes," he said. He tried to keep his face blank. How would he ever rid himself of this creature?

"Good. Because inspiring you is what will help me renew."

"Renew?" he said.

The muse smiled. Her teeth were that of the rotted old crone he had painted days before. He tried not to notice.

"Soon. Very soon. I will be beautiful and powerful again. But I need your help to get there."

Picasso said nothing. He kept his eyes on his brushes and turned his mind to the task, and away from the muse. It was the only way he could keep himself from running screaming from the room.

CHAPTER THIRTY-ONE

It's not like you to sleep in," said Chandler as he placed a mug of coffee beside the bed.

He was in Lauren's apartment. He was always there these days, rarely going back to his own house, his old memories.

"I'm tired," she said.

Chandler placed his hand on her forehead. "Are you sick?"

"A little woozy," she answered.

"Maybe you should cancel your appointments. Take the day off."

Lauren pulled herself up into the sitting position in the bed and reached for the coffee, but as she brought the mug to her lips the smell reached her nostrils and she was nauseated.

She put the cup down, pushed back the covers and ran for the bathroom.

She made the toilet bowl in time. Chandler followed her, then held her hair back as she vomited into the bowl.

When her stomach was empty and the dry heaving stopped, she sat by the toilet shivering and pale.

"I'm calling your office to tell them you can't come in today."

"No … I have to. I'll be okay."

"Lauren, you're sick. You aren't going anywhere."

Chandler helped her up and led her back to the bed. Then he took away the coffee mug and returned with a glass of water.

Lauren sipped the water.

"I guess I must have eaten something bad," she said.

"Could be, but food poisoning would usually work quicker than this. I think you have stomach flu. Want me to call a doctor?"

"No. I'll be fine. You go to work. I'll ring the office and cancel my appointments."

"You sure?" he said.

"Yes. I'm starting to feel better already."

Her color was improving as she spoke and so Chandler was reassured. He kissed her forehead then placed her cell phone on the bedside table.

"If you need anything, call me," he said.

"I will." She closed her eyes and turned her head into the pillow.

Chandler left the room, closing the bedroom door behind him.

"Cassandra?" said Juniper. "Are you getting up?"

Cassandra opened her eyes. She looked weary and the whites were bloodshot.

"I'm just a little tired this morning."

"I thought you needed to go into the office today?" said Juniper. "Your clients …"

"I do."

Cassandra pulled herself up from the bed. She was wearing a thin cream satin nightshift. The nightshift wasn't as fresh as it had been the night before. It was spotted with perspiration stains and Cassandra, normally immaculate looked as though she had woken after a heavy night drinking. But Juniper knew this wasn't the case as he had never seen her drunk.

She made her way to the bathroom, closing the door behind her, and a few moments later, Juniper heard her vomiting.

"Are you all right?" he said.

Cassandra didn't answer and so Juniper opened the door and went in. He saw her leaning over the toilet bowl and rushed to her side.

"You're sick," he said.

Cassandra dry heaved into the bowl. Then reached up and flushed away the evidence of her sickness.

"I'll be okay. It's just … I'm so weary."

"What can I do?" Juniper said.

"Nothing. Paint. That's all you can do. This thing will be sorted out soon."

"What thing?"

"My … it's nothing. Just a stomach flu."

He helped her stand.

"You should go back to bed."

"Yes. Just for a little while …"

She let him lead her back into the bedroom, then climbed back into the bed. She closed her eyes and turned over.

"Paint," Cassandra said. "As though *my life* depends on it."

"I haven't finished the women … I'm afraid to do their faces."

"I know," she said. "But you need to be brave. Then we will tell Chandler. You have his card?"

"Yes."

Juniper hesitated by the door. "Can I get you anything?"

"Knowing you're working will make me feel better," Cassandra said.

"Okay."

Juniper left the bedroom and made his way down the hallway towards the studio. As he opened the door he was greeted by the painting. All of the women's bodies were complete, except for the small gray patches that he couldn't seem to rid himself of in each of the figures. One had a gray outline for her left hand, another, whose back was facing outwards, had gray all the way down her spine. The fourth figure showed a scar on her torso, directly where her kidney would be. The fifth one had a huge gray patch over the left side of her chest, directly over the heart. The sixth and seventh women had marks over the face. One over an eye, the other over her mouth and jaw. Juniper knew what all of this meant and this was why he was afraid to paint the faces in.

He considered creating something new now. He felt an overwhelming urge to paint but Cassandra would be displeased if he didn't at least finish one of the women. He opted for the one that meant less injury. The girl could survive without her hand, but the others possibly wouldn't survive their injuries.

He picked up his brush and then a shudder ran down his spine. The dark thing was in the room with him, and now his hand was moving of its own volition. He raised the brush and began to outline the head of the fifth woman, rather than the first, as he had intended.

"No," he said, but his hand was out of his control. It swept over the canvas and the face came into view. Juniper recognized her but couldn't stop himself from completing the features.

"Not Marina," he said. "No. Stop."

He pulled himself back from the canvas. Marina was his first girlfriend. She would be in her late thirties now. But they had dated for a little while in Russia. She had also been the first woman that Juniper had painted.

He forced his fingers open and dropped the paint brush.

"She isn't in America," he said, "so leave her alone."

Laughter.

Yes. He was really hearing it!

"I won't paint anymore," said Juniper. "I won't let you kill Marina."

Chandler's card was on the side next to his jar of spirits.

Juniper picked it up, then took his cell phone out of his pocket. The painting wasn't finished and so he hoped this would mean that the creature couldn't attack Marina yet.

It took him three attempts to dial the number correctly because his hands were shaking so much.

In the corner of the studio the shadows watched him.

"Detective Chandler?"

"Yes?"

"It's me, Avgustin Juniper. I know who the next one is."

"You've painted another face," said Chandler.

"Yes. It is Marina Mikhailov. She is Russian. You need to protect her."

"Where will we find her?"

Juniper looked at the shadows. He knew then where Marina was, but could Chandler get to her before the creature did?

"Empire State Building," Juniper said. "But hurry. The thing will take her heart. She can't survive."

Juniper completed the call and then he picked up the paint-brush. He began to work on the second girl's face. Filling it in rapidly.

"Let's see if you can go after two at a time," he murmured.

When he had completed this figure, he returned to Marina and finished her face. Then he looked over to the corner of the room. The shadow was gone and there was no longer any dark-ness in the corner of the room.

He sent Chandler a text, telling him who the other girl was and where she would be. He didn't know if Chandler could reach them both, but he hoped he got to Marina at least.

Then he left the studio and returned to the bedroom. When he opened the door, he found Cassandra was gone.

She must have dressed and gone into work after all, he thought. Juniper shrugged. She could have left a note at least to say she was feeling better.

He sent her a text.

Are you okay?

A few seconds later she replied.

Feeling better. Busy now but be home around 7.

Juniper returned to his studio because he didn't know what else to do. He then spent the next few hours tweaking and perfecting the two new faces. He did not go onto the other women.

His cell phone rang just after one.

"Cassandra? How are you feeling?"

"I'm great. Never better. Listen let's eat out tonight. I have a lot of work to do, but I can meet you at the Italian restaurant at seven."

"Okay."

"How is work going?"

"I did two new faces," he said.

"Two? Why?"

"I wanted to make sure one of the girls survived."

"And did they?"

"I don't know. Detective Chandler hasn't called."

"I'll call him."

CHAPTER THIRTY-TWO

Chandler reached the Empire State Building in record time. Then he received the text about the second girl. What was Juniper playing at? He couldn't be in two places at once. But then perhaps that was the point. Neither could the attacker. He called Sarasvatī's mobile but his call was diverted back to the office.

"Sarasvatī's sick today," said the girl at the office. "She phoned in earlier."

It wasn't like Sarasvatī to take time off, so he suspected it might be pretty serious. Chandler asked for back up to both the Empire State Building and to the Jekyll and Hyde Club on 7th Avenue South between Barrow and Grove, where the other girl, Denise Miller, worked as an entertainer.

"How can I help you, Detective?" asked the supervisor at the Empire State when Chandler flashed his badge.

"Do you have any payment record for a Marina Mikhailov?"

"Russian, right?"

"Yes."

The cashier checked the computer. "I don't have any individual payments under that name but we did just have a group booking of Russian tourists go up to the top."

"Which way?"

"The elevator is on the left," the cashier said.

The elevator arrived just as Chandler reached it. He pushed his way to the front of the waiting queue of tourists, waved his badge and requested that they all wait there until further notice. Then he entered alone. It was a nightmare getting to the viewing platform at the top. Two lifts connected by a walk-through corridor. Chandler moved as quickly as he could, badge in hand to wave at the various attendants at each point.

As the elevator doors finally opened on the topmost viewing platform, Chandler looked around, wondering which direction to go in first. There were several groups of people. It was difficult to tell at a glance what nationality anyone was. Juniper had sent an image file of Marina Mikhailov's face from the painting. Chandler studied it for a moment, then began to walk through the tourists. Laughter and loud voices drew his attention. He thought the language he heard might be Russian but wasn't sure.

"I'm looking for Marina Mikhailov," he said to one man who seemed to be in the group.

The man glanced over his shoulder, saw Chandler's badge and began to talk rapidly to another man beside him.

"Uri doesn't speak English," said the second man. "How can we help you?"

The second man's English was good. Chandler explained who he was looking for, and he showed the picture of Marina's face to them.

"Yes. I know her. She is travelling with the group," he looked around. "There! She's by the telescope."

Chandler turned to see Marina alive and well and feeding coins into one of telescopes which were positioned around the outside of the viewing platform. He breathed a sigh of relief and hurried over to her.

A group of uniformed police officers came out of the elevator and Chandler led them over to Marina.

"She needs to be placed in protective custody. She's not to be left alone at any time, night or day."

"Would she be safer in Russia?" asked one of the uniformed officers. "We can get her on a plane home."

"For now, we keep hold of her. And anyone else that Juniper remembers he's painted."

"Juniper?" asked Marina. "*Avgustin Juniper*?"

"Yes. I'll explain it all to you as we travel to the station," Chandler said.

"Wait. What about my friend," Marina asked.

"Which friend?" Chandler said.

"The girl I'm travelling with. Her name is Sophia Resler. She was one of Juniper's models too."

"What does she look like?"

Marina pulled out her cell phone and retrieved a photograph of Sophia.

"You two, go and look for this girl," said Chandler to two of the uniformed officers. "Get her over here and we'll all go down together."

The doors of the elevator opened and Chandler hurried Marina inside. Surrounded by officers, Chandler felt she was at least safe for the moment, but where were his other two men with Sophia?

A loud commotion drew Chandler's attention. A piercing scream ripped through the air, followed by further screams as people rushed for the elevator.

Chandler ducked inside and pressed the down button, leaving Marina inside with four men as he dashed through the doors seconds before they closed. He barred the elevator doors as people rushed towards them.

"Police! Stop where you are!" he said. The elevator started its descent behind him.

"What's happened?" Chandler said. The people at the front

began to talk all at once. Hysteria was in the air, barely restrained by the one police officer barring them from leaving. But at least Chandler knew that Marina was safe for the time being.

"Detective Chandler," said a voice from the crowd. Chandler turned to see one of his officers approaching. "We need an ambulance."

"Sophia?" Chandler said.

"Yes."

"I'm afraid none of you are leaving," he said addressing the crowd. "There's been an incident."

He called for more backup and a paramedic crew. Then, he left the uniformed cop by the elevators and went to see what damage had been done to Sophia Resler.

The second cop was waiting beyond the telescope.

"What state is she in?" Chandler asked.

The cop shook his head.

Chandler looked behind him, saw the prone body of a girl lying face down. The back of her dress was ripped open, and so was her back.

"What the fuck … ?" Chandler said.

At that point the uniformed officer stepped away and duly lost his lunch by the telescope.

Chandler wasn't sure until the MD saw the body, but it looked like Resler's spine had been ripped out through her back. She was more than likely dead before her body hit the ground. The skin on her back was peeled back like the petals of some horrific rose, the edges red and cauterized, and inside her body he could see the ends of her ribcage and other organs, all pulsing gently as whatever life there was ebbed away. There was no way she could be saved even if medics had been there. What was more horrific was the lack of blood.

In the back of his mind Chandler remembered an exhibition he had once gone to, of flayed and dissected human bodies, somehow all preserved in a plastic resin. They were beautiful in their grotesquery, nerves and veins and bones all visible in the flayed bodies, which had been positioned in manners aesthetically pleasing to their creator, some German doctor who had invented the process.

Poor Resler's body reminded him of this. The complexity of the human body, open to display.

"All these people here and she's attacked like this. The killer has to be here. Somewhere. We'll work our way through them and see if we can find a connection," Chandler said. "You okay?"

"Yes," croaked the cop. "Never seen anything like that before."

"Me neither. Go and stay by the elevator. Make sure no one tries to leave. Back up will be here any minute."

The cop did as he was told, glad to walk away from the grisly sight.

The crowd was thinned down to the last dozen people when Chandler noticed a familiar face among them.

"Miss Awen, what are you doing here?"

"I was meeting a friend," Joy said.

"This is the second crime scene I've found you at this week," said Chandler.

Joy frowned. "It is purely a coincidence, Detective."

"Have you spoken to Juniper today? Did he tell you anything about his painting?"

"What painting?" asked Joy.

"Juniper is currently painting a picture that has seven women in it. All of whom have modeled for him in the past."

"So?"

"So. I came here after receiving a tip from him telling me that Marina Mikhailov would be the next victim."

"Is that the girl who was attacked?" Joy said.

"No. There was another one of his former models here too.

While we were looking out for Marina, our perpetrator went after Sophia Resler."

"I'm sorry to hear that. That's awful," said Joy.

"Did you see anything?" Chandler asked bluntly.

"No. I'm afraid I was waiting for my friend on the other side. I just heard the screaming and came to see what was going on."

"Okay. At least I know how to get in touch with you if I have more questions."

"Of course, Detective. And I wish I could help."

"You may leave now."

Joy turned to go.

"Just one thing … I assume your friend was a no show?"

"Yes. I received a text from her to apologize. She's sick today."

"Can I have her name?"

"It isn't relevant, Detective."

"I'll decide when something is relevant, Miss Awen. Who were you planning to meet?"

"You need to confirm what I'm saying is true, I suppose."

"The name?"

"Well I have no issue with telling you. I'm certain she will tell you I'm not lying. It was your colleague, Gemma Sarasvatī. We were going to meet for lunch, but she's had to take the day off work sick."

Chandler watched Joy leave. He was confused by her relationship with Sarasvatī. What did Joy and Gemma have in common? Would Sarasvatī, a cold fish by anyone's standards, actually be the sort of woman that Joy would be friends with? He couldn't imagine it. And yet it was true. How else would she know that Sarasvatī had called in sick that day? And why would Joy lie when she knew that Sarasvatī would tell him she had?

He wrote himself a note to speak to Sarasvatī when she was back in the office. It was a shame she wasn't well. He could really have used her efficiency that day. He also noted a text which told him that the other girl, Denise Miller, had been taken into custody. That was something at least.

His cell phone rang.

"Chandler," he said.

"It's Cassandra here. Avgustin told me he sent you a lead. Were you successful, Detective? Is Marina Mikhailov safe?"

"Yes," Chandler said. Though he didn't know why he should tell her anything.

"What about the other girl?" Cassandra said.

"In custody. Safe," he said.

"Oh, thank God. Maybe we can put a stop to this."

"Cassandra, could you ask Juniper if he painted another face today?"

"He told me he did two."

"Just ask him. And ring me back with the answer, will you?"

"Why?"

"Indulge me."

Cassandra said she would.

A few minutes later she rang back. "Avgustin said 'no.' He was tired after working on the other two, and so he went and lay down for a moment. Oh, hold a minute will you, I'm getting another call."

Chandler waited while Cassandra took her second call. Then she returned to him.

"Sophia Resler is dead, isn't she?" she asked.

"Yes," said Chandler. "So I assume that was Juniper on the other line."

"He has just gone into the studio and he found another face filled in. He swears he doesn't remember doing it. But he says it's in his style. Oh my God this is awful."

"We saved two women today," Chandler said. He was surprised to hear the stress in Cassandra's voice. "I guess we are going to have to be happy with that."

CHAPTER THIRTY-THREE

Denise Miller was anxious as the police car drove her towards the safe house. They had let her return home to collect some personal items, but she was never allowed to be alone in any room. Even the bathroom door had to remain slightly ajar as she took a shower. And a female officer stood there the whole time.

She had been dressed as the bride of Frankenstein—having only just started the job at the club, she was worried that her sudden departure with the police would mean they would find someone else. Denise needed the money, and had tried to explain this to the officer who led her away.

"Your life might be at risk," the female plainclothes officer had explained. "You have to come with us for your own safety."

She'd had no choice but to go with them, but now she was worrying how she would pay her rent at the end of the month, and what her mother would say when she learnt she had posed for an artist in the nude for money.

"Almost there," said the officer. "And you'll have company."

"Who?" Denise asked.

"A Russian woman. She seems nice. I took her there earlier today."

"She posed for Avgustin too?"

"Former girlfriend, it seems. And yes, probably."

Denise was more than a little jealous when she heard this, though it was crazy to feel like that when she had barely known Juniper. He had always been distant with her, though he had used her a lot for his art at the time so she had thought he liked her really. Then there was the nude picture she had agreed to pose for. After that he hadn't invited her back. Denise had always thought that this was because he had got what he wanted from her—he had been grooming her all along to pose naked.

"Here we are," said her escort as the car turned into a driveway.

They were in the suburbs, out of New York City and on the way to Long Island. The house was big. Bigger than Denise could ever dream of owning.

"So, you want to be an actress?" said the female officer, trying to make polite conversation.

"No. Why do you think that?"

"Well, the acting stuff. At the restaurant."

"Oh no. It just pays well. With the tips and all. I want to be a writer."

"Really?" said the officer. "What have you written so far?"

"A few stories. I'm working a lot. Don't have much time."

"My brother-in-law writes screenplays," said the male officer as he stopped the car.

"Cool," said Denise.

"Just wait in the car while we make sure everything is good inside," said the female officer.

"Sure," said Denise.

She was beginning to wonder if she could write a screenplay about her experience. It was all a little over the top. Surely the killer wouldn't know she was here?

The car was unmarked to avoid drawing attention to them

with the neighbors. Although Denise wondered how many had realized the police used this location as a safe house. She thought that she would be observant enough to see the strange comings and goings and might have put two and two together easily. But then, she always people watched, because she knew it was important if she wanted to be a writer.

The female cop had assured her that she and Marina were safe, and so Denise believed them. It didn't help her financial circumstances though and she couldn't push this fear away as she waited in the back of the car.

The front door opened and the cops exchanged a few words with the other cops inside.

The female cop turned around and nodded to Denise and beckoned her out of the car.

Denise opened the door and started to climb out. It was now night and quite dark, but she felt as though she were stepping into a void. The streetlights over the driveway weren't working and so Denise closed the door and, placing her right hand on the car, she used it to guide herself around the back.

She didn't know why she went around the back of the car instead of the front, but later she would wish that she had made a different choice.

She was only out of sight of the cops for a few seconds.

"Ouch," she said.

"What's wrong, Denise?" said the female cop hurrying towards her.

Denise emerged from the back of the car.

"My hand," she said. She was clutching it inside her jacket.

She removed her arm and then the female cop saw: Denise's hand had been severed at the wrist. The stump was neat, and in the circle could be seen the ends of her radius and ulna, neat ovals of bone, with the darker marrow inside. It was as though a laser had sliced through her arm. Neat, surgical, and effective.

"Get an ambulance," she said as Denise stumbled forward into her arms.

CHAPTER THIRTY-FOUR

Juniper was in the kitchen when Cassandra arrived home. He had told her he was too depressed now to go out, and he was drowning his sorrows in a bottle of vodka. Without a word Cassandra took a glass from one of the top cupboards and she placed it by the bottle.

Juniper poured some of the liquor into her glass.

Cassandra sat down next to him at the breakfast bar.

"I'm never painting again," he said.

"You have to. You can't stop now. No matter what. Any victory is a good one. As Detective Chandler said, two women were saved today."

"I didn't paint zhat third face. I went to sleep."

She took his hand. "Avgustin, there is something you need to know. This thing is controlling you. Whatever it does during those times, it is not your fault."

"But why? Why am I being used like this?

Cassandra sighed. She had no answers that she could give without freaking him out more than he already was.

"Just be aware that we all believe in you. This person will be caught. And stopped. But it will need you to take a leap of faith in order to achieve it."

"No. No more. I can't do more. What about these women? I can't put them in harm's way."

"They are all at risk until this … creature is caught. So you have to do it, Avgustin. You have to keep painting."

Juniper was quiet then he looked up and met her eyes. He was struck with how beautiful and perfect she looked. So much better than in the morning when she was suffering from some form of stomach upset.

"You *are* better?" he said.

"Don't worry about me. I'm tough. I've been through worse than a stomach bug."

"You look beautiful."

She smiled.

Juniper's heart lifted. She *was* beautiful. It was as though she had somehow renewed herself and there was a glow of energy and light around her. He had never noticed it before. He glanced down at his vodka glass, now empty. Maybe he had drunk enough for one day.

He pulled Cassandra to him, kissing her on the lips. "If I were to paint anyone, it would be you," he said against her mouth. "You inzpire me. More than anyone I have known."

"Maybe you should paint me," she said.

"No. I could not risk you."

"Come on," she said.

"Where?"

"To bed. Where else?"

She led him down to her room. Thanks to the housekeeping service the bed was now made. Cassandra pulled Juniper on to the duvet without drawing it back.

She stripped away his clothing and he helped her unbutton her blouse: peeling it from her body before dropping it to the floor.

There was no desperate tearing at each other, no hurried caressing. Only warm, slow, sensual lovemaking followed.

Afterwards Juniper felt calmer. Cassandra's touch had such a soothing effect on him. And her body looked wonderful. Her eyes were brighter, not blood-shot as they had been earlier. Her skin glowed with a new vigor. He saw "life" when he looked at her. His hope for the future soared.

When this is all over I will paint her. When this is all over I will ask her to marry me, he thought. The idea was no sooner in his head than he was shocked by it. How could he ever hope to hold onto such an amazing woman? She was everything he was not.

"You asleep?" she murmured now as she curled up against him.

"No," he said.

"Stop worrying. Everything will be fine."

He pulled her into his arms. She smelt wonderful: summer, vodka and sex. How could he ever think he could possess such a beauty? She was a work of art all of her own.

He closed his eyes pressing in the tears of joy that sprang from them. He *loved* her. He really did. She was his heart and soul. How had he ever thought those pathetic lusts and minor interests he'd had over the years were anything like love. *This* was love. This was regal. Magnificent. Unselfish. He would do anything for her.

The tears tried to force their way past his closed lids. He swiped his hand across them, hoping she wouldn't notice. How could he explain that they were tears of happiness? That he had realized he loved her more than even his own life.

Cassandra snuggled into him and her breathing leveled out. He was pleased that she was better now. He hated to see her ill, and he wanted her to rest.

When he was sure she was asleep he slid from the bed and left the room as quietly as he could.

His mind was racing. Sleep was impossible. So much had

happened in the last twenty-four hours. Sophia Resler was dead. But as Cassandra had reminded him, his actions had saved two others. They were safe now, in police custody. Even this bold attacker couldn't get to them now.

Marina, his first love, had once held his heart, but it now belonged solely to Cassandra. He would never give it away to anyone else.

In the kitchen, Juniper filled a mug with milk and cocoa. Then he placed it in the microwave. A few moments later the timer pinged and he took out the now hot chocolate.

He had on occasion enjoyed this at night to help him sleep. Sometimes with a shot of vodka or brandy in it. That night he didn't feel the need for the extra alcohol. Instead he drank the chocolate as it was. Then, finally feeling sleepy, he left the kitchen and began to walk back to Cassandra's bedroom.

He paused at the door, remembering that he had left his toothbrush in the other bathroom, in the bedroom he had once occupied. Juniper turned around and headed back to his old room but as he passed the studio, he noticed that the door was slightly ajar. He remembered closing it firmly earlier when he had received the news about Sophia. He reached in, turned on the light and loitered in the doorway, looking around the room for sign of intrusion. Then he noticed his easel.

The picture on it had changed. It was no longer the seven statues. It was the abomination!

Juniper took a step closer. Who had put this here? He *knew* he hadn't revisited it since he had put the blonde hair on the monstrous scalp. Now he saw that the figure had a new hand. He could also see the spine running through the otherwise grayed out torso.

"Oh God! Oh God!"

Juniper fell to his knees before the easel. Who had done this? What did it mean?

He knew of Sophia's attack. The spine was hers for certain,

but the hand? Did this mean that Denise had also been found by the creature?

If so, then Marina was still in grave danger.

He pulled himself back up to his feet and searched for Detective Chandler's card but found it wasn't on the sideboard where he had left it. Where was his cell phone anyway?

Paint, Avgustin.

Juniper was trembling now. Was he going insane? Had he completed this painting and then forgotten? What would Cassandra make of it when she saw the piece?

He reached for it, picking it up from the easel. His hands were shaking as he held it aloft. He must destroy it.

He placed it back on the easel and picked up his palette knife, holding it above the picture. But his hand wouldn't sweep down. No matter how much he tried the creature which rode him wouldn't let him destroy the image.

He dropped the knife. Then he placed the painting at the back of the room, duplicating, without knowing, the act of the long dead artist, Pablo Picasso, as he turned his painting face to the wall.

He couldn't bear it. It was an abomination because of what it meant. What it represented.

Paint, Avgustin.

Juniper hurried to the door of the studio, then paused. He had to destroy the piece now, before anyone saw it.

Paint.

He picked up the canvas of the seven statues and placed it back on the easel.

He was tired and his eyes blurred as he stared at the painting, trying to reassure himself that no other faces had been added.

There were four of the seven now. Maya, Denise, Marina and Sophia. How horrible—only three to go.

Only three more and you're free, Avgustin. Only three and I will release you. You can have the life you want with Cassandra. You can be happy. All it takes is three more faces.

The devil was talking to him. Goading him to finish, to sell his soul. And now that Juniper had everything to live for, he was tempted.

He stared at the canvas. Who would have the least damage?

Anna. Yes, Anna. She could survive losing an eye, couldn't she? That's all it would be....

No! Juniper thought. *I can't. No more please. I beg you.*

He backed away from the easel. Cassandra would help him. Cassandra would hold him and he could sleep.

He turned the light off and closed the door of the studio. Then hurried back to Cassandra's room, forgetting the toothbrush that he had come down to collect.

CHAPTER THIRTY-FIVE

"Come in," said Lauren as she opened the door to Joy and Cassandra.

It was after hours. Lauren's secretary was long gone. Chandler was working late and so she hadn't needed to make an excuse not to see him. It was something of a relief for all of them to gather again.

"You look well," Joy observed as she entered. "Positively glowing."

"Jake's recovery is proving to be rewarding," Lauren said.

"That's good," said Cassandra. "Avgustin has finally bonded with me. He even wants to paint me."

"It shows," said Joy her voice blank.

"And what about you?"

"I was renewed not long ago," she said. "A minor artist that came to the gallery and had some success, but I inspired him to go into the stock market with the little money he made. He's now a multimillionaire. It turns out he has a knack for knowing when to buy and when to sell."

"So. We'll all go on. For a while more anyway," said Cassandra.

Lauren led them into her therapy room. Cassandra halted at the doorway when she saw the fake Van Gogh hanging on the wall by her desk.

"Looks like we all have a sense of humor," said Joy.

Lauren glanced at the painting and shrugged.

"I called this meeting because we are going to have to face facts," she said. "One of us is the killer."

"There is a fourth one," Joy reminded. "She's pretty sick right now too. And has no inspiration to renew from."

"The detective?" Cassandra said.

"You recognized her then?" Joy said.

"Yes. When she came over to interview Avgustin. I wouldn't let her in at the time. I thought she was trying to inspire him."

"It could be her," Lauren said.

"She's also very close to the case. In a position to know who the women Avgustin painted were."

"But why has she latched onto him? Why not take parts from any female?" Lauren asked.

"She can't. There has to be a source to use, or inspire if you like, otherwise the parts wouldn't …" Joy said.

"Wouldn't what?" asked Cassandra.

"Meld. She's replacing the bits of herself that are failing. I wouldn't be surprised if she's done this before." Joy said. "You read the Picasso journal, didn't you?"

Cassandra nodded. Lauren said, "Yes."

"Picasso was touched by all of us," Cassandra pointed out.

"Yes," said Joy. "It could still be any one of us."

"Suppose we assume that we three are not guilty? Especially as we all want to help Avgustin. And that none of us is sick right now," Lauren said.

"I'll accept that," said Joy.

"But what are we going to do about Gemma Sarasvatī?" said Lauren. "Assuming there are only four of us left. If it's not one of us, then it's her."

"I reached out to her," Joy said. "Tried to meet with her. She said 'yes,' then called off sick."

"That was at the Empire State, right?" said Cassandra.

"Yes," said Joy.

"Whose idea was it to meet there?" Cassandra said.

"It was … Sarasvatī's," Joy said.

"Odd. Unless she already knew that Marina and Sophia would be there," Cassandra said. "Maybe she was setting you up."

"I don't think so. I had the feeling she was genuinely sick. She really didn't look good when she came to the gallery."

"And you didn't see the girl attacked?" asked Lauren.

"No. I told Chandler, I was over on the other side of the building. I heard the scream. Then got pulled along with the crowd as everyone panicked. I guessed what had happened when I saw Chandler standing by the elevator."

"Never mind *see*," Cassandra said. "What did you *feel*?"

Joy shook her head. "Nothing. Nothing at all. I suppose I should have felt the other one's presence."

"I need a drink," said Lauren. "Anyone else?"

Joy and Cassandra nodded.

Lauren walked around her desk and opened the bottom drawer. She extracted a bottle of Scotch whisky and three small tumblers. The other two didn't comment about her being prepared for them, it was a foregone conclusion.

Lauren poured a good measure of the amber liquid into each glass. She picked up two and held them out. Cassandra and Joy took the glasses and then they sat down on the couch that had been the resting place for many of Lauren's patients.

Lauren picked up her glass, then took a seat in the chair opposite them. She sipped her drink.

"What are we going to do?" Cassandra said again.

"We invite her to meet again. With all of us. Then we *look* at her. I mean *really* look," said Joy.

"And if she has those … parts in her?" asked Lauren. "What then?"

"Then we reason with her," said Cassandra. "What else can we do?"

Lauren sipped her whisky. It tasted bitter now, not the smooth Scottish single malt that it should be. Like poison. She put the glass down on the table between them. She felt a little sick again.

"It's a shame we can't get help from *them,*" Lauren said.

"We're on our own now," said Cassandra. "*They* don't even exist anymore."

"What's going to happen to us when we can't inspire?" said Lauren. Her voice was flat.

"The same as Sarasvatī," said Joy. "Then we might feel a little differently about the choice she's making."

"And if we can't go down that route?" asked Cassandra.

"We become human. And eventually die," said Joy.

The three muses fell silent and pondered their future. It didn't seem as promising as it had just a few hours earlier.

"There's one other issue we have to address," said Lauren. "What do we tell Jake?"

"He's been surprisingly open-minded about Avgustin's painting and the connection with the attacker," Cassandra said.

"But he's suspicious too," said Joy.

"I think he could handle a little more knowledge," Cassandra said. "We could tell him some of the truth. But not all."

"I don't want him to know about me," said Lauren. "But if you two want to reveal to a mortal that you're muses, have lived since man was first conceived, then go ahead. I'm not sure even his open-minded attitude will take that knowledge on."

"Then what do you suggest?" asked Joy.

"Tell him nothing. If we can't make the other muse see sense then we might have to take things into our own hands," Lauren said.

"He won't stop looking for the killer. He'll always believe that Avgustin's models are in danger," Joy said.

"Better that he gets a cold case than the truth," Lauren said.

"You know him better than any of us," Cassandra said. "But I think he'd probably prefer closure."

"What of Avgustin?" asked Joy.

"When he's finished the last three faces, he's done," Cassandra said.

"What do you mean by 'done'," asked Lauren.

"He'll be finished with this creature."

"How do you know she won't keep using him?" asked Joy.

"Picasso …"

The three grew silent again, because they already knew the answer.

Paris, 1917

Picasso had tried to rid himself of her but she wouldn't leave. Whenever he was in the studio, her dark presence followed. And when some of the women he painted disappeared he knew she was somehow involved.

Yes. He knew what she was. What she was meant to be. But something had gone wrong for her. And whenever she appeared to him, she wore different faces, all of women he had once known. A confused jumble sometimes of parts that he recognized, at other times she was stable, usually immediately after one of his models had mysteriously vanished. She glowed then. As though that tiny part of someone else had revived her deteriorating form and given her new life.

He thought he knew what was happening, began to recognize the signs. *She* was fine for a while and then, something would drive him to find a stranger—merely pick her up off the street and take her back to paint. His charm always worked for him, as though *she* inspired or fueled it, making him irresistible to women.

"I need to repair myself," she had whispered to him from the shadows. "Then you will be free."

"How long?" he asked.

"A few more. Just a few. Then one final piece will bring it all together."

He made a deal with her consciously—knowing that she would eventually free him, and so he went about business with more direction and determination than he had before. Finding those girls, even knowing in advance what she would take from them. Like her pimp he chose carefully for the best he could find for her. It occurred to him that he found something to make the work less horrible, and also, in some jaded way, pay homage to the sacrificial victim because she had something of value and beauty to give to the muse.

He didn't ponder on what would happen to each girl as they left his studio. *She* would use, or absorb the poor unfortunate in some way. Picasso felt no remorse. He knew he had been unable to refuse, or fight, because if he hadn't done as *she* wished, his close friends would have suffered and those women he had painted that he cared about would become fodder for her too. Better that the street girls died instead. No one would care. No one would miss them.

Then the day came. He had found a whore who was unusually young and untainted to pose for him. She was a sweet girl and still had a softness about her. Picasso noted that she had a mostly unspoiled heart when he saw her feeding scraps to an urchin on the street corner. It hadn't taken much to get her to come back to his house and pose for him.

"Go now," he said, when the picture was finished.

"What about payment?" she said.

"Take a painting. Any one you like. They are worth far more than the few francs you asked for," he said.

And because the girl knew who he was, she happily rifled

through the paintings and chose something that she thought she could sell.

She left. Picasso barely noticed. But the moment of his freedom happened shortly afterwards.

A hard thump to the chest brought him to his knees before the canvas. He looked up and saw that he had painted the area gray on the painting of the girl. And knew that she could not survive this sacrifice: her tender heart was her undoing.

For a moment he studied her pretty face, feeling a large amount of guilt, and then the pressure of the last year lifted completely from his shoulders.

The muse *had* repaired herself, as she had told him she would. He was free. *He knew it.*

He didn't know how long the renewal would last. Would it be weeks, months, years or centuries? Either way the bargain he had made with her—call her the devil for she might as well be—had been met. The final piece of her body jigsaw was in place and his talent had molded it together. She was now complete. He saw it in his mind's eye.

Horrible. Beautiful. Grotesque. Striking. Monstrous.

He could paint as he wished again—oh the joy that soared in his soul—and the stack of ugly artwork that was gathering dust at the back of his studio could now be destroyed.

He was aware as he sorted through them that he had survived a different kind of war, one far more personal than the one that still raged in Europe.

No one ever associated the spate of missing girls with Picasso. Why would they? He had kept all of that artwork in his studio, had never shown anyone these abominations. And if anyone had seen them, what would they make of it? The Crystal Cubism style made it hard to recognize any model unless he labeled the artwork. And he had no intentions of ever identifying any of these women.

Now to destroy them.

But "destroy" was a loose term for what he would do.

He took all of the canvases from the back and painted over them one by one. As he came to the end of the pile he realized that not all of the artwork was there. Something was missing. But which one, he couldn't remember. Maybe it was one of the muse herself? Maybe one of the many girls he had painted as a sacrifice to the creature?

But who had taken it?

The last girl …

Yes. He had said to her to take a painting. But where had this missing canvas ended up? If she had been the final sacrifice that meant … No. Too unlikely. The creature would not want a painting of herself. Especially *that* one.

He realized then which one was lost. And he remembered the day he had painted it. His heart was full of bitterness and hatred. He had shown her for her true ugliness and it was an abomination that he had promised never to show anyone. He had never let the muse see it, but then did she know what he had done anyway? Had she inspired the girl to choose this one deliberately so that she could retain it?

He rifled through the remaining paintings. Panic grew as he tossed aside his beloved canvases, and then … he found it.

He sighed with relief, not understanding how this one had become entangled in his regular pieces. But then, as he brought it to his easel, with every intention of painting over it, something stayed his hand. Not the muse who had been pulling his strings for the last few months, but his own self. He couldn't destroy it because this was the only thing he had to prove she had existed. It was a memory, even if it was a hideous one. He may have been forced into this awful union, but he had survived it and he would never forget what he had done. The picture would be a reminder. Even if he never looked at it again.

The painting was hideous. He hated it as much as he hated the subject. He stared at all of the other canvases, now white-washed over. Could he revive any of them? Probably with a carefully diluted solution. But he didn't want to. It was right to destroy them and leave them thus.

But not this one. Not this one ever.

He took the canvas to his bedroom and began to rip up even more of the floor where his money stash and the journal were kept. He buried the painting wrapped in a sheet under the floorboards, replacing and securing them over it.

Once this was done he penned an entry in his journal:

My torment is finally over. She's gone and there is nothing more she can force me to do. I made a bargain with a demon, though she claimed to be a muse. She did not inspire me, not as a muse might. She used me as her puppet and all the while she took parts from my models remaking herself. Elongating a life that I suspect should have been ended long ago.

Inhuman monster. I fell into her trap without ever knowing her. Who was she really?

Of course he had known her in the biblical sense, when she reeled him in, pretending to be Alice. And he admitted it in the journal. Telling the whole sordid story in the hope that it would relieve his conscience, but also knowing that no one would ever see it because he planned to destroy it all one day soon. Along with the painting that was evidence of his crimes.

My life can begin now. Truly begin. And I can change how I've lived until this moment. I can make amends.

He saw his life unfold before him. A future. Family. Happiness. He blamed his bohemian lifestyle for making him susceptible to evil. Being bohemian had meant freedom to him, but now he saw what had happened as punishment. He would, and could, change everything though.

I will marry Olga! Yes. And we will start a family. Life. We will make a new life together. Have the children that she so desperately wants.

At that moment he heard movement in the house and realized Olga had returned. Up to this point he had been afraid to paint her but now knew that Olga would become his new inspiration. His new muse.

He returned the journal to its hiding place and went out to her.

Life would become normal again.

First he would photograph, then he would paint Olga.

A short time later, with his new positivity flowing like the river of life through his veins, Picasso proposed to Olga.

They married in July 1918. Nothing could mar their future together.

But when they returned from their honeymoon in Biarritz, Picasso found his house looted. The floorboards were ripped up in his bedroom—the painting, journal and his remaining emergency funds were all gone.

Present Day

"Where did the German say he obtained the painting and journal?" Cassandra asked outside Lauren's office.

"He didn't," said Joy.

Cassandra knew she was lying but didn't ask any more. Let Joy keep her secrets. It didn't matter in the scheme of things. Soon, all of this would be over. For now, she had to return to Juniper and encourage him to finish the last three faces. His freedom, meant her freedom also.

CHAPTER THIRTY-SIX

The apartment was in darkness when Cassandra returned home.

She wasn't used to finding it so empty. She had reduced the security detail after Juniper's stalker had been killed, reasoning that all of that was now behind them. She wanted normality in their daily routine. Juniper needed to feel that his life was going to stabilize once he finished the last three faces.

Now Cassandra walked through each room, switching on lights as she went. The apartment was uncommonly vacant and she felt an intense absence as she found herself outside Juniper's studio.

"Avgustin?"

She opened the door and found the room was in darkness. Where was Juniper? He should be here. She reached into her pocket for her cell phone and dialed his number. In the dark Juniper's phone lit up and began to vibrate.

She turned the light on and picked up the phone. Where had Juniper gone?

"It can't be far," she said. "Otherwise he wouldn't have left his phone behind."

Perhaps he had run out of vodka and had gone out to buy some?

But no. The housekeeper kept a close eye on their stocks of food and drink. There were always several back up bottles in the walk-in wine storage at the back of the kitchen. Juniper needed nothing. There was no reason for his sudden departure from the apartment when he should have been here working.

She had spoken to him just two hours earlier, and he had been expecting her back at any time. So why had he gone out without her?

She placed down the phone and lifted her eyes to the easel. Standing on it was the painting of the patchwork figure. It was missing a heart, two areas of its face, and one kidney.

Marina Mikhailov was still safe.

Why hadn't *she* taken the Russian girl's heart?

It was a game. *Of course.* Cat and Mouse. The heart would be last and it would furnish the muse with the final piece of the jigsaw that Juniper would piece together.

The painting was ugly. Every bit as revolting as the Picasso piece was. Juniper had created his own reminder of what was happening to him. Would he, like Picasso, attempt to destroy it when this was all over? Would he too write a journal to relieve his pain?

Cassandra looked around the studio. If so, where would Juniper have hidden it?

She searched the studio looking for any obvious hiding place. There was a sideboard with drawers now full of tubes of oil paints and brushes, nothing more. And no secret panels or she would have known about them already. She had bought it, some years back, preparing the room for Juniper. Everything in here had been ready, poised, for him to come to her. She hadn't known then what circumstances would bring him to her. Just that it would happen. The premonition, her special skill, was never clear. It showed outcome, not the cause of it. But of course, when she had heard of his arrest, she knew the time was right. She had been waiting, poised, to take complete control of his life. And she had been able to do that so easily. He had handed himself over to her with complete trust. If only he had really known what she was.

"Where are you now, Avgustin?" she said. "I wasn't expecting you to disappear again."

She picked up the brush he had been using hoping to feel something from it. She received a sickening wave of fear and hatred. The brush fell from her fingers.

"Where are you?" she asked again. This time she ran her hands over the sides of the canvas, feeling for Juniper's invisible fingerprints. She received nothing but self-loathing and disgust.

Then she saw the other painting, resting face outwards against the stack of ones that Joy would be receiving soon. That was, when this awful business was done, and life returned to normal. Like Picasso, Juniper would regain his life. All he had to do was finish the painting. It was so simple. Why didn't he just do it?

She walked towards the canvas now, picked it up and saw that another face had been outlined. Though somehow, Juniper had resisted and hadn't finished it.

Even so, Cassandra could see enough to know who the girl was. Her foresight told her. She stared off into space searching the ether for more information. It would help if Juniper had actually finished the face properly. More of the girl's future would appear to her. She could narrow down where to go.

She thought of calling Chandler to tell him there was another attack forthcoming, but decided against it.

Then it came to her: Juniper's knowledge seeped through the canvas. It was like a beacon. A homing signal and suddenly Cassandra knew where he was. He had gone to try and save this girl himself.

Oh, the fool: to get in the way of the future. It was written that they would all die; there was nothing he could do about it.

A bridge. She saw it. Brooklyn Bridge. But why there?

She turned in a circle, gathering her bearings before she started to dissolve. Then a jolt. The dissolution halted. She *couldn't* change form. *What was happening*? Surely Juniper's love of her had given back all of her powers now?

But no. Something was wrong. There was cramp-like pain in her abdomen. She felt that nauseating sickness wafting over her again.

What was wrong with her? She was better now, healing, renewing. She had the *glow*. Even Joy had said so!

Her hands went to her stomach.

"Avgustin!" she gasped. "It isn't possible!"

Cramp again. A change in her DNA for certain. And *something* was in there, growing inside her.

A life! A child!

"It isn't possible," she repeated.

But it was. It had happened. She had managed the impossible. She was pregnant. And how could this happen unless she truly was becoming human?

A dark fear paralyzed her for a moment. Humanity meant mortality. Ultimately death. Not pregnancy and birth. This was a new anomaly. Surely it had never happened to any of their kind before.

That was the fun of their sexual freedom. Promiscuity without any of the pitfalls: they couldn't catch any diseases, nor could they become pregnant. But that had somehow changed.

And it meant that Juniper was going to become a father, too.

She thought of calling Joy and Lauren, sharing this news with them, but abruptly she was afraid.

Mortality meant she was no longer one of them. She was at risk.

How would they react to this news that she was carrying a child? Doing the impossible … It would be like a slap in the face to both of them. It would have been to her if this had happened to one of them instead of her.

She had to get to the bridge by normal means now, which meant travelling through the rush hour traffic.

Damn it. Damn it all.

She had to stop Juniper from saving this other little whore. The muse had to be renewed, only then could Juniper be freed. It was more important than ever that he could live a normal life now. And, that he should never learn who and what she really was. Who she had been—for those days were over now weren't they?

Cassandra turned to leave the studio, then she remembered Juniper's phone. Should she leave it here, pretend she hadn't seen it? Or should she take it with her to the place he was heading.

She shrugged, placing it back where Juniper had left it. She looked around the room, making sure that everything was as he would expect. Then she turned the light off and closed the door.

At the front door she paused. How would she explain her sudden appearance at the bridge? It wasn't as though she could hide in the shadows. Or could she?

She shook her head. She couldn't worry about that now, all she could do was get to Juniper, pull him away from the scene and let it unfold as it was meant to. The girl's cheek and jaw would be harvested as it was supposed to. Then Cassandra and Juniper would be one step closer to the end of this whole sordid business.

Her phone rang. She retrieved it from her pocket and stared at the number. It was Lauren's.

Trembling, she answered it. *Did she know*?

"Joy told me to call you. Stay away from the bridge," Lauren said.

"Avgustin is headed there."

"He'll be too late. Sit tight until he returns to you."

Cassandra hung up. She didn't ask Lauren how she and Joy had known about Juniper's attempt to save his next victim. She didn't want to have to answer questions in return. Not for the first time she began to suspect that Joy and Lauren knew more about this business than they were letting on.

What was going on?

When she had left the two of them alone at Lauren's office she was satisfied that they would not interfere for now. At some point they would tackle the muse who would likely explain the motivation for their crime. Whether they accepted what she said or not a decision would be made as to what to do about it.

Their job was to inspire. They should never use their power for anything but that. But Cassandra, in the light of impending mortality, still wanted to live forever. She still wanted to inspire.

She placed her hands around her waist. Now there was something else at stake.

Oh God! What was she so afraid of? Was immortality really that good? This endless cycle of having to motivate, living in a world that you are never really part of.

Until now I've always been alone.

The muses had never socialized. They were always in competition for one creative are another, so how could they truly be friends?

Something else occurred to her now.

Her "glowing" state had nothing to do with renewal. She had deluded herself. Juniper had not bonded with her. He hadn't bonded with anyone. It was why he could still be used. Just like Picasso …

We'll all just disappear. Fade away as though we never existed. And what would take the place of the muses and their inspiration then? Nothing. Humanity needed none in this world of self-motivation.

She thought back to one of the first people she had enthused. She had fed for years on it. Renewed, and renewed as this person's myth passed down through a generation of religious fanatics. Then the world had changed and belief in the supernatural waned.

Noah.

Oh, yes, he told his wife that God had spoken to him—when all the time Cassandra was laying with him, whispering her inspiration into his heart and soul. Ultimately this man would have fallen into obscurity without her. She pulled his dull and boring ass right up and made him into the leader he became. All she had to do was create the flood to prove him right. His frigid wife took all the glory for her husband who "spoke to God" when really he had been fucking a muse in their own stable while she slept.

Cassandra smiled as she recalled how Noah liked to be ridden. Was he one of the first she'd met who liked to be dominated? Probably.

And when she had renewed to full capacity, she had been happy to leave him to his glory. The rewards for it continued to find their way to her for years to come.

Smiling, Cassandra, went into the kitchen, poured herself a drink, but the liquor didn't taste good and she recalled then, from a surgeon she had inspired in the early part of the 21st Century, that pregnancy and liquor weren't a good thing.

She pushed the drink aside. It was early days. She was perhaps … she felt her stomach. A few weeks. Yes. The baby was still little more than a blob. Eyes and limbs would form soon. The miracle of reproduction: nature's own incredible magic was working inside her. *Wow*. So unexpected. She could never have imagined how great this would feel.

It was a girl. She knew already. Was shocked that she hadn't realized it had happened at the moment of conception.

What would the baby look like?

Cassandra felt a surge of joy pushing up through her normally stable emotions. Joy and fear in the space of a few moments. Was this how humans lived, in a constant state of emotional flux? She was so afraid for her unborn child. Afraid of her own impending mortality.

She opened the fridge and glanced inside. She was hungry, and thought she ought to eat something. She pulled out some chicken pieces, and a pot of potato salad. She turned some of it on to a small plate.

Her appetite hadn't been good recently, now she knew why. The chicken and potato was basic enough not to turn her stomach and she ate a small amount of each.

She had always been able to eat whatever she wanted without any weight change. Choosing to eat salad for appearances sometimes rather than necessity as it had never affected her figure even if she ate the most fattening and unhealthy foods. Her metabolism just used it. And often as the renewal wore off, she found herself eating more, as though the nutrients in fatty foods would help her hold on longer.

Of course this would now all probably change. Her figure, for the first time, would alter without her influence. The thought made her feel peculiar and vulnerable. Was this how normal women felt? And if so, how did they ever just ignore it and get on with their lives regardless?

Being beautiful was easy for her now. But what would it be like when she really had to work at it? What would it feel like when her face began to wrinkle, her breasts sag, her waistline expand?

She heard the front door open and leaving her half-eaten plate of food on the side she hurried to the kitchen door. It opened before she reached it and Juniper entered with his bodyguard Marcus. Of course! Why hadn't she realized that he wouldn't go alone? Marcus was her most trusted and loyal guard, which was why she had retained him. He wouldn't have let Juniper go anywhere without an escort.

"Where have you been?" she said. "I was worried."

"Sorry, Ms. Moúsa," Marcus said. "I should have called to say I'd taken Mr. Juniper out for a drive at his request. We went towards the Brooklyn Bridge but had to turn back as there was an incident."

"She's dead and it's all my fault …" Juniper said.

"Thanks, Marcus, that will be all."

Marcus left the room and Cassandra took Juniper's arm and led him to the breakfast bar. He sat down and she passed him the glass of liquor she couldn't drink earlier.

"What happened?" she said.

"Another girl. I started another face. Then I knew where she would be."

"So you took it on yourself to go there, instead of calling Detective Chandler?"

"It zeemed like the right thing to do."

"Oh, Avgustin. Don't you know that you have to take care of yourself now? And me … What if you'd gone, and the thing attacked you. Where would I be then?"

"What do you mean? It won't attack me. It needs me."

Cassandra sighed. She was on the verge of telling him she was pregnant, but something made her hold back. She was incredibly insecure. What if Juniper rejected her?

This is silly! she thought. *Even my thought processes are becoming human. And more female. I will look after myself like I've always done. I don't need anyone.*

Her phone vibrated in her pocket. She withdrew it to see that she had received a text from Lauren.

The girl was a no show. Rogue didn't appear.

"The girl is safe," she told Juniper now. "Apparently there was an accident on the bridge. So even if you thought she would be there, she was probably stuck in the same traffic as you. And more than likely so was her potential attacker. So you see, this isn't all written in stone. It can still be fixed."

"I didn't complete the face," Juniper said. "Maybe that's why she was okay today. But it will only be a matter of time."

"Look, Chandler has managed to secrete Marina away. She's one you saved. You have to think about yourself now. Finish the faces, let's get this over with."

"How can you be so cold? *You.* Who are so beautiful in every way …"

"I'm not cold, Avgustin, I'm practical. That's all."

"I love you," he said.

Cassandra's heart leapt in her chest. "You do?"

"Yes. I want this to end so I can paint you. So we can have a life together."

"We will. That will happen."

Still, she couldn't tell him. That stupid insecurity. A fear or phobia of opening herself up, probably for the first time. Besides she had to digest this herself, didn't she? She had to consider what it really meant.

"You want a life with me?" he asked. His eyes glowed with hope.

"Yes … Haven't I already shown you that?"

"This?" he said looking around. "Bringing me to your home. Creating a life for me that I never thought was real."

"It is real."

"It zeemed so fairytale. So constructed."

"I suppose it would look like that."

Tell him!

She shook her head pushing aside the inner argument. *Not yet. When this is all over.*

"Come to bed," she said instead. "I'm tired and we both need to rest."

CHAPTER THIRTY-SEVEN

Jake Chandler was in shock.

Only that morning he had learned that their safe house had been compromised. Marina Mikhailov had been moved, even as Denise Miller was being taken to hospital. Marina was now being monitored twenty-four hours a day. Even he didn't know where: no one in his office did because there was obviously a leak.

He had made the call to the FBI himself, asking them to take Marina in. It was unusual for any cop to willingly give their case over to the feds, but Chandler believed their investigation had been compromised. It meant, of course, that they were now under close scrutiny, and a federal officer would be looking into all of their personal affairs as well as their work schedule. He didn't mind. He had nothing to hide, and it was better than the alternative: that more women died while they were chasing their asses because someone inside was corrupt.

Even so, Chandler couldn't imagine who that might be. And why? Why would any of them help this sick bastard to harvest body parts?

As he travelled back to his house in Queens, stuck in rush

hour traffic, cars bumper to bumper, he considered his case. It was getting colder all the time. Even though Juniper was purported to have some form of psychic ability that manifested itself in his art, Chandler wasn't sure how much of Cassandra's story he really believed. It was too fantastical. Was the man psychic or did he know perfectly well who the killer was and where he would strike because he was an accomplice?

A few months ago, the latter would have been what Chandler thought most likely. But he *knew* that Juniper was innocent. He was the foil of the bastard who was doing this. He believed that part, even though it was difficult to say why. But why Juniper? And why these girls? Juniper himself could not think of a single enemy that would and could do these terrible things.

Chandler had to admit that there was no way a normal perpetrator could have attacked Sophia in broad daylight in a crowd without anyone seeing it. The perp would have had to have carried something that could operate with accuracy and efficiency within the space of a few minutes, to neatly rip out Sophia Ressler's spine, while cauterizing the wound. Then what had happened to the body part itself? They had searched and interviewed everyone who had been there. No sign of anything that could do it. No sign of Sophia's spine either. There was no logical explanation. No one human could have done it, which was what Cassandra had implied to him that day when she told him of Juniper's ability.

He found it difficult to believe and was erring towards caution with this whole pre-warning thing, but so far, Juniper had been right. The attack on Denise confirmed it even more—especially as it had happened right under the noses of his own cops.

Chandler left the highway and turned down a street into his estate. Soon he was pulling up onto his driveway.

He felt as though he was arriving at a stranger's house and not his own. For weeks he had been staying at Lauren's. When she told him she was busy tonight, he thought it a good opportunity to drop by the house and check that all was well and to collect some more clothing. He was constantly washing and wearing the few things he had at Lauren's.

Chandler was halfway through his house before he halted. He hadn't thought of Jules on the doorstep but he thought about her now. He tried to feel guilty for being with Lauren, but he couldn't summon up the regret. He was somewhat detached from the events that had occurred in this house, recalling it all like some long ago, vivid nightmare.

He tested his emotions. He was numb to them. Like a tooth that had been pulled, he could feel the hole, but the pain was gone.

He went into the kitchen, opened the fridge and extracted a bottle of beer. Lauren had introduced him to the delights of wine in recent months. Now he craved a cold glass of dry white. The beer, unfortunately, would have to do—he didn't have any wine in the house. He didn't even have any milk or food in the fridge worth eating.

He emptied out the rotting contents now and left a note for his housekeeper to clean the fridge when she next came. He also left an envelope containing her wages.

The house being so unused now didn't really need her, but Chandler was cautious. He didn't know where things were going with Lauren. Perhaps one day they would get married, but for the moment he wasn't thinking that far ahead. It would mean a huge change, selling his house and buying something together for certain. Chandler wasn't sure he was ready for that yet. It was all too new. All too soon.

Sometimes he felt that he should pinch himself to see if he was dreaming. Lauren was a mystery he still had to solve, and their relationship had progressed so quickly that, he had to admit, it scared him.

She was a dedicated shrink though. The amount of times when she was called away to help one of her patients—like this evening no doubt. Even though she said she was meeting friends for drinks. He wasn't convinced because Lauren worked too hard to have a social life and he had never been introduced to any friends.

He sat down in his empty living room and stared at the TV. It was switched off and he didn't pick up the remote and turn it on, because his thoughts were elsewhere. Like Lauren's lovemaking. It was perfect. She always seemed to know what he needed.

Chandler sat backed and closed his eyes. He imagined her there with him, kneeling between his legs, unzipping his trousers and extracting his eager cock: just as she had the other night. So exciting, so intuitive because there was nothing like a good blowjob to take your mind of the gruesome aspects of the latest murder case you were working on.

Somehow, they had quickly graduated from cautious lovers to full trust. They hadn't used condoms for weeks. Lauren was taking care of all of their contraceptive needs. He'd even seen the pills in her bathroom cabinet, so it didn't concern him. Lauren was too efficient and intelligent to take any risks.

His mind went away from sex and back to the idea of Lauren's unknown friends.

"You're pretty friendly with Joy Awen," he had remarked after she had appeared at the airport with her.

"I have a lot of interest in art," Lauren said. "And she's quite an inspirational lady."

They had been unlikely friends but Chandler knew that friendships sprang up in the oddest places. Like he and Lauren. He could never have known, the day he walked into her office, that she would become so much a part of his life.

He opened his eyes as a loud ringing echoed through the house. For a minute, he didn't recognize the sound or where it was coming from. It was such a rare thing for his house phone to ring: everyone he knew always called his mobile.

He stood, hurried into the hallway and picked up the receiver.

"Hello?"

"Jake?"

"Yes?"

"It's Gemma here. I need to talk to you. Are you alone?"

"Yes."

"Good."

"There hasn't been another attack, has there?"

"No. It's not really about work. It's personal."

"Oh."

"Can I come round? I'm not far from your house right now."

Chandler glanced at his watch. It was quarter past ten at night. "Sure. You okay?"

"I will be. But it's important or I wouldn't bother you."

Sarasvatī ended the call by saying she would be there soon.

Jake was tired and so he made himself a coffee and then returned to the living room to wait for Sarasvatī.

When she arrived, he offered her a drink.

"Hard liquor?" she said.

"I have some Jack in the kitchen. You've changed your hair," he said.

Sarasvatī was usually a dark brunette, now her hair was loose over her shoulders and she had changed the color. It was blonde, slightly wavy and longer than it appeared when she had it tied up. She wasn't wearing a coat but carried with her a large backpack.

"Oh this?" she shrugged.

"Go in the sitting room. I'll be right back with that drink."

Sarasvatī sat down on the sofa and placed the backpack on the floor by her feet. Chandler returned with two glasses. One had a double shot of Jack Daniels, the other had several ice cubes in it.

"Didn't know if you wanted it on the rocks."

"Neat is fine," she said taking the glass.

Chandler placed the glass of ice cubes down on his coffee table beside the TV remote control and his cooling cup of coffee. Then he sat back down in his chair.

Sarasvatī took a large swallow of the drink.

"So. What's wrong?"

"I'm sick, Jake."

"I know you've needed some time off recently."

"I'm really sick. It's not just a stomach flu. I'm … dying."

"My God! *Gemma*!"

"It's okay. You don't have to say anything. In fact, I'd rather you didn't until I've told you everything first."

"I'm listening."

Sarasvatī sipped the whiskey again. She looked surprisingly well for someone who had just said she was dying. But now Chandler noticed the raised spots and boils under the carefully applied make up. Make up that Sarasvatī usually didn't wear. He noticed too that the blonde hair, which didn't really fit her olive skin tone, was in fact an ill-fitting wig.

"I guess you could say its old age," she said. "Finally catching up with me. I'm a lot older than I look. I've been around for many years. Though I don't expect you to believe that. Not without evidence."

She leaned forward and opened the rucksack at her feet. Then she pulled free something that Chandler was very familiar with: a thick brown file.

"It's not everything," Sarasvatī said. "But I hope it will provide you with enough proof that what I'm saying is the truth."

She placed the file on the table. Chandler's eyes followed the movement and placement of the folder, then went back to Gemma. They gleamed with curiosity. She met his gaze and for the first time he noticed how watery her eyes were. They were the eyes of a much older person.

"I'm a muse," she said.

"Huh?" said Chandler.

"We were devised by the gods of Olympus when they first created man in their own image. This was because they did not believe that the clay shells that the first human was created from would be anything more than a toy. A doll if you like. They wouldn't be able to think much for themselves. Or so they thought. As man is now creating AI, this was the gods' equivalent. Humans were walking, talking dolls to them. Nothing more. The first shock was when they learnt they could, and did, reproduce. Nature took the blueprint of man and woman and added its own spin."

"Gemma …" Chandler interrupted.

"*Please*. Hear me out."

Chandler sat back in his chair and nodded. If the woman was dying how could he deny her this fantasy? Maybe it was part of the illness?

"This is going to be like mythology 101 but bear with me. I and my sisters, nine of us in all, were created because Zeus refused to believe that his toys were anything more than cattle. We were the only thing that could inspire man or woman to achieve their best. To develop and grow beyond mere animals. They couldn't do this alone. Later, Hera also made nine male muses, as she believed that they would better inspire the female creatives. Humanity became sexual playthings too. They were inferior to the inhabitants of Olympus but the male gods, and Zeus was the worst of them, lusted after the female 'toys' who nature gave great and natural beauty to. They used humanity any way they could. They were pawns, encouraged to fight wars for the Olympians' sport, because they saw these futile deaths as nothing more important than the breakage of a plaything. And because the gods were trying out and impregnating human females, it wasn't long before the goddesses themselves decided they would lie with man. He was an interesting variant on their ever-demanding male equals. The one thing both gods and goddesses had in common was that they both loved being worshipped. They loved to be seen as superior. They were immortal, and humanity craved the one thing that their gods denied them—to live forever."

"Gemma, I don't know much about Greek and Roman mythology, but …"

"It isn't mythology, Jake. I was there. I was one of them. I'm giving you this background to better explain our purpose. The muses' purpose that is: it was to make beautiful things happen in the world. From the first discovery of fire, to the invention of science. We have been there inspiring every new and big idea. That is until man became self-motivated. This occurred as his intelligence grew. At the same time the gods were telling man they needed them, humanity never realized that the gods had found they couldn't live without worship. When it stopped, they faded away."

Chandler was intrigued despite himself. And if Sarasvatī was using her story as some kind of metaphor for her own impending mortality then he decided he was prepared to listen.

"What happened to them? The gods."

"I don't know for certain. But I suspect they began to age. They lost their miraculous power. They grew so old that they forgot who they were. And then, they died, like all life must in the end. It is easier for me to believe this than consider the alternative."

"Which is?" Chandler asked.

"That they abandoned us. That they grew bored of their game with man. And that we muses were left behind to rot. You have to understand, they were our creators too. We their children you might say. And they left us to die," Sarasvatī said.

"But you say you didn't die. You lived on?"

"I lived on and so did the others for a time. But one by one we began to fail. You see our purpose is to enthuse, inspire, motivate. When we were no longer needed we couldn't renew. Oh, some found other methods by which to live. The males failed sooner. They were created on a whim and Hera had not given them the resilience that she and Zeus had infused us with. Perhaps it was spite. She always played games with Zeus. Always tried to prove to him that the female was stronger." Sarasvatī paused as though she were remembering all of this.

"Whatever happened, the males all died some centuries back. It was rumored that each of them fell in love and settled down with the human they were meant to inspire. They, like the gods, succumbed to humanity's charm. But us, the nine originals, were colder, more distant. Took what we did as a job. The reward for inspiring was so great, you see. If you could only feel a fraction of the elation we have when the magic happens …

"Some years ago, I felt the first five sisters born begin to fail. They couldn't inspire any more. They failed to *connect* with a creative. The last four, including myself, only survived because we adapted. I diversified from musicians, which was my main strength. And I went into different ways of encouraging. Emily Pankhurst was one of mine. My calling changed. I would be a driving force in the growth of women through the ages. Men no longer interested me."

She picked up her whiskey and took another drink. Chandler said nothing as he waited for her to continue. He was hypnotized by her narrative, and as he looked at her, he saw her face change, youth bloomed briefly there.

"You are affected by me, and so I am helped by you," Sarasvatī said. "As I give, I receive. It is how it works. Thank you. Thank you so much Jake. You are so receptive to our kind. This little bit gives me strength to continue and may even make it possible for me to do what must be done. If there were more men and women like you we wouldn't be in this mess."

"Please go on," he said not knowing how else to respond. Could anything stranger happen in this case?

"I suspect my three remaining sisters adapted their skills too. But quite a few years ago now. At the turn of the century, when humanity moved into the start of the modern age, and science grew in strength, as did your medical ability, we four were drawn to a very special talent. Oh, artists came and went. They were food for one or the other of us for a while, kept us ticking over you might say. But none were like Picasso. None called with such power as he. He was the last.

"Oh, he didn't need inspiring in the true sense, though his womanizing ways would have proved a distraction if we hadn't kept him on track. And every one of us tried him out. Became his muse for a while, but he was so fickle that often we were forced to concede to another until such a time as he grew tired of them too. I was his first inspiration.

"He was a mere boy of four years old when I put a paint brush in his hand. I whispered to him that he would be great and his brush went to the canvas as though he had painted since the day he was born. His father tutored him by day when he realized that he was special. I enthused him by night. He was soon becoming a man and I had stepped back, letting him taste the delights of mortal women for fear of spoiling him completely. Then Cassandra whisked him away from me and into her bed before I had the chance to completely make him mine."

"Cassandra?" said Chandler, but Sarasvatī knew that he was thinking of the prophetic and tragic female of Troy, whose prophesies were never believed, and not the obvious—Cassandra Moúsa.

"She stole Picasso from me. Then merrily stepped back and took the renewal that poured her way. And though my early years' inspiration had given me some of my vigor, she took most of the magic that I had created. All she did for him was to advise that his success would come in France. She planted the seed that he should leave Spain. And he did."

"You were Picasso's muse and he was taken from you?" Chandler said as though he were confirming the facts before she moved on.

"She opened the doorway for the others too. And they came and went, sweeping into his life under different guises. Almost all of the women he painted in his early years were us, in one form or another. Picasso was a flame to us moths. He would use us up and spit us out, growing in his own strength while we withered from lack of sustenance."

"You fed on him. You sound like vampires."

"Perhaps we are something far worse," said Sarasvatī. "We were immortals with the ability to change shape, even gender if we wished to. We could be anyone we wanted, but the power for this came as a reward for our work as inspirers. If we failed to generate the creativity used by a human then we couldn't renew. I guess this was the joke that Hera and Zeus played on us. It made us work harder to inspire. Or …"

"If you don't renew, you die?" Chandler asked.

"We become mortal for a time. That state may exist, with some remainder of power for a while. When that power fades, we age rapidly. Then we die. There is always the ability to inspire there though. Even close to the end. And Jake, this is why I'm here. I want to help you bring this to a conclusion."

"How?"

"One of my sisters is harvesting the body parts from Juniper's models. I knew it, almost immediately when Annabel Linton was attacked. She does this because the source of inspiration from an artist is the only element that can be used to help us renew. Jake, she is three parts from reaching full renewal. If she does this, she'll disappear and we'll never find her. For the rest of us we have barely one lifetime left. Me, even less. She could live for another century before she needs to harvest again."

"You're saying that the person we're looking for is also a muse?"

"Yes. And she is using Juniper's talent to exact her revival. I should have stopped her in 1917. There was a spate of girls going missing. Street girls mostly and so no one really cared about them. I didn't understand what was happening then but it all went on around Picasso. He was used, just as Juniper is being manipulated now. The thing is, if I don't stop the killer this time, I won't be alive when she next resurfaces. It has to end now."

Chandler's mind was opened to the possibility that Sarasvatī was telling the truth. His logical brain tried to resist it even as his heart knew it was reality. All along he had been chasing his tail. Nothing added. All of it was implausible, and so he was beginning to believe in the impossible. What Sarasvatī said made as much sense as anything else he could come up with. So why not? Maybe muses did exist. She had definitely changed before his eyes. Or was he going insane?

"Wait," he said. "There were only three of the seven models attacked. We managed to save Marina Mikhailov."

"Not saved, Jake. She's been set aside for last."

"What do you mean?"

"Marina represents the heart. She is the last element. She was never meant to be anything but the last victim. She's been produced now because she makes Juniper feel that some of them can be saved. But they can't be, Jake. Not by humankind anyway. Once her heart is harvested the muse will absorb it. Juniper's talent will meld it with her body. Then it will pump new life into her. She will be renewed."

"Like some grisly Frankenstein monster being sparked by lightning," Chandler said.

"It's one way of seeing it," Sarasvatī said. She smiled as though the idea amused her.

"But that still doesn't explain the fourth woman," Jake said. "You said there are only three left."

"Juniper painted another face which sent the other muses on a wild goose chase this evening. Then, in his sleep, he painted another. This woman is still alive but she no longer has one of her kidneys."

Sarasvatī finished her Jack Daniels.

"You'll receive a call about it before the night is out."

"How do you know about it already?"

"Each of us has a talent. Cassandra always had foresight—prophecy if you prefer. I have hindsight. I saw it after it had happened."

"Who is she? Who is the muse that's doing this?"

"I don't know," said Sarasvatī. "But with your help I intend to find out."

"You know everything else but not this?"

"I know it is one of three women. All of whom you and I have had a great deal of contact with recently."

"Who?" Chandler said, pushing for the answer.

"One is Cassandra Moúsa, another is Joy Awen …" Sarasvatī said.

"And the third?"

"For this you need to brace yourself," Sarasvatī paused. "It is Lauren Michaels. Your lover."

Chandler laughed then. How absurd to think that Lauren was some kind of supernatural entity. "You almost had me, Gemma. Who put you up to this? The boys at the station?"

"This is not a joke, Jake. I wish it were," Sarasvatī said. Her face had grown grave, and the glow he had watched appear earlier, was beginning to fade. "I need you to believe me, or I won't be any use to you when the final battle comes."

"You can't really expect me to believe that Lauren is …"

"I wasn't sure of her myself at first. She isn't carrying the name. We change our faces so often that the name is our calling card. You must understand that we never work together. We are competitive, and solitary. Each new person that one of us inspires is another that we cannot touch."

"What do you mean your name is a calling card?"

Sarasvatī explained the meaning of hers, Joy's and Cassandra's surnames.

"Lauren was Laurel Muse some years ago. Not Lauren Michaels," Sarasvatī explained. "The name makes us look closer at each other and then we recognize our sisters. See who they really are. I have the evidence here that might make this easier for you to accept."

Chandler's attention was brought back to the folder that Sarasvatī had placed on the table between them.

"What evidence?" he asked. He was suddenly afraid of seeing

it and so made light of their conversation again. "I expect I'm going to open that folder to see 'Sucker' stamped across the first page."

Sarasvatī opened the folder. She rifled through a pile of old documents until she found a photograph.

"You see, whatever face we are wearing, the creative that we choose to affect always sees our original one."

"I don't get it?" said Chandler.

"Look at this photograph, Jake. It was taken in 1943, during the Second World War. Who do you see here?"

Chandler looked at the photograph. It was old and yellowed and he had no doubt it was authentic.

"The face Lauren is carrying is not the face you'll see. It's not the face that the photographer took. It is her true face. The one she was given on the day of her birth. Look at the photograph."

Chandler picked it up. He brought it closer, then squinted at it. The photo included several women. He looked at each face in turn. Four among them were familiar. He saw Cassandra, Joy and Gemma and then, in the front row …

"It's not genuine. Somehow you've Photoshopped this … aged the paper."

Sarasvatī sighed. "Look again Jake. I need you to believe. I don't have long left."

CHAPTER THIRTY-EIGHT

Chandler's cell phone rang and Sarasvatī picked it up. She glanced at the caller ID.

"It's the station," she said.

Chandler took the phone.

"Shallit here. There's been another one, Boss."

Chandler listened to Dan Shallit as he explained about the latest victim. She had lost a kidney but was otherwise alive and well.

"You were right," he said as he closed the call.

Sarasvatī nodded.

"If I am to believe what I'm seeing here. Why were you all in this same picture? You said you didn't work together."

"Sometimes we have a 'gathering.' Inspiring bravery was very lucrative. I was travelling with an all-girl singing group. Cassandra had made a name for herself as a soloist. Joy and Lauren were backing singers for a male vocalist and his band. We all ended up in an army camp where a show had been organized to entertain the troops. I remember seeing them, but we all deliberately avoided each other. We never even spoke in those days. After that picture was taken we went in separate directions, each following a lead that might give us yet another cycle of life."

Chandler buried his head in his hands. "What do I do?"

He *believed* it but he still had so many questions.

"Now you know the truth, Lauren will no longer inspire you," Sarasvatī said. "She'll realize before too long."

"Then what will happen?"

"That depends."

"On?"

"Whether she is our rogue or not."

"And if she is?" Chandler asked.

"Then she isn't inspiring you anyway. She's taking her renewal elsewhere. And if it isn't her, then she may opt to go the same way as our rogue."

"No! Why would she?"

"The rogue is trying to recruit us. She already tried me."

Then Sarasvatī explained how the muse had contacted her through a telepathic link. She couldn't tell which of them had whispered to her, explaining how she could save herself.

"Yet you resisted. Even knowing that your end is coming?"

"I was made to inspire. When I am no longer needed I am meant to end. I cannot stop the natural order of things. This is what I was taught to do. Besides, I still have hope that there is an Olympian homecoming waiting for me. For many lifetimes of service to man, it is the least I deserve."

"Heaven?" Chandler said.

"My version of it at least," said Sarasvatī. She stood then. "I'll leave the folder for you to look through. If you are still in any doubt then the proof in there will help you realize that I'm telling you the truth."

He went to thank her but it felt inappropriate. How could he thank someone for taking away the illusion of his life? He had been happy before this. Oh yes, he wanted to catch the killer, but when that killer might be his own girlfriend? Lauren had saved him from himself. Surely she had inspired him, and so, whatever renewal she was experiencing was down to that. Wasn't it? And why couldn't that keep on, even though he now knew what she was?

"Goodbye for now, Jake," Sarasvatī said. "I will call you when it's time."

"Time for what?" he asked but he knew already that she referred to a final showdown. A time when he would bring about the end of the rogue, whoever she may be and expose the others for what they really were.

"We have to prevent her getting the heart," Sarasvatī said. "You're sure that Marina Mikhailov is safe?"

Chandler nodded. "At least for now. I handed her over to the feds. I don't even know where they have her."

Sarasvatī frowned. "Oh no. That will make things very difficult for us."

"Why?"

"The final stages will happen when she goes after Marina. Jake, can you find out where she is? We'll need to know in order to keep her safe."

"She'll be surrounded by feds, this thing can't get to her," Chandler explained. "She's as safe as she can be."

"No. She isn't. She's in grave danger. The rogue probably already knows where she is. And certainly, when the final face is painted, as Juniper obtains the information, so will she. You have to get me on protective detail with Marina. If I'm there, the rogue can't hurt her. She'll just pass by the feds like a ghost, take what she wants, completely unseen. But she can't hide from me."

"My God. Just like on the Empire State Building." His rational mind fought against his acceptance of the information Sarasvatī gave. It was crazy but he *knew* it was the truth.

"Exactly," said Sarasvatī. "Which means that I'm the only person capable of protecting her."

Chandler thought about it. "Okay, I'll contact them tomorrow and recommend you. Though I'm not sure if they will use you or not."

"If you can find out where she is, I'll do the rest," Sarasvatī said.

Chandler didn't ask her to explain. He couldn't take any more that night and it was with a great deal of relief that he closed the door behind her as she left.

Alone again in his house he was acutely aware of the silence. He didn't turn on the television, he merely sat back down and stared at the blank screen.

A movie was playing across the back of his mind and he couldn't shake it regardless of how insane it all was. Sarasvatī's story was too real and Chandler had seen so much in the past few months that didn't add up. Now he began to question everything that Lauren had ever told him. And what of Cassandra? How could he even trust that she really wanted him to help Juniper, or the leads she had given him? Did she know who each of the victims were because she was the one pulling Juniper's strings? It seemed likely as she was the closest to him.

And what of Joy? She had the most to gain from Juniper's success as an artist, but did she also have an extension to a life that was coming to an end at stake too?

His mind was racing and full of questions and doubts. He believed Sarasvatī but he still struggled to make any real sense of her tale. She had given it to him in a nutshell. Typical—no gloss delivery. Just like the efficient cop she was.

His cell phone vibrated on the coffee table. Chandler looked at it and saw it was a text from Lauren. His heart thudded in his chest. Did she know that he knew who she was?

He picked up the phone and read the text:

Home now. The place feels empty! Missing you xxx

He didn't know what to respond and then the answer came and he typed a response back to her:

Missing you too xxx

Easy. Then he started to type another text. *Where did you go? Who were you with?* But he deleted it and placed the phone back down on the table. He had to act as normal as possible. He didn't own her and would never have questioned her under normal circumstances, but now he was wondering where she had been all night. Obviously, another girl had been attacked and Lauren was one of the suspects. He still struggled to believe it though.

Chandler's emotions were in turmoil. He was angry. Vulnerable. How had he fallen for all of it? Had she been playing him? Shit! He had even brought her in as a medical consultant on the case. He had practically handed her all of the case notes. Even discussed the victims with her including the models of Juniper who may be at risk. Had he unwittingly given the perpetrator all the information she needed?

God, he hoped not.

He stared at the brown folder as it lay closed on the coffee table. All the information and evidence he needed was inside. But he was scared to look.

He pressed his thumb and finger onto the bridge of his nose. What good would it do knowing more? All he could think about was how wonderful Lauren was. How she had rescued him from a pit of despair that he had been unable to climb out of alone. Surely she had done her job of inspiring him well. He had to have been the reason she was going on.

He remembered the sickness then. Only yesterday, though it felt like longer ago. She had been really sick. Very weak. He had worried about her. Was this a sign that she wasn't inspiring him after all? Was it possible that Lauren was only a short way behind Sarasvatī, that she wasn't inspiring anymore? That she was a murderer? Could Lauren be an immortal that was slowly becoming human too?

It was insane. All of it. And such a mess. A mess that Chandler just couldn't extract himself from. Especially when the outcome would confirm which of these three was really the rogue. Part of him hoped that it was Lauren. Wasn't that better than thinking she would fail and die? Though he couldn't imagine that scenario either. She was so young and vital.

Are you all right? X

Chandler looked at his phone seconds before it vibrated. Some instinct, or connection with Lauren perhaps, made him realize that she would ask this very question. Especially as this was his first night alone for some time, and he was back in his house with all of his memories.

He considered his answer. He could type that he was fine, or he could call her. Isn't that what a caring, unsuspicious boyfriend would do?

On impulse he pressed call. She picked up almost immediately.

"Hi," she said. "Everything okay?"

He deep sighed into the phone. "We've got another victim."

"Oh no! When did this happen?"

"About an hour or so ago."

"Would you like me to come over?"

"No. That's okay. I'm pretty tired. Think I'll go to bed soon."

"It's quite late. . . ." she observed. "You should get some rest."

"I will. Just wanted to hear your voice."

Lauren's tones softened at his words. "I'm glad you called. It's nice to hear your voice too."

"Anyway, I'll see you tomorrow . . ." he said.

"Sure. And I think I'm going to take real good care of you."

He closed the call after a few moments of sex talk. He was stimulated by it despite himself and he went to bed thinking about her naked, writhing under him.

Sleep was slow to come after that. He tossed and turned in a state of arousal after talking to her. He stroked his semi-hard penis thinking about Lauren and hoping that cumming would make him stop thinking and let his mind and body rest. His sex drive had certainly increased since she had come into his life, and now he missed her warm and lust-filled touch.

This is ridiculous, he told himself. *I can't be without her for even one night. Even after what Gemma has revealed.*

In fact, it made him want her more.

Chandler considered getting in his car and going to Lauren's or even taking her up on her offer to come over. Only that, he thought, might be weird. He had never brought her to the house. It didn't seem right to do that somehow.

Failing to relieve himself he climbed out of bed. His cock was standing up and he caught sight of his naked body in the mirror on the dressing table.

He was horny. Too horny.

The bedroom door opened and he turned, surprised, to see Lauren standing there.

"You called?" she said.

"But how …?"

She placed her fingers on his lips, then traced a line down his body with her hand.

"So this is how I inspire you" she said.

Chandler gasped as she gripped his cock. Then she rubbed it back and forth until he thought he would explode in her hand.

He pulled her to the bed and stripped off the simple shift dress that she was wearing. He found her naked underneath.

It's true, he thought. *She's a muse and she holds my life in her hands.*

The thought didn't terrify him as it should. Instead he grew harder. He pushed her back down against the pillows, spread her legs beneath him and plunged into her, even though he knew she wouldn't be ready.

Lauren arched against him, wrapping her legs around his waist so that he could get into her as deep as possible.

She gasped against his lips, "Please, Jake. Please."

It wasn't the love-making they had done before. Chandler fucked her. He wanted to make her his. Keep her forever, no matter what the consequences, and now was the time to bind her to him. Bond her forever, even if she was a cold-blooded monster.

"I'm no monster," she gasped.

"Come for me," he said pounding her harder until she was breathless beneath him.

He pulled away, flipped her over, pulling her up onto all fours. Then he rammed himself into her, deep and hard. Lauren screamed as her orgasm ripped through her body. Normally she controlled what they did in bed, and how they did it, now Chandler's change forced her to react out of character. She gave herself to him. Let go of all of the control she held changing their relationship completely. He inspired her. He became the muse, she the creative. She saw him blossoming as he turned her over onto her back and buried himself back into her warm depths. And then Jake came too, pouring his seed into her eager womb.

Afterwards, he pulled her into his arms and held her.

"I'm sorry," he said.

"What for? That was wonderful."

"I didn't hurt you?"

"Not beyond the realms of pleasure," she laughed.

He fell silent.

"You *know* what I am," she stated.

"Yes."

"And you still wanted me?"

"Even more."

"I love you. I'm not supposed to feel like that," she said. "But, I'm becoming human."

"And what do you intend to do about it?"

"Enjoy it, I suppose. Though the morning sickness isn't so good. I believe it only lasts for part of the time," Lauren said.

"Morning sick … Oh my God. Are you telling me …?"

She nodded.

"But. The contraceptives …"

"There to reassure you. I never actually needed them. I didn't think I could …" she struggled to say it for a moment, "get pregnant."

Chandler's heart pounded in his chest. What did this mean?

"You don't have to worry. I can afford to have this alone …" she said.

"You're misunderstanding my silence," he said. "I'm overwhelmed with … joy."

He felt her tears against his chest and hoped it meant her happiness too. Though he was afraid, a new emotion rose and filled his heart full of hope: she wasn't the perpetrator. She couldn't be.

"I'll have to be gentler with you in future," he said. "I wouldn't have been so … vigorous if …"

Lauren laughed. He felt her run her hand over her eyes, wiping away the tears.

"Sleep now, darling," he said.

"We have a lot to talk about."

"Yes. But not now. You need to rest if you're going to be mortal."

She relaxed and sank into him. Soon afterwards he heard her breathing change. Chandler closed his eyes and rested, though sleep still eluded him. He felt protective of her and relieved. He knew now that two of the women were in the clear: Gemma and Lauren. So, who was the person behind the deaths? Who was controlling Juniper? There were only two choices left: was it Joy or Cassandra?

CHAPTER THIRTY-NINE

Avgustin Juniper looked at the canvas as Cassandra placed it on the easel. She was pushing him hard to finish and he was trembling from the exertion of his resistance.

"I don't vant to condemn another girl," he said now.

"I wouldn't be asking this of you if I didn't feel it was the only way forward."

"Forward, vhy? It's murder and I'm an accomplice every time I paint."

"We've gone over this already. Avgustin, please. I can't explain until this is done but I need you to believe me."

Cassandra held out his brush. Juniper took it.

"Finish it today," she said. "Then it'll be over. You want to be free, don't you?"

She ran her hand down his back and Juniper was soothed. He began to see the logic. Paint and be damned, or don't paint and still be under the control of this creature. It wasn't much of a choice.

"We can be free …" she said.

"Free …"

"Yes, Avgustin. Free us."

She stepped back as he fell into a trance. His brush swirled onto his palette and then to the canvas, working faster than usual.

He finished the girl who he had tried to save on the Brooklyn Bridge first. Her name was Carla Rodriguez. The girl's name thumped into Cassandra's mind as the last brush stroke fell. There was a gray patch where Carla's jaw and cheek should be but the picture was as finished as it was going to be.

"The next one …" she urged. "It's only an eye. She can survive that."

Her voice and promise soothed Juniper and the outline of the sixth girl now took shape. She had pretty eyes and Juniper focused on them for a while, though one eye remained grayed out. The seventh girl was already drawn in, though the picture was incomplete. Juniper went on to this one with more enthusiasm.

"She's already been taken," he said. "Her kidney."

"I know," said Cassandra.

Juniper finished the painting in record time. Then he removed it from the easel, placing it up against the wall with the others.

"What are you doing?" asked Cassandra as she watched him put another painting on the easel.

"Time to finish this," he said.

She stared at the horrific jigsaw painting of the muse. Now it was almost finished, Cassandra was reminded of Picasso's horrible painting of the same model. She knew that Juniper would begin to fill in those gray-toned areas as the parts were harvested by the muse. So far he hadn't completed the kidney, and now he took great pains to add this to the painting, creating first a hideous wound in the side in which he now inserted a life-like painting of the stolen kidney. Cassandra had no doubt that if she had a photograph of this missing part it would be identical to Juniper's painting.

"So. Are you just going to fill all those in?"

"When the parts are taken. Yez."

"How do you know when they are taken?" she asked.

"I feel it. Here." He indicated his heart.

Cassandra turned and left the room. It was time. She had agreed to meet Joy and Lauren and the end of this would be soon.

By standing so close to Juniper as he painted she had seen what he saw. She knew where Carla Rodriguez would be and so the final lap of the harvest would be done. It was already written who would win, but Cassandra could not see that result no matter how hard she looked.

"Marcus? I want you to make sure that Avgustin doesn't leave the apartment today," she said to her bodyguard. He was waiting in the kitchen for her instructions.

"Of course," he said.

"Make sure he eats. And keeps working."

Marcus nodded and Cassandra left the room and the apartment.

After she had gone, Marcus switched on the kitchen television and found the football. Juniper wouldn't need feeding for a while and Marcus kept the volume down so that he could listen out for any sign of the artist coming out of his studio.

"Not a pretty sight," Dan Shallit said as he uncovered the body of Carla Rodriguez.

She had been a good-looking girl. Shining dark hair, smooth skin. Her eyes were closed as though asleep. But below her eyes … the head was mutilated. Part of her cheek and all of her jaw had been taken away, leaving smooth surfaces through which the bone, cartilage and flesh could be seen. Her upper jaw and teeth jutted obscenely, and her tongue lolled lifelessly over her neck. It was horrific.

"For her sake I'm glad it killed her," said Chandler. "She wouldn't have lasted long with those injuries."

"Is it me or has the perp speeded up a little?" Shallit said.

"They are coming closer together," Chandler said. "They were weeks apart, now days. Maybe it will be hours before they strike again."

Chandler thought about the morning and his parting with Lauren. He had agreed to meet her later at Joy Awen's Gallery. Where he knew the other muses would be gathering to take care of their problem. Part of him wished this to all be over, and if Juniper continued to work on the final faces, it was likely to be very soon.

Shallit dropped the sheet back over Carla's head and Chandler walked away. That morning he had called his FBI contact and asked for Sarasvatī to be posted to the detail protecting Marina Mikhailov. He knew that her help would be crucial if Marina was to survive, as the last piece in the muse's body parts puzzle. He couldn't let the monster have her. Things had changed.

He wanted Lauren to be safe, and a showdown with the killer that she, Cassandra and Joy planned, didn't please him, or reassure him that she would be. After all the other two were now his main suspects. Maybe they were even working together? Either way the odds weren't good for Lauren.

He didn't tell her about Sarasvatī's visit to him the night before. Or about the folder of evidence that he had hidden in the bottom drawer of the guest bedroom chest of drawers. Lauren wouldn't find it; he was sure she would respect his privacy and not snoop around his house. Besides, she had left before him that day, hurrying off to her needy clients and Jake, who had planned to have the morning at home, had been called to the crime scene soon afterwards.

He kept telling himself that it was just a normal day, as though it would help him to accept that he had stepped out of the real and safe world he knew and into the *Twilight Zone*.

There was only one other victim standing between Marina Mikhailov and the rogue.

"She'll swoop as soon as she can," Sarasvatī had said after he called to tell her where to go to protect Marina. "Try and find out who the other girl is from Juniper."

He had tried. He had rung Cassandra's apartment and only received the rather unhelpful response of one of her bodyguards.

"Mr. Juniper is working. He is not to be disturbed."

"Very well," Chandler has said. "When he breaks for lunch have him call me."

Somehow, he had a feeling that the guard wouldn't tell Juniper, and now that he knew who Cassandra really was, Chandler was loath to have any contact with her until the meeting later. He didn't want her to realize he knew until he was in a position to stop her or Joy from taking Marina's heart.

It was late afternoon when Chandler finally climbed into his car and headed off towards the Gallery. He was just early enough to avoid the late traffic, and he arrived a few minutes before the time he had agreed to meet Lauren.

Periodically throughout the day he had recalled Lauren's revelation. Chandler had given up on the idea of ever being a father when Jules had died. Now he was contemplating a future he had not considered possible.

Of course he had to marry her. There was no question. But after Sarasvatī's astounding disclosure, he had another concern that Lauren herself didn't seem to have. How long did she have left? How quickly would the aging process start? From what Sarasvatī had told him, it took over rather suddenly, aging the muse until they died of old age.

It was a discussion they would have to have when all of this was over, and Chandler hoped that it would be over soon, maybe even that evening.

He saw Lauren walking towards him. As she reached him he peered at her intently, looking for signs that her body was failing, but she looked beautiful and fresh.

"Hello, darling," she said. Then she kissed his lips before taking his hand and leading him towards the gallery entrance. They walked in and Lauren confidently headed towards Joy's office.

The door was open and Cassandra and Joy were inside waiting.

"Detective Chandler!" said Joy surprised.

"I didn't expect to see *you*," Cassandra said.

Chandler noticed how sullen she was. She didn't look too well either. There were blue circles under her eyes and she looked thinner than usual. As though she hadn't been eating much recently.

"Jake knows *everything*," Lauren announced as they entered.

She then turned and closed the office door, shutting them all away from the gallery. "You were the one who didn't want him to know …" Joy pointed out. "Now you just bring him here and announce he knows everything. *What* do you *know,* Detective?"

"I know that one of you is the rogue," Chandler said.

The three of them laughed.

"And how do you deduce that?" asked Cassandra. "What evidence do you have to support this claim?"

"I know it isn't Lauren," Chandler said. "So it has to be one of you two."

"So why isn't it Lauren?" said Joy. "You seem pretty convinced."

"I'm turning human," said Lauren. "I'm also … pregnant."

"What?" said Cassandra. "Well I guess that rules me out too then. Because that's two of us."

"You're pregnant?" asked Chandler. "Is it Juniper's?"

"Yes. I'm also fairly sure that I'm turning human too."

"I may need to have a doctor verify your pregnancy," Chandler said.

"Fine. But I haven't told Avgustin yet. He's enough to worry about at the moment."

They all turned to look at Joy.

"Well, isn't this fine and dandy?" she said. "You've got it all worked out. But I'll tell you now. You're wrong. I'm not the rogue. I have plenty of life left in me, I'm not turning human and I'm not harvesting. Look at me!"

She held out her arms, flashed her legs.

Cassandra and Lauren squinted at her.

"She seems solid. Strong. A full muse," Lauren said.

"Then we're no closer to the truth?" Cassandra said.

"Our suspect hasn't changed," said Joy. "I'm sorry to tell you this but your colleague Gemma Sarasvatī is also one of us."

"I know," said Chandler.

All three muses turned to look at him in one move. It was eerie how they appeared to be one and the same when they did that.

"How?" said Lauren.

"She came to see me last night, before you arrived. She told me everything. What was happening to her. How she is dying. She wants to help us find the rogue before it's too late for her."

"She's deteriorating that fast?" Joy said the color drained from her. "That's not a good sign."

"How do you know?" said Lauren and Chandler simultaneously, "What do you mean?"

"I suspect that she's dying until she harvests the remaining parts. Once she has them, there's no way to stop her."

"Gemma told me that the heart is always the final piece …" Chandler said.

"I expect she knows that better than any of us," Joy said.

"You're saying she's the rogue?" Chandler said.

"I think that's obvious now. Don't you?"

"At least the last face hasn't been painted," Chandler said. "I'll call my contact and have them bring Gemma in for questioning."

"The last face *has* been painted," Cassandra said. "Avgustin finished the entire piece this morning."

"Why didn't you call me? I thought we had a deal?" Chandler said.

"We had decided to take care of it … in house," Joy said. "That was why we are meeting this afternoon. Surely Lauren told you that?"

"I didn't think the painting was finished. I thought there was still time," Lauren said.

"We agreed to hurry Avgustin up," Cassandra said. "I did what was agreed."

"There's no point in arguing about this right now … excuse me," said Chandler as his phone started to ring. He answered.

"Chandler? It's Shallit here. There's been another one …"

"Jesus Christ!" said Chandler. "Shallit, I want you to get over to this address," he read out the information he had on Marina's safe house. "Gemma Sarasvatī will be there. Arrest her."

"What?" said Shallit. "*Arrest* Detective Sarasvatī?"

"That's what I said. I'm on my way there now."

Chandler turned to face the three other muses. "You heard?"

"Jake. I'm sorry. But if Gemma is over there. Then it's too late for Marina," said Lauren.

"It can't be," Chandler said. "I have to go."

"You won't take her," said Joy. "She's too strong."

"She didn't look strong last night."

Then he hurried out of the office.

"What should we do?" Cassandra said.

Joy shrugged. "It's too late."

"I'm going with Jake," said Lauren before she hurried after him.

"I'd better get back to Avgustin," said Cassandra.

"Wait, Cassandra. I've something to tell you," said Joy. "I'm afraid I haven't been entirely truthful with you."

CHAPTER FORTY

"About time you showed," said the male cop who opened the door to Gemma Sarasvatī as she arrived at the safe house. "My partner has to go. She has childcare issues today."

Sarasvatī nodded to the female cop who rushed past her and out of the door to the car parked up in the drive.

"How's our potential victim bearing up?" Sarasvatī asked as she entered the large hallway.

The male cop shrugged. "She's taking a bath right now. We aren't supposed to leave her alone but she kicked Angie out, demanding privacy."

"I'll go and check on her," said Sarasvatī.

"Yeah. Rather you than me. She's a little temperamental."

The cop pointed towards the door along the corridor.

The house was a one-tier structure, with several rooms off the main corridor. Sarasvatī walked down the hallway.

"Third door on the left."

"Thanks."

"Hey. Tell her to hurry up. It's a lot easier when we're all in the same room."

Sarasvatī found the bathroom door half open and she rapped lightly on it.

"Miss Mikhailov, I'm Detective Sarasvatī. Can I come in? I need to verify that you are safe."

"Can't I get any privacy around here?" Marina called. "It's bad enough you locked me up like this."

Sarasvatī heard water sloshing as the girl climbed out of the bath.

"I'm just getting dry," she said. "Right. Come in."

Sarasvatī opened the door and she found herself face to face with Marina.

So this was Juniper's first love. It was obvious really, why the heart of this one would do the job of saving the life of a muse. There was no magic more powerful than love. Sarasvatī wished she had experienced this emotion firsthand but even though she had started to become human several years ago, she had chosen to isolate herself rather than let anyone in to see her disintegrate.

Her legs trembled as she entered the bathroom. It was almost over. She had made it.

Then the unthinkable happened. The front door to the house burst open and a team of cops poured in. Sarasvatī heard the commotion and she turned to face the door of the bathroom, ready to defend the life of Marina Mikhailov.

But the next person that entered was a colleague. It was Shallit.

"Dan? What are you doing here?" Sarasvatī asked.

"Gemma, I'm sorry. I have to do what he says," Shallit said.

"Who?"

"Chandler told me to arrest you."

"What?"

"I'm sorry Gem, but you need to come with me. I'm sure it'll all be straightened out."

"Dan. Please. You're making a mistake. I have to stay here and protect Marina."

Sarasvatī backed up; her body barred Marina from the door.

"Gemma. Don't make me do this...."

Shallit raised his gun.

"Come quietly," said another officer behind Shallit. "You know the drill."

"I haven't done anything wrong," Sarasvatī said. "I *have* to protect Marina. You don't understand."

Four more men came into the bathroom. Marina had backed up as far as she could away from the door.

"What's going on?" she cried.

"Look. I agree. This will all be straightened out. But guys, you know me. You need to trust me," Sarasvatī said. She held her hands up. "I'm unarmed. So let's keep calm. Is Chandler on his way? I'll talk to him. All will be fine."

Despite his orders Shallit found himself lowering his gun.

"Let's just get Marina into the living room. You guys need to stay near her. Don't let her out of your sight. But let me stay in the room too, okay? At least until Chandler gets here."

"How are you doing that?" said Marina behind her.

The Russian girl had noticed that the cops appeared to be calming down and doing as Sarasvatī said.

"Call it a skill," she answered. "Now go with them."

Wrapped in a towel, Marina moved around Sarasvatī and walked towards the men. She glanced at Sarasvatī as she passed, noticing how sick the woman looked.

"What's *wrong* with you?" she asked.

"Don't worry. It'll all be over soon," Sarasvatī slumped against the bath as Marina passed through the doorway and out into the hall.

Two cops took her arm and led her back towards the sitting room.

"Come on," said Shallit. "You better stay where I can see you."

Sarasvatī nodded her head quickly, "I just need a minute, Dan. I'm not strong right now."

A commotion outside the room drew Shallit's attention. He turned away from Sarasvatī and hurried out into the hallway.

"Hey! Who are you?" he called.

Sarasvatī slid to the floor.

I have to get up now or it's all over, she thought.

She pulled herself up on the bath edge. Using the edge of the sink she began to walk, gaining strength as she reached the door.

"One step. Then the other," she murmured. "You can do this…."

"It's finished, Gemma," said a female voice as she staggered from the bathroom.

She looked up to see Joy Awen. She was holding the arm of Marina Mikhailov.

"Out of all of them, I didn't think it was you." Sarasvatī said.

"Me?" said Joy in surprise. "Don't try and twist this onto me. I came here to save her."

Chandler entered the hallway with Lauren running close behind.

"Let go of her, Awen," Chandler said.

Lauren pulled Marina free of Joy's grip. "I've got you. Don't worry!"

"It's my duty to take care of this," Joy said. "What she's done is against everything we were created to be."

"Jake. It isn't me. I'm here to protect. You know that," said Sarasvatī.

Chandler's gun was in his hand and he looked from one to the other of the women.

"Time's running out for me," Sarasvatī said. "I can't hold on. Don't let her take Marina."

Marina was becoming hysterical.

"What's going on? Who are these women?"

Lauren put her arm around Marina. "I'll take her in here," she said and she led Marina towards the living room door.

The door opened. Cassandra was waiting there, and the cops

inside were standing frozen as though time had stood still in the room.

"Not so fast," Cassandra said.

"Don't get in my way," Lauren said. "It's over."

"Not until the fat lady sings," said Cassandra. "And since I'm the only pregnant muse, then I think that qualifies me as the 'fat lady.'"

Chandler could see it all unfold before his eyes. One moment he was convinced that Sarasvatī was the rogue, then he had changed his mind and Joy became the focus of his suspicions.

"Believe in your instincts," Sarasvatī murmured to him.

He could barely move, but he turned slowly, as if he was chest deep in mud, and he saw Cassandra blocking the door to the sitting room and the tussle between her and Lauren for Marina.

Marina broke free of them both suddenly and she ran towards Chandler as Cassandra yelled a warning. Joy tripped the Russian woman up as she made to pass her and Chandler's gun twisted towards her.

Then out of the corner of his eye he saw Lauren's outstretched hand.

But Marina fell and Chandler felt a line burn through his shirt and searing the skin on his forearm. He dropped his gun.

"Lauren!" he gasped in shock.

Sarasvatī screamed as she threw herself in front of Chandler. Lauren's invisible beam hit her full in the chest. Chandler dived to the floor, scrambling for his lost weapon. His hand fell on it as Lauren approached Marina who was cowering and crying on the floor at Joy's feet.

Joy threw herself over Marina in an attempt to guard the woman with her own body.

Lauren raised her hand again. Joy's coat parted as though a

zipper was being pulled open from inside the back. Light bounced off Joy as Lauren's power reached the skin beneath. Lauren fell back, temporarily blinded by the fierce light that struck her. Her hand flew upwards and a precise hole was cut through the ceiling above. Joy remained unharmed, covering Marina; she was what both Lauren and Cassandra had said—a whole muse who had renewed, because she still had the ability to inspire.

"Shoot her, Chandler!" Cassandra's voice came to him through a fog of white noise.

He turned his weapon upwards to Lauren but he couldn't shoot. His heart was breaking. Besides, how could he kill this being with such tremendous supernatural power?

"She's mostly human!" one of them shouted. "You can do it, Jake!"

He turned then to see Sarasvatī beside him. She was glowing and changing before his eyes. No longer did she appear to be on the verge of collapse.

"You have the strength inside you," she said and Chandler knew that he did. Sarasvatī was inspiring him to be a hero. She was renewing before his eyes.

He turned his gaze back to Lauren. But then he faltered again. She was carrying his child....

"No," said Sarasvatī. "She lied to you, Jake."

Her hand touched him, he felt the heavy fugue lift from his eyes and he saw for the first time the horror that Avgustin Juniper had seen that night, not long ago, at the gallery.

Lauren was made up of different body parts that joined together with thin red healing scar lines. He recognized all of them, and now could see the watch that Maria Matthews had described as being on the lower arm that had been stolen: a mosaic of a Picasso masterpiece, somewhat ironic. Lauren was not Lauren. Her face was a collage of other women, her torso a devastating patchwork horror all supported by a shapely ballerina's legs.

"Lauren …" he said.

How had he not seen this? How had he been so blind?

She turned her eyes to him. One blue, the other, newly taken, was a deep hazel. And Chandler could see the scar of the other triangular piece taken from the first victim, Annabel Linton.

It was a horror freak show of the worst kind.

Lauren glared at him with hatred. "I will live on!" she said and then she raised her hand and pointed it towards him. In the center of her palm he saw a spark ignite and knew he wouldn't survive the invisible blast from it.

Gunfire. Slow motion as her body jerked and bounced backwards. She fell hard—a corpse before she hit the ground—Chandler glanced down at the gun in his hands still smoking from his execution of the woman he loved.

Sarasvatī was holding his hand still. He dropped the gun and she caught it.

All hell broke loose then, and the other cops, released from their paralysis, were spurred into action. As the others came out of their fugue and ran into the hall, Chandler noticed that Joy and Cassandra were nowhere to be seen. Sarasvatī remained at his side.

He stood and walked towards Lauren's body. Now that he could see her flaws, he couldn't unsee them.

"Jesus. What is that?" said Dan Shallit. "She's got some kind of flamethrower in her hand."

"A laser cutter. New technology," Sarasvatī said as she moved forward.

Chandler felt her using some form of magical hypnosis on the other cops. They saw what she wanted them to see. For a minute Chandler saw it too. Lauren, looking like normal, but holding something that resembled a cattle prod in her right hand. The watch was still there though and when he closed his eyes and reopened them again he saw her for what she really was.

"Looks like we bagged our killer," said Shallit. "Hey, Sarasvatī! The drinks are on me tonight."

Chandler and Sarasvatī stepped away as they let the other officers take over the crime scene.

Chandler was trembling and in shock.

Sarasvatī looked down at her hands, then she ran her fingers through her hair, pulling off the blonde wig and revealing rich and lush locks of chestnut brown.

"I'm your muse," she said. "You have no idea what you've done for me."

Sarasvatī supervised Marina until the paramedics arrived. They gave her a thorough examination in the back of the ambulance. She had suffered nothing more than a few cuts and bruises. But they were concerned about her memory loss, believing she must have hit her head as well. And so the Russian woman was taken to the hospital for further tests.

Sarasvatī and Chandler left the others and they climbed into Chandler's car.

"Of course now I don't need this. I can be anywhere I want in the blink of an eye."

Chandler inserted the keys into his ignition and started his car. His hands hadn't stopped shaking. Sarasvatī reached over and touched him again. The shock receded and calm came over him.

"She played you, but she also aided you. She couldn't help it," she explained. "She was one of us, after all. Had she really been able to inspire you, then she wouldn't have needed to harvest."

"I *didn't* love her …?"

"No. Or again the outcome may have been different."

"What of the others?" Chandler said.

Sarasvatī gazed through the windscreen of the car as though she could see. "A miracle has happened for all of us."

EPILOGUE

Cassandra found Juniper asleep in her bed when she returned to the apartment.

"Avgustin," she said as she slipped naked under the covers and wrapped her arms around him.

"Yez," he murmured half asleep.

"It's over. Your demon is gone. Everything you ever wanted can now be yours."

Juniper opened his eyes. Cassandra had left the light on in the bathroom and it glowed into the room reflecting on her skin. She looked beautiful.

"Marina is dead?" he said his eyes sad.

"No. The police caught the killer. Marina is fine. We are fine."

"I want you," he said. "I love you and I want you to marry me."

"Not the most romantic of proposals," she said kissing him on the lips. "But since I'm pregnant with your child, I guess I should say yes."

Avgustin pulled himself into a sitting position and reached for the lamp by the bed. He switched it on and looked at her.

"You're …"

She nodded. "Early days."

"Oh my God. I never expected …"

He pulled her to him and kissed her lips and then, realizing that he had been a little too rough, he stroked her long blondc hair back from her facc.

"It zuits you. You look stunning. Perfect."

"Human," she said. And then she snuggled up to him, thinking of the miracle that had not only happened to her body, but had also granted her a full and normal mortal life to live out. She was full of beautiful emotion. Tears almost came to her eyes as she wondered what their baby girl would look like. Which of them she would resemble more.

"I *love* you," she said and she really felt it.

"That's the first time you've told me," he said.

"It won't be the last."

Joy Awen pulled open the secret storage cabinet behind her desk and she gazed at the painting that had been completed by Picasso so long ago.

For the first time she did not see hatred in the brush strokes. She saw wonder, fear, and bewilderment instead.

Joy had hated this painting for so long it was difficult now to see it for what it was: a warning.

She had posed for it. Had always known she was the muse who had used Picasso to find another source of renewal when her time had been so close. She had been failing. Dying. Then she had stumbled on this way of helping herself. How could she ever admit such failure to her other sisters?

The time had been approaching again. She had felt it, but when she bonded with Juniper, before the death of Annabel, she found herself becoming the source of his secret inspiration. Even Juniper had not known that Joy was his real muse all along.

But Lauren had piggy-backed on that inspiration and manipulated Juniper to help her to live and prosper. Joy hadn't known it was her—it could have been any of them. She had pulled the women all together in order to bring the rogue out of the woodwork.

She stared at the painting now. Oh, the horror of it when she had found it under Picasso's floorboards. She had sniffed it out when he ran away with Olga to Biarritz. She had taken the journal in a fit of anger, but had left the picture there, too hurt to know what else to do. Then, a German soldier, a deserter, had stumbled into Picasso's empty house. He'd taken the painting along with a stash of money Picasso had left there. It had taken years before the painting found its way back to Joy, like a bad penny coming home.

Joy had detested it, but she had kept the artwork ever since —along with the journal. It was a reminder of how low she had stooped. A reminder that she must never again take the lives of humans in order to prolong her own. She had sinned, but repented, and help had come at the eleventh hour.

Her sacrifice to save Marina, and stop Lauren, had not gone unnoticed. She had fully renewed and so had Gemma.

Cassandra's reward was the biggest surprise though. Who would have thought that the coldest one of them all would find the deepest love?

The gods had spoken from Olympus and now the muses knew they were no longer alone.

Joy pulled the painting down from the secret cupboard.

The buyer would be here soon to collect his new purchase and Joy was happy, finally, to let it go.

She needed no more reminders of the days when she posed for Picasso.

ABOUT THE AUTHOR

Award-winning author Sam Stone began her professional writing career in 2007 when her first novel won the Silver Award for Best Novel with *ForeWord Magazine* Book of the Year Awards. Since then she has gone on to write 15 novels, 5 novellas, and over 40 short stories.

Sam's first screenplay, *The Inheritance*, which is the first story in *White Witch of Devil's End* (a *Doctor Who* spin off anthology movie about white witch Olive Hawthorne—first seen in the Jon Pertwee era, *The Daemons*) made its DVD debut in November 2017.

Sam has since written two more screenplays which are currently in pre-production.

She was the first woman in 31 years to win the British Fantasy Society Award for Best Novel (*Demon Dance: Book 3 The Vampire Gene series.*) She also won the Award for Best Short Fiction in the same year (2011).

Sam loves all genre fiction and enjoys mixing horror (her first passion) with a variety of different genres including science fiction, fantasy, and Steampunk.

Her works can be found in paperback, audio, screen and, ebook.

Sam currently resides in Lincolnshire, United Kingdom, with her husband David and cats Leeloo and Skye.

For more information visit www.sam-stone.com.

IF YOU LIKED ...

IF YOU LIKED THIS BOOK, YOU MIGHT ALSO ENJOY:

Empty Rooms
by Jeff Mariotte

The Fly Guy
by Colum Sanson-Regan

Pockets of Darkness
by Jean Rabe

OTHER WORDFIRE PRESS TITLES

Our list of other WordFire Press authors and titles is always growing. To find out more and to see our selection of titles, visit us at:

wordfirepress.com

Printed in Great Britain
by Amazon